Praise for the novels of
New York Times and *USA TODAY*
bestselling author

shannon
stacey

"Books like this are why I read romance."
—*Smart Bitches, Trashy Books*
on *Exclusively Yours*

"This is the perfect contemporary romance!"
—*RT Book Reviews* on *Undeniably Yours*

"Sexy, sassy and immensely satisfying."
—*Fresh Fiction* on *Undeniably Yours*

"*Yours to Keep* was a wonderful,
sexy and witty installment in this series....
This was a truly magical book."
—*The Book Pushers*

"This contemporary romance
is filled with charm, wit, sophistication,
and is anything but predictable."
—*Heart to Heart, BN.com,*
on *Yours to Keep*

shannon stacey

undeniably *Yours*

HQN™

Recycling programs
for this product may
not exist in your area.

ISBN-13: 978-0-373-77685-6

UNDENIABLY YOURS

Copyright © 2010 by Shannon Stacey

This edition published by arrangement with Harlequin Books S.A.

For questions and comments about the quality of this book
please contact us at Customer_eCare@Harlequin.ca.

® and TM are trademarks of the publisher. Trademarks indicated with ® are registered in the United States Patent and Trademark Office, the Canadian Trade Marks Office and in other countries.

www.Harlequin.com

Printed in U.S.A.

Thank you to my editor, Angela James, for your support and for your tireless work in making my books stronger. And thank you to every member of the Carina Press and HQN teams for your dedication to bringing good stories to readers. I'm honored mine is one of them.

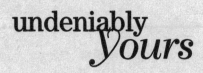

undeniably *Yours*

CHAPTER ONE

October

EVERY TIME THE NEW ENGLAND Patriots chalked one up in the win column, Kevin Kowalski got laid.

A score for them was a score for him. Not that he was always looking for a companion on a Sunday night, but the offers weren't scarce. As he slid a foaming mug of Sam Adams down the polished surface of the best damn sports bar in New Hampshire's capital city—which just happened to list his name as proprietor—he caught a blonde watching him. The Pats were lining up at first and goal on the big-screen, but her eyes were on him, letting him know the New England quarterback wasn't the only guy in scoring position.

But tonight he was having a hard time concentrating on the blonde with the chemically enhanced lips, surgically enhanced boobs and alcohol-enhanced sex drive giving him the *you could go all the way* look.

He was too busy keeping his eye on the brunette at the other end of the bar. It wasn't just the fact she was pretty, with a mess of dark brown hair falling to her shoulders and eyes to match. Or that her fisherman's sweater and jeans hugged her body in all the right places, though that certainly didn't hurt.

Mostly he was keeping an eye on her because her date was going downhill in a hurry. Either the guy in the uptight, button-down shirt and khakis had had a couple before he'd walked into the bar or he had the alcohol tolerance of a high-school freshman, because it had only taken a couple shots of Scotch for Drunken Asshole Syndrome to kick in.

Now there was some body language going on between the couple, and her body wanted away from his body. His fingers would start looking for a soft place to land. She'd deflect. Rinse and repeat.

Jasper's Bar & Grille had three rules. No smoking. No throwing beer mugs, even at the Jets fans. And when a lady said no, it meant no.

The Patriots scored, and the glasses shook on the shelves as a triumphant roar filled Jasper's. The blonde hopped up and down on her bar stool, her boobs testing the bungee ability of her bra straps.

And the jerk with the wandering hands raised his empty glass to wave it in Kevin's general direction.

He made his way down to the couple but ignored the glass. "We won't be serving you any more alcohol, but you're welcome to a coffee or a soda, on the house."

Uptight Guy's face turned as red as a Budweiser label, and Kevin sighed. He was going to be one of *those* guys. Jasper's had a zero-tolerance policy, so as the guy's ass lifted off the stool, Kevin gave Paulie the signal and watched her roll her eyes as she reached for the phone.

"I'm not drunk and I want another goddamn Scotch!"

The woman put her hand on the guy's arm, as if to push him back onto his seat. "Derek, let's—"

"Who the hell are you to tell me I can't have another goddamn Scotch?"

Uptight Guy's badass act was diluted a bit by the weaving. "I'm the guy who reserves the right to refuse you service."

"Beth, tell this asshole to gimme another drink."

Kevin shook his head. "You're cut off."

It happened fast. Kevin wasn't sure if the guy was throwing a punch or reaching in to grab him by the shirt, but his elbow hit his date and knocked her backward. She didn't fall, thanks to the guy sitting next to her, who was pleasantly surprised to find himself with an armful of brunette, but it distracted Kevin enough to allow the guy to land a weak, glancing blow to his jaw.

Uptight Guy, whom the woman had called Derek, sucked in a breath, as if he just realized what he'd done. Kevin watched as the guy's fight-or-flight instinct kicked in and wasn't surprised when he chose flight. Sadly for him, Kevin was six-two and had some experience collaring yahoos, whether they were crooks back when he'd worn a badge or his four rowdy nephews. He reached across the bar, grabbed the guy by the scruff of the neck and yanked him back.

Derek was struggling like a pickerel on a hook and, when Kevin's grip almost slipped off the guy's collar, he jerked hard. Derek's head snapped around, and his nose exploded on the edge of the bar. Oops.

The guy screamed like a girl...and the crowd went wild. Jasper's didn't attract a real rough crowd, but everybody loved a good fight.

"Good fight" being relative, of course. Derek cupped his hands over his face, trying to staunch the blood and let out a high-pitched keening sound that made more than a few of the patrons wince.

"Shut up or I'll knock your ass out," Kevin

yelled at the guy which, of course, got everybody in the bar chanting. *Do it...do it...do it...*

"Oh, my God, his nose!" Derek's date untangled herself from her neighbor and grabbed a couple of napkins off the bar. She tried to get to Derek's nose, but he kept pushing her away.

The crowd quieted when a couple of police officers walked through the front door. Derek's keening changed pitch when he saw them, from a pain-filled squeal to an *oh, shit* desperation.

"Hey, Kowalski," the older of the two cops said.

"Hey, Jonesy. Your old man like those tickets?"

"Are you kidding me? Tenth row, fifty-yard line? He was in heaven. Said to tell you thanks and give you his best."

"Glad to do it," he said easily, still holding on to Derek's collar. He fostered a friendly relationship with the local P.D., not only because he'd been on the job once down in Boston, but because any good businessman did. Especially businessmen who served alcohol. "Got a live one here."

"What happened to him?"

"Hit his face on the bar. You know how it is."

In the split second between Kevin releasing him and Jonesy grabbing for his wrists, Derek stupidly decided to make a break for the door.

The rookie made a move to stop him at the same

time Beth did. She accidentally—at least it *looked* accidental—tripped him, and the young cop fell on his face. Jonesy jumped over his partner and did the nearing-retirement version of a sprint after Derek.

Beth was practically hyperventilating.

The rookie scrambled to his feet as Jonesy took down his prey in a half-ass diving tackle that made the crowd roar in approval. Rookie had his handcuffs out, but it looked as if Uptight Guy was going all-in on a resisting charge.

"Why are you doing this to him?"

Kevin's gaze swiveled to the woman, who looked almost as pissed as her date. "I didn't do jack to him, lady. Did you forget the part where he hit *you?*"

"He didn't hit me. He bumped me trying to hit you."

Yeah, that was so much better. "How about the groping? How many times were you going to tell him no?"

She actually rolled her eyes at him. "I had it all under control."

"No, now it's all under control."

"Look, it's not what you... Forget it. You have to help him, though."

Since Derek had two hundred pounds of veteran

cop kneeling on his head while the rookie tried to secure the cuffs, there wasn't much Kevin *could* do for him, even if he wanted to. Which he didn't.

"It's not what you think," she insisted.

"I'm going to sue you for everything you've got, asshole," Derek screamed over his shoulder. "And you, you dumb bitch, you're fired!"

Oops. Kevin looked at Beth. "I thought he was just a bad date."

She climbed onto a stool and dropped her forehead to the bar with a thunk. "You just cost me my job."

Only several years of fine-tuning his brain-to-mouth filter behind the bar kept him from pointing out she was maybe better off without it. "Want a beer?"

A BEER? RAMBO THE BARTENDER here thought a beer was going to fix the mess he'd gotten her into? Beth Hansen curled her hands into fists to keep from reaching across the bar and shaking him like a martini.

So Derek was a drunken ass. So what else was new? It was nothing she couldn't handle. She handled it once a week or so, as a matter of fact, and had been for three months.

After work, Derek would leave the office and

walk down the street to have a drink. He'd call his secretary—that would be her—with some bogus excuse requiring her to stop by the bar. A paper that needed signing. A fax he'd forgotten to read but absolutely had to before he went home. She'd show up, he'd try to get in her pants, she'd put him in a cab and the next day they'd pretend it didn't happen.

Sometimes, like today, he'd even drag her out on a weekend. Maybe not ideal working conditions, but she'd suffered worse.

But this time Derek's usual bar was closed for renovations, so he'd kept on walking until he'd come to Jasper's Bar & Grille. Now her boss had a broken nose, and she had no job.

A beer wasn't going to help.

She lifted her head and propped her chin on her hand. "Did you have to call the police?"

"Yup."

"You could have let it go."

He rested his palms on the edge of the bar and looked her in the eye. God, he was tall. And that wasn't all he had going for him. Besides the height and the blue eyes and the dimples, he had broad shoulders straining the seams of an ancient Red Sox T-shirt and thick brown hair that had that careless style of a man who didn't want to fuss with it. Probably mid-thirties.

"Lady, he punched me in the face."

"It wasn't much of a punch," she muttered, since she couldn't deny it. "I almost had him talked into a cab, but you had to go and make it a big deal."

"Hey, Kevin," a younger guy called out. "Can we make a mimosa?"

"This is a sports bar, not Easter brunch." He turned back to her, shaking his head. "All I did was tell him he was cut off. Not only do I have the right, but when a patron's visibly intoxicated, I have the obligation. And I ain't exactly a turn-the-other-cheek guy when it comes to getting punched in the face."

Kevin had a point. It wasn't his fault her boss was a jerk, so blaming him was probably a little unreasonable. But the only difference between the previous times and this time was him. "You didn't have to break his nose."

"*That* I didn't really mean to do. He slipped. Kind of." The sheepish, dimpled grin he gave her was so irresistible she could feel aggravation's hold on her temper loosening.

She was about to respond when he reached his arms up to a high shelf. Muscles rippled under his T-shirt, and when he stretched for a stack of folded towels, a gap opened between its hem and the waistband of his low-slung jeans. The tantalizing glimpse of abs made her mouth go dry, which was okay because she'd forgotten what she was going to say anyway.

When he moved out from behind the bar to mop at Derek's blood, she grimaced and moved over a stool. Not that she was queasy but because Kevin smelled as good as he looked. And the closer he got to her, the better he looked.

Then, without warning, her view was blocked by a busty blonde whose outfit made Daisy Duke's look like going-to-church clothes. The woman handed Kevin what looked like a Jasper's napkin with lipstick smeared on it. The same shade painted on the woman's plumped and puckered-up mouth.

"Hi, Kevin," the blonde said in pretty much the same breathless, baby-doll voice Marilyn Monroe had used to wish President Kennedy a very, very happy birthday. "Here's my number. You know… in case you want to call me…or something."

He winked at her as he took the napkin. "Thanks, doll. I just might do that."

Beth managed to hold it in until Hooters-wannabe Barbie had simpered out the front door, then she rolled her eyes. "Doll? Smooth line, Mickey Spillane."

"Hey, makin' the ladies happy is good for business."

"Yeah, and I bet you're just the man for the job. You should go after her. She seems just your type."

That wiped the naughty-boy charm off his face. "What makes you think you know anything about my type?"

She shrugged, making it clear she didn't really give a damn. "Careful you don't smear your napkin. And speaking of business, I need to go find another job now."

"I feel bad about that, even though it wasn't really my fault."

"I'll get over it." She slid off the stool and started toward the door. "Have a nice life. *Doll*."

KEVIN SMILED FOR THE WOMAN wielding the camera. Then he smiled again. And again and again and again.

"Okay," the bossy photographer said. "Now a few of the bride and her ladies, and then we'll do the groom and his brothers."

With matching sighs of relief, Kevin and his brothers Joe and Mike, along with their brother-in-law Evan, moved away from the gaggle of women.

They'd been at the picture-taking thing for twenty minutes already, and, early October or not, it was hot in a tux.

Joe's reception was at some swanky hotel-slash-banquet center that specialized in wedding receptions. As far as Kevin could tell, that meant they had a shitload of places to take pictures. In front of the garden. In front of the rock waterfall. Under the gazebo thing in front of the pond. His cheeks were starting to ache.

Mike tugged at his collar but not so much the drill sergeant with the camera would bark at him. "I'm ready to hit the bar."

Kevin nodded, though he didn't fidget because their mother was giving them the *I'm watching you* look. "Joe, I swear, if they don't hurry up, your wedding photos are going to look more like a Chippendales' photo shoot."

"If I'd known you two were going to whine like a couple of girls, I would have had you be bridesmaids instead of my best men. You'd look good in a dress."

Kevin snorted. "Don't make me kick your ass on your wedding day."

"Terry sure looks good in her dress," Evan said. "Kinda makes you want to—"

"No," Terry's three brothers said in unison.

Their brother-in-law scowled. "I hate that. I never get to share the good stuff."

Mike laughed. "Joey and Danny are old enough to watch the younger two in a room of their own. I'll be doing the good stuff to Lisa later."

Must be nice. After the wedding, they'd all be heading upstairs to their rooms to do the good stuff. Joe and his gorgeous new bride, Keri. Mike and Lisa. Evan and Terry.

He, on the other hand, was stag at his own brother's wedding, so the only good stuff he had to look forward to was losing the cummerbund and penguin shoes.

It had been a couple of years since Kevin's marriage had exploded in a cloud of toxic flames, torching his career along with the relationship, and since then his libido had survived on a steady diet of bar bunnies. Less satisfying but also a lot less risk, like eating a microwave meal instead of preparing a five-course feast. A lot less painful to throw away if it sucked.

He'd gone through his share of willing companions after the divorce, when he bought the bar, but lately he'd been making the trip upstairs to his apartment alone more often than not. The kind of women willing to spend one night with a guy they didn't know just because he filled out his shirts well—or so he was told—and owned the bar weren't the kind of women he wanted to have breakfast with the next morning.

And definitely not the kind of women you brought to your brother's wedding.

Unfortunately, thoughts of his type of woman led to thoughts of Beth, the pretty brunette who'd passed judgment on his type and been totally wrong. It had been two days since he'd busted her boss's nose, and it irked him he kept thinking about her. It also irked him she'd left with the impression he was some kind of player.

If she wasn't so prickly—and if he knew her last name or where she lived—he'd probably like an opportunity to show her she was wrong about his type. He wasn't sure why he cared, but it bugged him she'd left with such a bad opinion of him. He wasn't used to that.

"Almost our turn," Joe said, jerking him out of his thoughts. "And then we should be able to go inside. And do more…girly wedding stuff. Whatever. Keri's so happy she's gonna bust, so it's worth it."

"So are you," Mike pointed out. "I still don't know how you pulled this all off."

Joe snorted. "It's called a blank check, my friend. Keri wanted fall foliage and I wasn't waiting a year for her to be my wife, so I said the magic words—*money's no object.*"

His brother didn't usually make a big deal about the money the sick horror novels he wrote earned, but a blank check from him was a pretty big blank check.

The drill sergeant bellowed for them. "Okay, I want groomsmen lined up behind the groom, four inches between you and slightly angled away from the camera. You, the tall one—you're in the back."

Screw that. Kevin threw his arm around Joe's shoulders and pulled him into a headlock. Joe jerked to the right, trying to escape, but he moved right into Mike's waiting noogie. Evan laughed and added rabbit ears to the back of Joe's head.

The photographer almost dropped her big, fancy camera, but the mothers of the bride and groom were hitting the shutter buttons as fast as their compact digital numbers would fire.

"Kowalski Wedding Photo of Doom," the bride shouted, and Mike's four boys and Terry's almost-teenage daughter joined the pig pile.

They were all still laughing, a little breathless and more than a little sweaty, when the wedding planner finally pulled them apart and ushered them inside. Thankfully, the black tuxedos hid the grass stains, but his niece Stephanie's dress was missing some lace around the hem.

They were supposed to go to the head table, but there were still toasts and formal dances and more freaking pictures to survive before the party could begin, and he wasn't getting through all that with nothing but a sissy glass of champagne. With beer on his mind and a possible redheaded dance partner in his peripheral vision, he made a quick detour to the open bar.

And came face-to-face with Beth.

CHAPTER TWO

OF ALL THE WEDDINGS in all the world, she just
had to be working this one. Beth took one look at
Kevin in his tuxedo and knew it was going to be
a very long night.

Tuxedo meant wedding party, which meant he
was not only going to be there for the entire event,
but he was a VIP. That meant she had to smile and
make nice with the pain in the ass whose fault it
was—kind of—that she was manning an open bar
from six in the evening until one in the morning
instead of sitting with her feet up after a fairly mild
day answering Derek's phones and syncing his calendar.

She felt a hot flush spread across her chest as
his blue eyes met hers. She'd been kind of bitchy
the day they met, and she felt bad about that. But
mostly the hot flush came from the memory of
what he'd done to her in her dreams last night.

This morning she'd blamed it on the microwave
burritos she'd devoured too close to bedtime, but

now, with the man once again in arm's reach, she had to reluctantly admit—but only to herself—she might be attracted to him. Just a little. Since, even if she *was* looking for a relationship, it wouldn't be with a guy who collected numbers on napkins, she'd prefer to blame the hot and sweaty night on nuked pseudo-Mexican food.

"What can I get you, sir?" she asked, hoping he wouldn't remember her.

The way his dimples flirted with the corners of his mouth said no such luck. "Sam Adams."

She grabbed a chilled bottle and popped the cap. "Glass?"

"Bottle's good." Instead of letting her set it down, then picking it up, he took it out of her hand, which caused his fingers to brush hers and her to shiver. "Glad to see you found another job."

She shrugged and tried not to make too big a deal about pulling her hand away. "Part-time and temporary, but better than nothing."

"Gimme your cell phone for a sec."

"Don't have one." Not that she'd hand it over to him. She didn't need him punching his number into it because she wouldn't be calling him.

"You don't have—"

"Uncle Kevin!" A teenage boy in a tux rushed over and took hold of Kevin's elbow. "If you're not sitting down in ten seconds, Grammy said she'll drag you over by your earlobe and make you cry."

Kevin laughed, then winked at Beth. "I'll be back."

That's what she was afraid of. Unfortunately, things would be slow at the bar until the toasts were done and people felt free to get up and move around, so she had plenty of time to watch the goings-on.

When the DJ announced it was time for the best man's toast, she saw Kevin laugh, which made the groom look nervous. Intrigued, she stood tiptoe, trying to see around the guests jostling for video-taping space. Kevin accepted the microphone from his dad, and a few people snickered when a guy she assumed, based on family resemblance, was another brother was handed one, too.

"Did I ever tell you you're my hero?" Kevin asked Joe, and then he got down on one knee in front of him. The other brother stood behind him with his four sons—or so she assumed after watching them—gathered around.

Then they started to sing, and laughter rippled through the crowd. It seemed that besides blue eyes and dimples, not being able to carry a tune was a strong family trait for the Kowalskis.

But watching Kevin sing the worst off-key rendition ever of "Wind Beneath My Wings" to his brother, with his other brother and nephews singing backup, Beth felt the first alarming stir of a bad case of the warm and fuzzies.

It just got worse watching him interact with his family, especially dancing with his mom and a teenage girl Beth thought might be his niece. It was a big, affectionate, loud family, and their laughter was the soundtrack of the night.

Once the duty dances were over and then the dinner dishes cleared away, Beth lost track of time handing out mimosas to the women and mostly beer to the men. Once the older folks and kids went off to bed, the drinks would get stronger, but for now it was easy work.

"So you really don't have a cell phone?"

Or it would be easy work if her body wasn't tuned in like a quivering antenna to the vibe Kevin was broadcasting. "I really don't. Another Sam Adams?"

He held up a half-full bottle. "I'm set. Mike grabbed me one."

Then why are you over here? "Okay."

"Even my mom has a cell phone, and she can't figure out how to check her email."

"Why are you so hung up on my not having a cell phone?"

"Hung up?" He laughed. "Hung up. Cell phone. Get it?"

She rolled her eyes, but couldn't stop herself from laughing with him. "That was bad. And I washed my cell with my jeans and haven't gotten around to replacing it yet."

"Got a phone at home?"

"Yup." She turned away to make another mimosa for the beaming woman she'd figured out was the mother of the bride.

When she was done, Kevin slid a cocktail napkin toward her. "Got a pen?"

There was one next to the register, but when she held it out to him, he ignored it. He just grinned at her, with the pretty blue eyes and the oh-so-charming dimples.

"Oh, hell, no," she said. "I'm not writing my number on a napkin so you can add it to your collection."

"I don't have a collection because I don't want their numbers. I want yours."

Before she could respond, another of the boys ran up and yanked on his arm. "Uncle Kevin, it's time for the cake!"

Beth used the blank napkin to wipe down the bar, then tossed it in the trash. She was there to work, not dodge advances from a guy who thought his dimples would make her throw herself at him.

The dimples wouldn't. The whole package might—the looks and the sense of humor and the very sweet way he was with his family, along with the steamy way he looked at her—but she wasn't going to be a number on anybody's napkin.

IT WAS ALMOST TWO in the morning before the staff got the go-ahead to call it a night, and Beth sighed in relief as she yanked out the elastic holding her hair back and tossed it into the trash. It had been one hell of a night.

Kevin Kowalski was persistent, she'd give him that. She'd sucked it up and presented him with nothing but bland professionalism until he'd seemed to catch the hint. Still, every time her gaze had landed on him—which had been a lot more often than she cared to admit—he'd been watching her. When they'd dropped the lights, signaling to the stragglers the party was over and it was time to get the hell out, he'd given her one last inviting look. She'd turned her back, making busy with a bus pan, and when she turned around, he'd been gone.

The pay phone beckoned, waiting for her to call a cab to take her home to her bed, but first she snuck out the back door and walked down toward the water. The grounds were beautiful, and now, with the twinkling party lights off, the moon dancing across the water beckoned. It was quiet, soothing her frazzled nerves.

"You look beautiful in the moonlight."

She didn't scream, but her heart seized in her chest like a blown engine. Because he startled her, of course, not because of the words Kevin said in a voice a man usually used with a woman who was naked under him.

He was sitting on one of the stone walls with a half-empty bottle of beer, his long legs stretched out in front of him and crossed at the ankles. The jacket, bow tie and cummerbund had been abandoned somewhere, and the white dress shirt was unbuttoned, baring his chest to the chilly night air. She tried not to give him the satisfaction of looking, but the expanse of chest led to taut abs she'd have to be dead not to want to run her hands over.

To his credit, he didn't gloat at being so obviously ogled. He reached down under his legs and picked up an unopened beer. After twisting off the top, he held it out to her.

She shouldn't. Even though she was off the clock, she was an employee and he was a guest. But there was something so lonely about the way he looked—unlike his usual life-of-the-party self—she couldn't bring herself to refuse and walk away.

"Thanks." She sat farther down the wall and took a sip of the ice-cold beer. Cloaked in the shadows, watching the moonlight ripple across the water, she had no idea what to say.

Then he grinned at her, and even in the dark, she could see those impish dimples. "Did your boss tell you we tried to get you free for a dance?"

"Oh, my God, what did you do?" Though it wasn't *really* his fault she'd lost her last job, if she got fired again because he stuck his nose in her business, she might need a restraining order just to stay employed.

"Joe—the groom and my oldest brother—asked your boss if you could leave the bar long enough for a dance. She refused, so he offered to pay extra. Then she got really snooty and informed us, 'this isn't a dance hall and the young ladies in her employ are not for private hire.'"

His fake, snooty old-lady voice made her laugh, despite her utter disbelief at what they'd done. "And why would Joe do that?"

"Because I wanted to dance with you."

The stark simplicity of his response made her shiver, and the tingle of desire mixed with leftover warm and fuzzies made for a dangerous combination. "I counted at least a dozen women who would have danced with you free of charge."

His eyes were serious when he looked at her again. "I'm not that guy."

"What guy?"

"The guy you think I am."

The only thing she knew for sure about him was that she was trying like hell not to want him and doing a piss-poor job of it. "I don't think anything. I barely know you."

"Dance with me now."

She laughed, and it sounded loud in the still night. "I haven't danced in years."

He put down his beer, then took her hand and pulled her into his arms. She set her bottle on the wall so she wouldn't spill it down his back. She'd tried resisting him, but it was a lost cause. Wrapping her arms around those broad shoulders was inevitable.

As her hands clasped behind his neck, his arms circled her waist and pulled her close. "You don't dance in your kitchen? You know, when you're all alone?"

"No. I don't dance in my kitchen, even when nobody's looking."

"You should. It's good for the soul."

No, good for the soul was swaying in his arms to the rustling, chirping music of the night as the water-reflected moonlight rippled over them. Okay, maybe not good for the soul, but it sure as hell was good for her body.

"Are you going to get all prickly on me if I try to kiss you?"

She tilted her head back so she could see his face. "I guess that depends on how well you kiss."

Kevin's eyes smoldered at the challenge—and invitation—and he threaded his fingers through her hair so he could tilt her head to just the right angle. Her eyes slid closed, and she sighed—a soft, breathy sound she couldn't believe she'd made—as he touched his mouth to hers.

The man could kiss, and as the aching desire of the present wrapped up with the steamy memory of her dreams, her body practically trembled with need.

"Stay with me tonight," he whispered against her mouth.

Some logical voice in the back of her mind wanted to argue against staying, but she didn't want to hear it. "Yes."

He took her by the hand, and, after they grabbed their beer bottles, they raced across the manicured lawn. They slowed down in the hall, where she hoped they wouldn't run into any of the staff as they dumped the bottles in the trash, and then tried their best to behave in the elevator.

Kevin managed to unlock and open the door to his room one-handed, his other hand still holding hers, then he closed it behind them and pressed her up against the wood.

"Watching you tonight and not being able to touch you was killing me," he said, and then lowered his mouth to hers.

She wrapped her arms around his neck and lost herself in the kiss, aware that even as his tongue danced over hers, he was slowly and not so stealthily trying to unbutton her shirt one-handed. It had been way too long since she'd been kissed, never mind had a man's hands on her, so she pushed his hand aside to hurry it along. As his tongue brushed hers and their breath mingled, she unbuttoned her shirt and then slid her fingertips under his, feeling the solid muscles twitch under her touch.

Then his hands were on her shoulders, sliding her shirt off, and she let him go so it could drop to the floor. She dropped her bra after it. His gaze raked over her, the look in his eyes as smoldering hot as his touch.

His shirt joined hers at their feet as he stripped down to just his pants, and then, before she was quite finished admiring the broad expanse of naked chest, his hands and mouth were on her again. When he lifted her off the ground, she wrapped her legs around his waist and held on to his neck.

His kiss grew more urgent, and she couldn't stop her moan when he backed her up against the door. With the cool wood against her skin and his hips between her thighs, her body trembled in anticipation.

Kevin licked his way down to her breasts, where his tongue flicked across one nipple and then the other. "You are so…freakin'…hot."

She didn't want to talk. She wanted those hips moving against hers as they had while they'd danced in the moonlight, but without any clothes between them.

As if he could read her thoughts, he turned and started toward the bed. She laughed when he dropped her onto the mattress, but the sound died in her throat when he dropped his pants and boxer briefs in one smooth motion.

Oh, yes, staying was *definitely* the right decision.

Ten minutes later, he had her naked, too, and so desperate she was horrified when a frustrated growling sound tore from her throat. He only chuckled and kept right on teasing her—kissing and licking and touching her, but never quite enough to give her what her body yearned for.

Finally, just about the time she was sure she'd go mad, Beth heard the telltale crinkle of a condom wrapper being torn open.

He settled himself between her thighs and rested his weight on his forearms so he could look down at her. His smile was warm, but his face was flushed, and naughtiness lurked in his gaze.

For a second she thought he was going to tease her some more, which might make her scream, but he kissed her instead. Beth threaded her fingers through his hair as he reached one hand down between their bodies and finally gave her what she wanted.

They both moaned as he slid into her, the sound mingling on their joined lips. He moved slowly, with short, gentle strokes, and she raised her hips to meet them. She savored the sweet friction of every thrust as he murmured in her ear—telling her how hot she was and how amazing it felt and how he never wanted it to end.

As his pace quickened, Beth ran her hands over his back, reveling in the light sheen of sweat and the way his muscles rippled under her touch. She was drowning in the intensity of his blue eyes, and she closed her eyes as the long-awaited orgasm took hold. He thrust harder, and she heard him groan as he found his own release.

As the tremors faded, he lowered himself on top of her, a hot, heavy weight she didn't mind at all. He kissed the side of her neck, and she smiled, stroking his hair. They lay like that a few minutes, catching their breath, before Kevin rolled away. She felt the bed shift under his weight, and then he was back, pulling her against his body.

"I'm glad you stayed," he said into her hair.

"Me, too." Very, very glad.

A NIGHT ON HER FEET followed by a night on her back under Kevin without sustenance had Beth awake at too-early o'clock, her stomach rumbling in protest. Doughnuts, she thought. She'd sneak down to the continental breakfast nook, filch some doughnuts and coffee, and be back before Kevin woke.

It took her a few minutes of rummaging to find her clothes, and, when she was dressed, she went digging through Kevin's clothes for his hotel key card.

And found napkins. The cocktail napkins she'd handed out with drinks, though they hadn't had names and phone numbers scrawled on them at the time. Oh, and fun notes, too. *I'm a former gymnast and I can still hook my ankles behind my head. Call me!*

When she snorted, Kevin rolled over, barely cracking his eyes open, and muttered, "Make sure you lock the door when you leave."

Beth froze as all the warm afterglow left her body in a disappointed whoosh. So much for him not being *that* guy.

She didn't waste any more time hunting for his key card. Slipping into the hallway—and making sure the door locked behind her—she told herself she'd never see the man again.

And this time she meant it.

CHAPTER THREE

THREE WEEKS LATER, Beth was doing laps of the drugstore. She'd spent ten minutes analyzing lip balm. Another five smelling cheap air fresheners. Fifteen picking a card for her mother's birthday, which was still three months away.

Anything to avoid her real destination—the feminine stuff aisle. The one with the tampons and freshening-up things and creams. And home pregnancy tests.

They'd used a condom. And she was only a week late. It could be stress. She should just take her lip balm, birthday card and paranoia and go home.

But her cycle ran like Swiss clockwork. And condoms were ninety-eight percent effective, which meant they had a two percent failure rate. She had a gut feeling statistics were about to kick her ass.

It only took her a few minutes to find the test

that promised to be accurate as early as her first late day, and five more to walk home.

The smell hit Beth as she reached the top of the second flight of stairs and turned down the hall to her apartment—old cat urine and stale poverty. She should be used to it by now, since she'd lived in the building for three months, but she'd yet to acquire immunity to the smell of cat piss. It was a good thing she planned to be on to the next city before summer came around again.

But what if there was a blue plus sign in the window?

Her key was ready in her hand, minimizing the time she had to stand in the hall, and she closed the door as quickly as she could once inside. It wasn't a lot warmer, thanks to a landlord who seemed to think ancient furnaces and a lack of insulation were sufficient for a New England winter, but it smelled a lot better. And that was thanks to a whole lot of elbow grease, *not* her landlord.

She tossed the drugstore bag on the card table that passed for a dining-room table, then crossed to the ancient rocking chair she'd rescued from the sidewalk to take off her shoes. The only other piece of furniture in the apartment, besides the metal folding chair that made the card table a dining room *set,* was a twin bed she'd picked up cheap at the Goodwill store. And it would all be donated back to Goodwill when she was ready to get on a bus again in three or four months. Whenever the mood struck.

Unless there was a blue plus sign in the window.

She couldn't have a baby. A baby meant a home. A real home, not a cheap apartment or by-the-week motel room. And a minivan. Moms drive minivans.

Beth didn't even have a car, never mind a Mommobile. She liked the bus—it was somehow reminiscent of hoboes riding the rails. She'd land in a small city she liked, find a job and a place to live, then earn enough money to move on to the next place.

It made income tax time a horror show, but she loved her life. Landing in a new place with nothing but a backpack and one suitcase was like starting over once or twice a year. Nobody to answer to, especially her parents. Leaving their nest, and keeping her nest on the move, kept them from hovering too much.

She wasted as much time as she could. The apartment was spotless, but she had a coffee mug and a spoon to wash. She sorted her laundry, checking her pockets carefully since she'd washed and dried her last cell phone. It hadn't been a big deal because Derek the drunken asshole had supplied her with a BlackBerry, but he'd demanded that back. She always had a landline, though, just to please her father. He'd also coerced her into keeping one low-limit credit card she rarely used along with the landline so at least she'd have something on her credit report should she ever grow up and buy a house. What he didn't seem to understand was leaving them behind, living the way she did, was the only way she *could* grow up.

When there was nothing left to distract her, she opened the home pregnancy test packaging and unfolded the directions. And…her telephone rang.

Credit report be damned. She wasn't paying for caller ID, but it was either her parents or her boss. "Hello?"

"Were you planning to come home for the holidays?"

Her mother never said hello. She just opened her mouth and let her train of thought run loose. "I'm not sure yet."

She wasn't sure of anything with that damn plastic wand sitting on the table. She usually took the bus down to Florida at least twice a year for a visit, once usually being for Christmas.

"Adelle and Bob want us to go on a cruise with them because the Donaldsons were going to go with them but had to cancel last minute. They can transfer the tickets to us, but it's in six weeks. Can you believe that? *Six!* Whoever heard of such a thing?"

"Who's going to cover your line dancing classes? And knitting class? And the other billion classes you teach?"

A patented Shelly Hansen sigh. "Your father thinks I should slow down a little. We're not getting any younger, you know."

"You're only fifty-two, Mom." Just like that it hit her. She was twenty-six. The exact same age her mother had been when she gave birth to her only child who'd survived to term. "Crap."

"What's the matter? Is something wrong?"

"No, I...stubbed my toe." It was on the tip of her tongue—the urge to lean on her mother's shoulder, even by phone.

But she'd put off doing the test, so now she didn't know for sure, and she'd hate to get their hopes up. Though she'd disappointed them by dropping out of business school to be a nomad, they loved her unconditionally, and a grandbaby would make them ecstatic. And they'd rejoice at her having an irrevocable reason for growing up.

There was also a possibility they'd drop everything and show up on her doorstep. The problem with being the only baby to survive five pregnancies? Smothering. Crushing, suffocating micromanagement and hovering. With the amount of time they'd spent coddling and hugging her as a child, she was surprised she'd gotten enough oxygen.

Then came her teen years. Where was she? When would she be home? The constant checking in. It only got worse when she started business school, and that's when she'd first packed a suitcase and gotten on a bus. Not to sever her claustrophobic relationship with her parents, but to save it.

"About that cruise..."

Beth smiled, picturing her mother picking at her thumbnail. "You should go, Mom. Really. Where I work now gets busy with Christmas parties and stuff."

"Are you sure? We can go another time."

"I'm sure. Go with Bob and Adelle while you can. You know you and Dad will get bored with each other if it's just the two of you. Send me postcards."

"You won't move while we're gone, will you?"

That made her laugh, which got another sigh. "No. I'll stay put so you don't need to worry about me."

They chatted a few minutes about life in a Florida retirement community. Her parents were on the young side, her father being a wise and lucky businessman, but it suited them as well as her wandering suited her.

"Your father's waiting for me now. He's got a coupon for the salad bar, but it's only good during early-bird hours."

After her mother assured her several times her cell phone would work on the ship, they said goodbye, and there was nothing left for Beth to do but pee on a stick.

Three minutes later, there was a blue plus sign in the window.

Her future flashed before her eyes. Diapers. Minivans. And Kevin Kowalski.

I CAN SUCK A GOLF BALL through a garden hose. Call me!

Because he was a gentleman, Kevin gave the woman a wink and a wave instead of letting her know claiming a level of suction that would turn his balls inside out wasn't really all that sexy. And he waited until she was gone before tossing the napkin in Paulie's direction.

It was almost a full minute before she stopped laughing. "Be cheaper in the long run to stick your dick in a vacuum hose."

He shuddered, then took the napkin back and tossed it into the basket Paulie kept next to the register for that purpose. The guys would like that one.

"You should keep her number," Paulie said. "She might come in handy if the sink gets clogged again."

She was still laughing when she walked by, balancing a tray of drinks, and he slapped her on the ass as she went.

Paulie Reed was his assistant manager-slash-bartender-slash-waitress, and she brought in the big bucks. Flaming red hair, breasts that mounded into cleavage so spectacular a man could suffocate in there. Slim waist, legs that went on forever and she knew the ERA for every pitcher to take the mound at Fenway. She was a walking, talking, stats-spouting wet dream for a sports-bar-frequenting kind of guy, but if you laid a hand on her, chances were you wouldn't be able to hold a fork for a while.

She'd come with the bar when he bought it a couple years back, and it had taken him all of about five minutes to realize she was worth every penny Jasper had paid her. It had taken another few days and one misguided, mutually disappointing kiss in the kitchen pantry to realize she might be one of the hottest women he knew, but they had zero sexual chemistry.

And speaking of sexual chemistry, he looked up just in time to see Beth walk through the front door, and the memory of their chemistry had an immediate effect on his anatomy.

She was either on her way to or from work, but even in a stiff white blouse and black pants, she would have turned his head. But unfortunately, she'd already turned his head and then turned him upside down with her little Cinderella act. Before he'd even opened his eyes the morning after Joe's wedding, he'd been looking forward to taking Beth out for breakfast. And maybe breakfast the following morning, too.

Instead, she'd been gone. No note. No phone number jotted down on the notepad next to the phone. Nothing. The people she worked for wouldn't give him a damn thing. It had crossed his mind a few times to give Officer Jones a call. If her info was on the police report from her boss's arrest, maybe Jonesy would trade it on the sly for another pair of Celtics tickets.

Pride had kept him from picking up the phone, though. If she had wanted to see him again, she would have given him a way to contact her. But now, almost a month later, here she was.

"Hey, stranger," he said, maybe too pointedly, when she'd hoisted herself onto a bar stool.

"Hi. Sorry I didn't leave a note on my pillow. I didn't think there was much of a point since it wasn't going anywhere."

It might have gone somewhere if she hadn't dumped him like a bad blind date. "I'd hoped it would at least go as far as breakfast."

She gave a short, barking laugh. "If you wanted me to stay for breakfast, you shouldn't have told me to lock the door behind me when I left."

He said *what?* "I don't remember that."

"You couldn't even be bothered to wake up all the way. You kind of mumbled it at me and capped it off with a snore."

He would have slapped himself in the forehead if she wasn't standing there, watching him. "Listen, I was asleep. I swear, my plan was to take you out to breakfast. Get to know each other better and find out how soon I could see you again."

She didn't believe him. He could see it on her face. "I'm supposed to be happy you didn't *mean* to send me on the walk of shame?"

It was a trap. Not an obvious one, but her tone and her body language suggested he had one foot hovering over a spear-lined pit. "I don't know if it will make you happy to hear it, but I wanted you to stay."

"Uh-huh. Makes me very happy to know I slept with a man who sends so many women on the walk of shame, he gives the exit line in his sleep by habit."

"Beth, come on. I'm a single guy. I own a sports bar. I live right upstairs. You knew I wasn't a virgin."

"No, but I didn't know you were a—" She stopped and raised an eyebrow at him. "Never mind."

Never mind *what?* He didn't want to never mind. He wanted to know what he'd done to deserve her low opinion of him. Unfortunately, Paulie chose that moment to appear at his elbow, obviously angling for an introduction. He never should have told her about that night.

"This is Paulie," he said obediently. "She's my assistant manager. Paulie, Beth. She's... Well, you remember her. I broke her boss's nose a couple weeks back."

What was he supposed to say? *This is the woman I told you about. The one I thought maybe was special, but she obviously didn't feel the same. And no, I won't say she broke my heart, but, yeah, it hurt a little.*

He watched the two women shake hands, each giving the other a speculative look, and gave a sigh of relief when Paulie walked away after mutual nice-to-meet-yous were exchanged.

"I guess I deserved that," Beth muttered.

"What did I do?"

"You couldn't just introduce me as a friend? Or an acquaintance, at least?"

Paulie didn't need to know she was the woman he'd thought might be special. "Was trying to avoid making you feel awkward. Failed, I guess."

"No, I… Sorry. I'm a bit out of sorts. Can we talk? Privately, I mean. Or should I come back another time?"

He couldn't imagine what they had to talk about, but he'd play along. His office had stacks of paperwork on every flat surface except his chair, though. "Paulie can handle the bar. We can go upstairs where it's quiet."

Her expression was grim, and, having some experience with rowdy patrons, he wondered if Derek the drunken asshole boss was making good on his threat of lawsuits.

He'd find out soon enough, he thought as he signaled for Paulie to take over for him. And he'd find out her damn phone number, too.

KEVIN DIDN'T TALK ON THE WAY up to his apartment in an elevator that looked more like a decrepit, oversize dumbwaiter. His silence made Beth nervous, but it also gave her more time to rehearse what she was going to say. Of course, she'd been rehearsing for two days and still had no clue what was going to come out of her mouth. She'd talked to her mirror, to herself, to her ceiling in the middle of the night. Didn't help at all when she was standing here next to the man whose life she was about to turn upside down.

As he unlocked his apartment door and gestured her inside, her hands started to shake. He pointed to the couch and told her to have a seat, but she chose to sit in the single armchair. If he sat next to her—close enough to touch her—she might chicken out.

"You look awfully serious." He sat on the couch, across from her, and propped his elbows on his knees. "And it's not like you can lecture me on not calling you, since you didn't leave your number. Hell, you didn't even leave behind a glass slipper on the front step."

"Sorry for leaving like that, but I didn't see any point in staying." He looked as if he was going to respond, and she didn't think she had the patience for explaining her Cinderella act, so she blurted it out. "I'm pregnant."

That shut his mouth with a snap.

"I know you used a condom," she continued when it became obvious he wasn't going to say anything, "but I… Let's just say I'd been in a bit of a drought and I haven't been with anybody else since, so, somehow, it's yours."

"A baby."

"Yes."

"My baby."

"Yes."

"Wow." He leaned back against the couch, rubbing his hands on the tops of his thighs. "You're sure?"

"I haven't been to the doctor yet, but I took a home test and…yes, I'm sure." She braced herself for whatever was to come. Denial. Accusation. Maybe he'd even throw her out.

And if he did that, she'd go. And if he still felt the same way after taking some time to digest the news, she'd be just fine. Having done the right thing and informed him of the situation, she'd be free to get on that bus to Albuquerque. Or maybe Florida, just to be closer to her parents.

"Are you okay?" he surprised her by asking. "I mean, are you feeling okay?"

She nodded. "I think it's still too early for morning sickness. I got a book from the library yesterday and it said between four to six weeks. But some women don't even get it. I'm hoping I'm one of the some."

He still looked a little shell-shocked. "You're keeping the baby, then?"

Even as she opened her mouth to tell him she was, her subconscious coughed up another alternative. She'd seen the Kowalski family dynamic at his brother's wedding. They were close. Loving. She could stick it out nine months, then give the baby to Kevin and get on a bus.

Even as the thought snuck into her brain, she looked down and watched her hand come to rest on her stomach, as if it had a mind of its own. She didn't know what would happen in the next nine minutes, never mind the next nine months. But she wouldn't be walking away from her baby.

She watched horror creep into his features and anger tighten his jaw. "No."

"No what?"

"Don't do it," he said, and there was a pleading note in his voice that didn't make any sense.

"Don't do *what?* I didn't say anything."

"Don't have an abortion. Please."

Frustration had a way of shortening her fuse,

but she took a deep breath and realized she hadn't said anything when he'd asked if she was keeping the baby. He'd assumed the worst. "I never considered that, Kevin. I swear."

He blew out a breath and scrubbed his hands through his hair. "I don't know what you want from me."

"I don't want anything from you. I thought you had a right to know, that's all. Now you know."

"I didn't mean that the way it sounded. I meant more like...I don't know what to do."

She gave a short laugh because it was either that or cry. "Join the club."

"Do you need money?"

"I'll make do." She always did.

"You don't have any insurance, do you? Not being temporary part-time."

The last thing she wanted to do was have this conversation with him. "No, I don't have insurance, even though I have a second job at a family restaurant now. And my mother had three miscarriages before she had me and one after, so I'm scared I'm going to lose this baby because I can't afford a really good doctor. So after years of telling my parents moving around a lot doesn't make me irresponsible, I'm going to have to ask them for money."

Crap. She hadn't meant to tell him that much, but when she'd opened her mouth, the panic that had kept her up the night before had just sort of spilled out. Inside, Mister Happy-family-with-enough-money-to-throw-a-fancy-wedding-bash-with-an-open-bar was probably recoiling in horror.

The tears spilling onto her cheeks were the last dollop of whipped cream on the whole steaming hunk of humiliation pie.

"You don't have to ask your parents for money." Kevin handed her a few paper towels, which she used to hide her face as much as wipe her eyes. "They're not having a baby. We are, and we'll be fine."

We. Part of her was relieved to have a partner in panic and uncertainty, but *we* was also a level of togetherness she hadn't expected to share with anybody for a while, especially with a guy whose Rolodex was filled out in Do-Me Fuchsia lipstick.

"Sit here and relax a few minutes," he told her. "I've gotta run down to my office, but I won't be long."

"I should go." She was tired, and emotionally, she was as wrung out as a cheap chamois cloth.

"Just give me a few minutes. I need to check on something and I'll be right back."

How could she say no? The poor guy not only

had a weeping heap of drama dropped in his lap, but the news he was going to be a father, too. He was doing pretty well, she had to admit. "Okay. I'll stay."

Halfway to the door, he turned back. "Promise me you won't leave."

"I promise. I'll be here when you're done."

When he closed the door behind him, Beth collapsed onto the couch with her wadded-up paper towels and sighed. She wasn't going to see Albuquerque anytime soon. She'd be too busy staying here and being part of a *we* with Kevin Kowalski, whether she wanted to or not.

CHAPTER FOUR

KEVIN CLOSED THE DOOR of his office behind him,
shutting out the din of the bar, and sank into his
desk chair.

Holy shit, he was going to be a father. Dad.
Daddy. Holy shit.

Sure, he'd been thinking maybe it was time to
settle down. Find a woman who wouldn't screw
him up the way the first one had and maybe have
a couple of kids.

But not necessarily today.

Leaning back in his chair and folding his
hands behind his head, he tried to absorb it. Condoms weren't one hundred percent, a fact he'd
had drummed into his head by his father the first
time he borrowed the car to go on a date. But why
couldn't he be one of the two percent who won the
lottery or bought a fancy French painting worth
millions for fifty cents in a yard sale?

No, he was getting a baby. Less than nine
months from now he was going to be a father. He

took a deep breath, heard how ragged the exhale was and took another. Didn't seem to help.

But now wasn't the time to panic because Beth seemed a little shaky, and they couldn't both be shaky at the same time. He could handle this. He was ready to have a kid. He hadn't thought much about it, but he must be because during those awful few seconds after he'd asked her if she was keeping it and she hadn't answered, the thought of losing that baby had made his gut clench up so bad he'd thought he was going to puke on her.

For now he had to keep his shit together and come up with a plan. He had a nice savings account. The bar was running well into the black. He could get his hands on whatever money she needed. Hell, worst case, he'd hit up his brother. Those twisted books Joe wrote had him rolling in cash. For now he rifled through the filing cabinet until he found what he was looking for. Taking another deep breath that didn't seem to help, he picked up the phone and punched in the numbers.

It took longer than he'd thought, and he feared he'd walk into his apartment and find her gone. But when he finally made it upstairs, he found her curled up on his couch, munching on Cool Ranch Doritos and watching country music videos.

"I hope you don't mind," she said, holding up the bag.

"'Course not." He sat in the chair opposite the couch and propped his elbows on his knees. "So I made a phone call and my insurance company is totally run by a bunch of dicks. Even if we got married this week, I don't have a pregnancy rider and your pregnancy would be a preexisting condition anyway, so no coverage. Although the baby will be covered as soon as it's born."

Beth had frozen, a Dorito halfway to her mouth, but then her eyes widened. "Married? No, Kevin, I—"

"For the insurance," he interrupted. "Which is a moot point, I guess."

"Oh. Okay."

What did *that* mean? "Unless you think we should."

She looked at him as though he'd just suggested they have a quickie on the bar during a big game rush. "I don't think so."

He tried to ignore the unwelcome pang of disappointment that made no sense. He was like a freakin' roller coaster. Scared she'd say yes. Bummed she said no and at the way she'd said it. Must be the shock. "You're probably right. My brother and his wife got married because she got pregnant. She had like a total meltdown a while back. Thought he'd only married her because of the baby and all that."

Beth nodded, then munched on another chip, her gaze shifting to the television screen. Some guy in a John Wayne hat was leaning against the bed of a beat-to-crap old pickup wailing about something. He hoped she didn't get the baby hooked on that shit. He'd heard babies could hear stuff like that before they were born and you should buy them classical music CDs or something like that. He wasn't a big Beethoven fan, but no kid of his was going to be singing *yee-haw*, either.

"So..." He had no idea what to say.

"My due date's June 28."

He opened his mouth, but nothing came out. June 28. A deadline. A little less than nine months to get his shit together.

"I'm sorry," she whispered, staring down at the empty, crumpled bag she was twisting in her hands.

"I can buy more." She gave him a funny look, and he realized she didn't mean the chips. He moved over to the couch and put his arm around her. "Hey, there's nothing to be sorry about. We took precautions, but nothing's a hundred percent."

She scooted away—not far, but enough so he got

the message and dropped his arm. "You're taking this awfully well."

"Trust me, I'm totally freaking out on the inside."

She snorted. "So am I."

Sick of the harsh crinkling sound, he took the empty chip bag from her and tossed it onto the coffee table. "We'll freak out together. To really bad music."

"There's nothing wrong with country music."

"Sounds like somebody stepped on a hound dog's tail."

She laughed and shoved him away. "It does not. What do you listen… Oh, my God, I don't even know what kind of music you listen to and I'm having your baby."

"I don't even know where you live."

"In a third-floor apartment. Like you."

Two third-floor apartments. Two flights of stairs. They'd need safety grilles on the windows. Check the fire escapes. Jesus, neither of them had a yard. You couldn't raise a kid with no yard.

A kid needed a house. A yard. Fences and toys and a bike and a dog. Plastic plugs in the electrical outlets and…all that shit Mike and Lisa had raising four boys. They'd even put some kind of Velcro strap on the toilet lid.

"Holy shit."

"Are we starting to freak on the outside now, too?"

He hadn't realized he'd said it out loud. "I think so."

"You sure know how to turn a girl's life upside down, Kevin Kowalski."

"Feeling a little sideways myself, Beth…" *Shit.* He didn't even know her last name, and it was too late to hide the fact. Smooth.

Her laugh was short and cynical. "Guess I should have written it on a napkin for you."

THURSDAY NIGHTS WERE PRETTY slow at Jasper's, but Paulie didn't mind. They always drew in enough of the regulars and the drop-ins to make the time go by, but not so much of a crowd people were shouting and getting impatient.

Usually Kevin took Thursday nights off, but tonight he'd stuck around. Or his body had, at least. His mind was someplace else, and wherever that someplace was, it wasn't happy.

Paulie wiped her hands on a towel and walked to the end of the bar, where he was sitting and staring into an empty coffee cup. "Want a refill?"

"Last thing I need is more caffeine."

Her boss—and best friend—wasn't the type to

dwell on things so she leaned her elbows on the bar and propped her chin on her hands. "What's up with you?"

"Gonna be a dad."

Okay, she hadn't seen *that* coming. "No shit. Anything to do with the brunette you took upstairs yesterday? The one whose boss's nose you broke a few weeks back?"

"Beth. She and the woman I told you about— the bartender at Joe's wedding? Same woman."

"So...wow."

"Yeah." He was tapping the empty mug on the bar, so she took it away and dropped it into a bus pan. "Guess that ninety-eight percent effective warning on the box wasn't just legalese."

"Tell your parents yet?"

"Nope. Nobody but you."

A guy down the bar was practically leaning over it, waving his mug to get her attention, but he could wait. "You okay with it?"

He shrugged. "I wasn't expecting it, but...yeah. I think I'm okay with it."

"Is *she* okay with it?"

"Hard to say." He laughed. "I think she'd be happier if it was some other guy's."

"Cut it out," she yelled at the thirsty guy who'd

moved on to banging his glass on the bar. "I'll be right there."

"Go," Kevin told her. "I'm just going to hang out and watch the game for a while."

"No problem," she said, giving him a sympathetic look before wandering down the bar to check on her customers.

She gave the glass-banging idiot a refill with a side of dirty look. A group came in and took a table in the corner, in Darcy's section. A few regulars came in on their heels, dispersing to their usual spots, mostly at the bar.

"Boston suits at table ten," Darcy said. A petite, quiet brunette, she was Paulie's opposite in almost every way. And she was a great waitress with a sunny personality that made up for her total lack of interest in sports.

Paulie nodded, giving the group a once-over from behind the bar. Like other groups of businessmen from the city, they'd go one way or the other—they either wouldn't tip for shit or it was Darcy's lucky day. Couldn't tell from looking at them which type they were.

Dick Beauchamp was sitting with them, though, and he wouldn't let the staff of his favorite watering hole get stiffed. Odd to see him so early or in his suit, though. One of his companions threw back his head and laughed.

Paulie's heart stopped.

"Oh, shit." She dropped to the floor, hiding behind the bar.

"Paulie?" Darcy must have climbed onto a stool because she peered over the bar. "You okay?"

"No," she whispered, waving for the waitress to go away.

This wasn't happening. Of all the sports bars in all the world, Samuel Thomas Logan the fucking Fourth had to walk into hers?

"Go away," she barked at Kevin's kneecaps when he walked over to investigate.

"Tell me those aren't FBI agents hunting a tall, redheaded fugitive."

"Of course not, dumbass." It was worse. So much worse.

"Dick's bringing one of them over here," he told her. "Must want to show you off."

"Shit." She tried to scramble away on her hands and knees, but Dick's face popped over the bar.

"Hey, Paulie, you hiding back there? Got somebody here I want you to meet."

Before Paulie could strike a hurried bargain with a higher power, Sam Logan's face appeared next to Dick's. She froze, as did his expression for a long moment.

He looked a lot like he had the last time she'd seen him. Because he loved being outdoors, his tanned skin set off his green eyes. He kept his dark hair clipped short because he didn't have the time or patience to fuss with it or make salon appointments, so he simply ran a clipper over it as needed.

The suit was different, of course. The last time she'd seen him, he'd been wearing a tux, standing at the end of the rose-petal-strewn aisle with his best friend at his side. Their boutonnieres had been pale blush blossoms to match her bouquet. The same bouquet she'd dropped as she'd turned and fled, tripping over the long train of her wedding gown before she'd managed to gather it all in her arms and run.

His expression was similar, though. Stunned. "Paulette?"

"Paulette?" Dick echoed. "Hell, we just call her Paulie. How do you two know each other?"

"Please don't," she mouthed at Sam.

When he arched an eyebrow at her, she knew the gig was up and felt a pang of mourning for the awesome life she'd lived for the past five years. "How do we know each other? Very, very well, as a matter of fact."

Dick seemed to expect him to say more, but when Sam didn't elaborate, he laughed and slapped his shoulder. "Small world, huh?"

He could say that again. Jasper's Bar & Grille was the last place in the world Sam Logan should have shown up. Yet there he was, looking down at her as if she was a bug and he was wondering whether or not she was worth the effort of stepping on. Hopefully he'd decide she wasn't and she could scurry away and find a dark corner to hide in.

But Dick Beauchamp wasn't done yet. "Since you moved in just around the corner, you and Paulie will have plenty of time to catch up."

Moved in? Around the corner? Paulie's stomach somersaulted as she tried to push herself to her feet. If Sam was going to get revenge by spilling her secrets, she could at least try to salvage some of her dignity.

"Yes, we will." Sam gave her a smile that didn't reach his eyes. "I'll be in touch."

Paulie watched him walk back to his table, the knot in her stomach pulling tighter and tighter. She didn't want him to be in touch. He was from her old life, and there was no place for him in her new life.

Once they were alone, Kevin stepped close and

leaned against the bar. "You want me to throw him out?"

Yes, she did. And she knew he'd do it, no questions asked. "No. He won't cause any trouble."

Not to anybody else. Only to her. There was no doubt in her mind Sam Logan was going to cause her all kinds of trouble.

KEVIN DELIBERATELY WAITED until Sunday evening to make the drive to his parents' house.

The lives of Leo and Mary Kowalski revolved around their children and grandchildren, but Mary had declared those few Sunday hours off-limits to them. He was breaking the rules, but it was the only time he could be sure none of the others would be around.

Because it was off-limits hours, he rang the doorbell. His parents were getting up there, but no way in hell was he taking the chance of walking in on something no amount of Sam Adams would wash from his psyche.

"Kevin!" His mother looked happy to see him, but the worry was there around her eyes. "Your father and I were sitting on the back deck. It's getting chilly, but winter's coming so we're getting some fresh air while we can. Grab a drink and come on out."

He grabbed a bottle of iced tea from the fridge and zipped his sweatshirt before heading out onto the deck. His parents each had a lounge chair, so he pulled up the wicker rocker and eased into it. "You guys remember the woman who ran the bar at Joe's wedding? Beth?"

"How could we forget?" his mother asked. "They almost threw us all out into the street after Joseph tried to hire her to dance with you."

"Pretty brunette," Leo added.

"Yeah." He turned the bottle in his hands, then settled on picking at the corner of the label with his thumbnail. "When the reception was over I went for a walk and... She's pregnant."

They were both quiet a moment, exchanging one of those old-married-people looks he still couldn't decipher, but which made him squirm. He and Beth were both adults, but that didn't make telling his parents he'd accidentally gotten a woman pregnant any easier.

"Lot easier to walk with your fly zipped," Leo grumbled.

His mother swung her legs off the side of the lounger so she could sit up straight. "I didn't realize you were seeing her."

"We're not really seeing each other. We just *saw* each other that once, more or less. But I guess the… Well, the dates and all… She took a test. She's due at the end of June."

"And you're sure it's yours?" His father was always the practical one.

"I'm sure, Pop. She's not really a big fan, so I doubt she'd tie herself to me for the rest of her life if it wasn't mine."

Mary made a *tsk-tsk* sound that made him want to grind his teeth. "You didn't sneak away in the middle of the night, did you?"

"No, Ma." He swallowed past the lump in his throat that was probably his pride. "She snuck out. Didn't even leave a note."

"What are you going to do?" they asked at the same time.

He shrugged. "My insurance won't cover her, even if we got married. The baby will be covered, of course, as soon as it's born."

"Married?" Leo shook his head. "I may be old, but even I know having a baby's no reason to get married anymore."

"We're not. It only came up because her mother had a history of miscarriages, and she wants a good doctor, so if my insurance would've covered her, it would have been worth it."

"Surely she could get some kind of assistance," Mary said.

"Probably, but then she's limited to what doctors they'll pay for her to see. And she doesn't need assistance, Ma. She has me."

Her eyes warmed. "You're okay, then?"

"I am." He was, and he was sure Beth would come around, eventually. "To be honest, even though it's something neither of us planned—and yes, Ma, we used protection, not that it did any good—I'm more than okay. I think I'm a little bit happy about it."

"And Beth?" she asked.

"She's… Beth wasn't really thinking about settling down, so a surprise baby's tougher on her, I guess. But she wants to keep the baby and we're going to do this."

Leo raised his glass. "Congratulations then, son."

"Thanks, Pop."

He was surprised when his mother got up and walked over to hug him. "You'll let us know if she needs anything. And we'll have you both over for dinner soon. When she's ready."

"I love you, Ma."

"I love you, too. Now where does Beth live? Is it a nice place for a baby?"

"I haven't been there, but I get the impression it's not very nice. She rents cheap places because she likes to move around, not places for raising a child. And she doesn't have a lot of money, so it's probably not great."

Leo snorted. "We'll fix the hell outta that, son. Don't you worry."

"She has tomorrow off."

CHAPTER FIVE

BETH PULLED THE COVERS UP over her head, but the knocking didn't stop. It was cold, and her cheapskate landlord wouldn't turn the heat up until November first. Whoever was at the door could just come back later. Like in the spring when it wasn't too damn cold to put her feet on the floor.

Then the phone rang. She snaked her arm out from under the warm covers and snatched the receiver. "Hello?"

"Hey, answer your door."

"No."

Kevin laughed in her ear. "Come on. It's even colder in the hallway than it is outside. Ma's already complaining."

Beth bolted upright in the bed, the covers falling to her waist. "Your mother's here?"

Great. At least if it was cold enough, maybe her baby's grandparents wouldn't be overcome by the eau de cat piss. Way to make a great impression.

"Pop's here, too. Answer the damn door." Then

he knocked again, just in case she didn't get the point.

"How did you find out my address?"

"I traded Celtics tickets for it. And I'm not telling you who."

"I hope whoever got them enjoys the game, but go away."

"Come on, Beth. They were really good seats."

"Not cool, Kevin," she said into the phone before she hung up on him.

He knocked louder. Dammit, he was going to upset the neighbors. And if they complained and she got evicted because of a disturbance, she wouldn't get her deposit back.

Beth sighed and hopped out of bed, pausing long enough to pull on her old, fuzzy bathrobe before unlocking the door. She left the chain on and opened the door a crack.

"Stop knocking," she seethed.

"Let us in and I won't have to knock."

"You can't just drop in unannounced this early in the morning."

He leaned in close to the crack and eyed her attire. "Beth, it's eleven o'clock."

"Oh." Sleeping in on her days off was her sole luxury, but eleven was pushing it, even for her.

When he knocked again, she jumped back away from the door. "Cut it out!"

"Let us in!"

Since the cold was blowing in from the hallway, she closed the door and slid the chain off before opening it again. Kevin walked in, followed by his parents, and she closed it again. Then all she could do was watch as they emptied the contents of several bags from the local home improvement store onto the card table she pretended was a dining room set.

"Okay," his father said in that loud voice she'd noticed at the wedding. "We got the lead test, the mold test, the radon test."

"Smoke and carbon-monoxide detectors," Kevin added, stacking up a pile of small square boxes.

"How are you feeling?" his mother asked her.

A little lost, since she had no idea what was going on. "Fine, thank you. How are you?"

"I'm so excited," she said, and then she threw her arms around Beth. "Another grandchild!"

"You told her?" Beth accused Kevin over his mother's shoulder. "It's bad luck to tell too soon!"

He shrugged. "Trust me, it's worse luck to keep secrets like that from my mother."

"There's no GFI outlet in the kitchen?" Leo was making himself at home, looking around. "Is that even legal? Holy crap, you don't have a couch! Who doesn't have a couch?"

"Kevin, can I talk to you for minute?" When he looked around, as if looking for a private spot, she sighed.

"One room and a bath?" he asked.

"If you say the whole word bath*room,* it's technically two rooms. We can talk in the hall."

"What are you doing?" she asked when they were alone, if chilly.

"An old building like this has all kinds of potential problems. We just want to make sure it's safe for the baby."

"You don't think I can keep the baby safe?"

He raised an eyebrow at her tone. "Of course I do. But this kinda stuff—testing and whatnot—that's guy stuff."

"Guy stuff."

"Yeah."

"And what am I supposed to be doing? Knitting him a blanket?"

"Him? You think it's a boy?"

She sighed. "You totally missed the point."

"Okay, look. Your place is—"

"Mine," she interrupted. It wasn't much. Nobody knew that more than she did, but it was hers and she'd be damned if the Kowalskis were going to just bulldoze right over her.

His crestfallen expression made her feel guilty. "Sorry. Maybe I'm overstepping. If you say I am, I must be. I just don't know what I'm supposed to be doing. I mean, don't I get to do *anything* before the baby's actually born?"

That was so sweet she melted a little on the inside. "This is new to me, too, Kevin, but—"

"You can't stay here."

"What?" Did he mean while they were doing the tests? "Where am I supposed to go?"

"The apartment across from mine. Holy shit, it's cold in this hallway."

"Back up, Kevin. I just woke up and your father's yelling at me because I don't have a couch and—"

"Why don't you have a couch?"

She sighed. "Because I could only bring things I could get up two flights of stairs by myself."

"Nobody helped you move?"

"No."

"That's why you can't stay here."

"Because I don't have a couch?"

"No, because you're alone with nobody else to help you out. I think I can see my breath, you know."

She was going to kick him in the shin. Hard. "I didn't know anybody when I moved here. I do now, so if I decide to buy a couch I don't want or need, I'll call a friend to help me carry it up."

"I want you to move out of here and live in the apartment across from mine."

Whoa. One hell of an ambush before coffee. "Sure, because you just hand out empty apartments at random."

"You're not random. There are apartments over Jasper's. Paulie lives in the big one on the second floor. I've got one of the two on the third floor. The other one's empty. And furnished, so all you need is clothes and food."

"I can't do that." She shoved her hair back away from her face. "I can't just move into your building, Kevin."

"Why not?"

That stumped her for a few seconds. Because… she just couldn't. There was Kevin across the hall, for one thing. It was bad enough her new pregnancy hormones seemed to be causing some pretty steamy dreams. Seeing him every day?

Even thinking straight was beyond her right now. She was supposed to be saving her money for a bus ticket and a new start, not diapers and a mini-van. Not thinking about moving into a fully furnished apartment that could end up being a *home*. Home meant building relationships with people who would want to know where she was and what she was doing. Home meant hovering.

Albuquerque. That was the dot on the map her eye kept landing on.

She could still go. There was time to escape the New England winter and start a new life before she even started showing. Sure, it was harder for a pregnant woman to find work, but she'd manage.

But even as a part of her was mentally leaving town, another part of her recognized those days were over. And the man standing in front of her was a big reason why. The only way she could have disappeared would have been not to tell him, and she couldn't live with that. So now she was stuck.

She jumped when Leo jerked open the door and waved a discolored cotton swab in Kevin's direction. "We got lead paint."

Her stomach dropped. Lead paint? Weren't there laws governing that sort of thing in apartment houses?

But that probably required somebody to report it, and the people who rented apartments there were people who didn't have a lot of residential choices. But lead paint…that was so dangerous for the baby.

"Jesus, it's cold out here," Leo said. "And whose cat's pissing in the hallway? This place should be condemned."

He closed the door on them, and Beth would have laughed if there wasn't a hot ball of shame in the pit of her stomach. The Kowalskis were one of those perfect Cleaver family types, and they probably didn't get she lived there by choice, not necessity.

Sure, it was a shithole, but it was *her* shithole.

"I'm sorry about him," Kevin said. "He's not trying to be offensive. He's just…honest. This is no place for you, Beth. I can borrow my brother's truck and we could have you moved today."

Tears of frustration shimmered in her eyes, and she blinked them back. It was too much, too fast. He was bulldozing right over her. But to knowingly spend another night in an environment that was toxic to the speck of baby she was carrying? "How much is the rent?"

"We can worry about that later."

"No. We can't."

"Fine." He gave her an amount that was less than what she was paying, and she shook her head. "Beth, come on. You get the *mother of my child* discount. You know I wouldn't charge you any rent at all if I thought you'd let me get away with it."

"I don't sign long-term leases. I only rent month to month."

"I can live with that."

She wasn't sure she could, but she didn't have a choice. "Okay, but only because of the lead paint."

His grin lit up his face, making her feel warm despite the temperature in the hall. "You might wanna get dressed then because I'm about to unleash my mother and she'll have anything not on your body packed before I get back with the truck."

HE WAS ALMOST RIGHT. There were still a few things left to pack by the time Kevin got back to her building with Mike's truck. Most of it was shoved in garbage bags. No points for style. They just wanted Beth out of there.

So that's what they'd done, so efficiently that his parents were gone by suppertime. He'd worry about trading vehicles back with Mike later. Beth still had a few odds and ends left to unpack, but she was more or less home. And judging by the sigh of contentment as she sank onto the cushions, she really liked the couch.

"I have to call the utility companies," she said. "And the phone company. But I'm not going to worry about it right now."

"Oh, the phone. There's one here. An unlisted

number and we mostly just had it so whoever was staying here could use it. Mike and Joe and the rest of them have cell phones, but not Pop. If you want you can just give that number out to your job or whoever instead of trying to get yours switched over."

She started to speak, but he held up his hand. "And every month I'll bring the bill over and you can write me a check."

"Promise?"

"I promise."

"Okay. It sounds easier than trying to get my number switched over here, especially since I still have to deal with the landlord. Since I left without notice, I probably won't get my deposit back."

"Actually, we ran into your landlord downstairs while we were carrying some bags down. Wanted to know who was moving. He wasn't very happy, but Pop had a little chat with him about lead paint and other health hazards and he'll be sending the check to this address. As soon as you get it and it clears, we'll find out who does housing inspections and turn his ass in."

She didn't look quite as happy as he'd thought she would. "Thank you."

"No problem. So, you want to go out and find

some food? We could go downstairs and grab
something or we could go somewhere else."

"I don't think so. I appreciate everything you
did today—more than I can say—but I think I'll
stay in."

"You don't have any food. Nothing worth eating
after a day of moving, anyway. And we could catch
a movie, or stop by the video store and rent one."

Judging by her expression, she was about to
shoot him down. "Kevin, I don't think we should
see each other anymore."

He couldn't quite wrap his head around those
words. "We'll see each other all the time, since
we live across the hall from each other now. Plus,
there's that whole *you're having my baby* thing."

She blew out a breath and folded her arms
across her chest in a defensive way. "I mean, see
each other like…a relationship."

"You mean no more sex." That sucked. Maybe it
was a hormonal thing, and she'd change her mind
in five minutes. A man could hope.

"No." She blushed and shook her head. "Well,
yes, I mean no more sex. But more than that. No
more dates. We're just going to be neighbors who
happen to be having a baby together."

He was surprised by the disappointment that
resonated through him. Most guys would jump at

the chance to be off the hook with a pregnant lady. "I don't get it. I thought we had a good time. And not just the sex part."

"I did have a good time, but…I can't explain it."

"Can you try, because I'm not really sure what I did wrong here."

"You didn't do anything wrong. You're just a little overwhelming. I know you're trying to help, but…" She shook her head, as if struggling for the right words.

"You're carrying my baby, Beth, and if you thought I was going to let you go through this alone, with nothing but a lumpy old mattress in a house that smells like cat piss, you don't know me very well."

"I don't know you at all. That's the point."

"I still don't get it. I think I've handled this whole thing pretty damn well."

"You have. You really have. And now you're trying to take care of me, but I take care of myself. I don't really do relationships and you're a little… suffocating."

"Suffocating?" What the fuck was she talking about now? "How the hell does wanting you and the baby safe make me a bad guy?"

"You're not a bad guy. You're a great guy, actually." Tears welled up in her eyes and spilled out onto her cheeks. She dashed them away with an angry swipe of her hand. "It's just...too much and I'm so overwhelmed and I...I..."

"Come here." He sat on the couch next to her and pulled her into his arms. "No kinky stuff. Just a neighbors-who-happen-to-be-having-a-baby-together hug. See? Not even copping a feel."

She laughed against his shirt with a hiccupping sound. "It's just...you're being so wonderful about this baby and you actually seem happy about it and you're so together and I'm just a mess."

"I am happy about it. But I'm not the one carrying the baby—you are. And maybe my life's more settled and ready for a baby than yours is." He leaned back against the couch, taking her with him. "I'm sorry I'm coming across as pushy. It's just the way I am—if something needs to be done, I do it. If somebody in my life needs something and I can provide it, I provide it. But I'll try to back off...some."

"I think the most important thing for the baby is that we're friends."

"We are. And I think a friend, at a time like this, would order takeout for another friend as a housewarming gift."

"Chinese?" she asked in a small voice.

He hated Chinese food. "Sure. Unless my mother

threw them out, the second drawer down in the kitchen had a bunch of takeout menus in it."

He let her go so he could check and to give her a minute to wipe her face. The menus, collected by the various family members who'd crashed in the apartment, were still there, and he sifted through them, looking for a nearby Chinese restaurant.

"Kevin?" He looked up, trying to remember what the only dish he liked was called. "Thank you."

Standing there in jeans and a faded, well-worn sweater, with her hair messed up and her eyes a little red, she was so beautiful he looked at her for a long moment. He didn't want to just be friendly neighbors who happened to be having a baby together. He wanted to pull her into his arms and kiss her until neither of them could breathe.

But he'd back off…for now. "You're welcome."

DURING JASPER'S POST-DINNER crowd lull, Paulie ran up the back stairs to her apartment to grab a yogurt and a few minutes of peace. Serving up burgers and fries night after night could seriously put a dent in a woman's junk-food cravings, and she wasn't in the mood for anything fried. But she'd barely peeled the top off a tub of key lime goodness when somebody knocked on her door.

She set the container on the counter and answered it, almost choking on her tongue when she saw Sam Logan standing in the hall. "How did you get up here?"

"Came up the stairs, same as you did."

"Did you miss the sign telling you stay the hell out if you're not authorized personnel?"

"Saw it. Ignored it."

"Sounds like you."

He just shrugged. "You going to invite me in?"

"No."

"That's too bad." She noticed how he subtly turned his body toward her so she couldn't slam the door in his face. "Guess I'll go back downstairs, then. Maybe chat with my waitress. Or the bartender. What's his name? Kevin? Funny how they all seem to think your last name's Reed. Why is that?"

She'd forgotten what a bastard he could be when he wanted something. "Maybe I got married."

"Or maybe you just changed your name."

Which he knew, of course. No doubt he'd had his people run a check on her as soon as he'd left Jasper's that first night. Maybe he'd even known before then. "What do you want, Sam?"

"I want to come in."

"I don't think that's a good idea."

"Wonder how your friends in low places would feel if they found out who you really are?"

It wasn't as though she was running from the law or anything. She hadn't done anything wrong, so she had nothing to fear from them finding out her real last name was Atherton. But she didn't want them to know. She wasn't that person anymore. "Fine. Come in and say what you want to say. But make it quick. I need to get back downstairs."

When he walked in and closed the door behind him, Paulie was almost staggered by the sense of how unreal the situation was. Sam Logan. In her apartment.

"Why are you harassing me?" she demanded when it became clear he was more interesting in looking around than talking. "Is this some kind of payback for not going through with the wedding?"

"You didn't just leave me standing at the altar, which would have been humiliating enough. No, you had to go and make the whole thing into a damn spectacle. Getting halfway up the aisle before you turned and sprinted out of there like there was a gold medal in the parking lot. God, Paulette."

Paulie tried to ignore the trigger word, but it was a hot button. *Paulette, stop fidgeting. You're making a spectacle of yourself.* "And there you go. If I thought for a second you would have been more hurt than embarrassed, I wouldn't have run in the first place."

"So it's my fault."

"You didn't love me, Sam."

"I asked you to be my wife." His deep voice was taut with a barely restrained rumble of anger. "Why do you think I did that?"

"Because our families expected it? Because I fit your criteria for Mrs. Samuel Thomas Logan the Fourth?"

His jaw tightened. She knew from experience that was as far as Sam losing his temper would go. Like her, he'd been taught not to make a *spectacle* of himself before he'd even been potty-trained. "Is that what you think? You think I'm so weak I'd just let my parents choose my wife from a list of most-likely candidates?"

She wanted to deny it, but she couldn't force the words out. Yes, that's what she'd thought. And when he got up and started for the door, she should have been relieved. He was leaving, and he probably wouldn't be back, which is what she'd wanted. She thought. But the thought of leaving this still unsettled—unexplained—had her going after him.

"Sam, wait…"

He turned on her so abruptly she almost crashed into him. "If that's what you thought, why did you even say yes in the first place?"

"I wanted to be Sam's wife."

"Yeah, I could tell by the way you sprinted out of the church."

"I didn't want to be Mrs. Samuel Logan the Fourth."

There went that tightening jaw again. "I don't even know what that means. But I do know you're way too hung up on my name."

"Not your name. What it represents."

"So…what? You wanted to be with me, but you didn't want anything to do with everything that's integral to my life."

That summed it up pretty well. "It's complicated."

"Let's simplify it."

"How?"

"Go out with me. Nobody knows who we are here. I'm just a businessman from Boston and you're the saucy serving wench who struck my fancy."

The surprised laughter bubbled up before she could stop it. "Serving wench? Buddy, if I strike you, it ain't gonna be in your fancy."

"Dinner. Someplace nice."

He was serious. After the very public humiliation she'd caused him, followed by five years of radio silence, he was inviting her on a date? "Sam, that's just…not a good idea."

He crossed his arms and gave her a look meant to intimidate grown men into caving to his terms, but it hadn't worked when her father gave it and it didn't work now.

"Now, Sam, don't tell me you've been pining for me this whole time." The lines of his face hardened, making her think she might have actually hurt him. "Look, I—"

"Dinner with me or your friends find out you're a fraud."

He said it so coldly she knew he meant it. "Don't you think blackmail's beneath you?"

"Nothing's beneath me when I want something."

A shiver tickled her spine as his gaze bored into hers, making it very clear she was the thing he wanted. And she realized, with a sinking feeling in the pit of her stomach, that part of her was thrilled to be forced into having dinner with him. Not that she'd let him know that. "When?"

"Soon. On a night you don't work late."

She didn't want him to know when she worked late and when she didn't. But she also didn't want him talking to her coworkers. Or Kevin. "Maybe."

He smiled—no, *smirked,* the bastard—and went out the door, leaving her confused, off-kilter and maybe just a little excited.

CHAPTER SIX

THE FIRST THING KEVIN SAW the following night when he finally escaped the paperwork hell that was his office was Beth. She was sitting at the quiet end of the bar where nobody liked to sit because you had to crane your neck to see the television, picking at the last of her fries.

She looked beat. "Hey, you."

When she looked up at him, he saw he was right. The exhaustion showed in her eyes the most. "Hey. What's the secret to your cheeseburgers?"

"It's a secret."

That got a smile. "I could have eaten at the restaurant but I was serving a cheeseburger and thinking to myself it didn't look anywhere near as good as a Jasper's cheeseburger and…here I am. This big, empty space on my plate is where the burger sat for about five seconds."

"How was work?"

"Slow." She shrugged, but he could see how it was weighing on her. "They keep telling me it picks up as we get closer to Christmas shopping time. We'll see."

"You want a refill on your soda?"

"No, thanks. I'm exhausted. Need to get my check and head upstairs."

"What check?"

"For my cheeseburger. The bill?"

Leaning his elbows on the edge of the counter, he shook his head. "We're not taking your money."

He hadn't expected the way her mouth got all tight and her cheeks flushed red. "I can pay for my dinner, Kevin."

"I know you can, but you're feeding my kid. I'm not charging my own child to eat. What kind of father would I be?" He gave her his best Kowalski grin—the one with the sparkling eyes and the dimples. "You can come in here and get your fabulous, one-of-a-kind Jasper's cheeseburger every night."

She was about to argue with him—he could see it on her face—but Randy happened by and tossed a napkin next to Kevin. Even in the dim lighting the bright magenta lipstick kiss shone like a beacon. Dammit.

Beth was not only stubborn, but she was fast and she snatched it up before he could. "I have whipped cream and cherry lube...want to make a sundae?"

Even though the words weren't hers, hearing them come out of Beth's mouth triggered a craving for ice cream so strong his mouth watered. Other parts of his body reacted, too, and he was very thankful he was standing on the other side of the bar.

"I never call them," he told her.

"Them? You get these a lot?"

He gestured over his shoulder. "There's a basket. I get a few."

She tossed the napkin at him with a snort of disgust. "A basket. Of course you save them."

"Paulie and the rest of the staff get a kick out of reading them. I've never called a napkin kisser and you can go look in the office and in my apartment and you won't find a single phone number written in lipstick on a napkin."

She looked doubtful, not that he could blame her. "When was your last serious relationship, and I don't mean with the women who kiss your napkins?"

And there it was. The only thing he didn't like talking about and there was no way to get out of it. More privacy would have been nice, but at least nobody was close enough to eavesdrop. "My last serious relationship would have been my marriage."

She doodled in the condensation on her glass. "You were married?"

"Yeah. We divorced a little over two years ago."

"What happened? Oh, wait…none of my business. Sorry."

That hurt. They were having a baby together. He'd think she'd want to get to know him a little better. "Before I bought Jasper's Bar and Grille, I was a cop. One of Boston's finest."

"You were a cop? Really?"

"Yup."

She propped her chin on her hands. "I can't picture you in a uniform, with a gun and everything."

"I've got a picture. I can show it to you later."

"I'd like to see it, but I think what you're doing now really suits you."

He smiled, looking her in the eye. "There's a lot about my life now that suits me."

"Charming." She rolled her eyes. "So you were a cop…"

Damn, she was a tough sell. "Yeah, so I always got shitty shifts in the bad parts of town, but I didn't think much of it. Then, one night, I went back to the house to pick up some paperwork I'd forgotten. I didn't usually bring paperwork home because the time I had with Vicky, I thought I should spend with Vicky. Found my captain there, banging my wife. And I guess it'd been going on for a while."

"I'm sorry."

"I beat his ass until I couldn't swing my arm anymore. Thank God the captain was married to some big-shot's daughter so he had to avoid the bad press. He didn't press charges, I dumped the wife and the job and came home. Bought Jasper's and here we are."

The way she looked at him told him he hadn't quite succeeded in making it sound like no big deal. Bullshit, of course. Losing his marriage and his badge—everything he cared about—at the same time had been a pretty big fucking deal. Even the memory of his captain's nose busting under his fist didn't make the memory of seeing the asshole's dick in his wife any easier to take.

"Did you have any children together?"

"No. That's about the only good thing about it." He helped himself to a sip of her soda, hoping to wash some of the bad taste out of his mouth. Didn't really help. "That Jasper-burger-craving bun in your oven is my first."

For a few seconds he thought she might dig deeper, but then she smiled. "If the baby's craving

Jasper burgers already, I'm going to weigh a ton by spring."

"And you'll still be the hottest woman in the bar."

He wondered if she was even aware of the pink creeping into her face from under the collar of her white work blouse. "Sadly, I'm never going to kiss a napkin for you."

"If you did, I'd not only keep it, I'd frame it and hang it right there, over the bar."

"Never gonna happen."

"EXCUSE ME, BUT I ASKED for this well done." Beth eyed the burger her customer was waving in her direction. It looked more like a hockey puck than ground beef. "See this fleck of pink here?"

No, she didn't see a fleck of pink. "I'm sorry. I can have them make you another one."

"No, I'll eat it."

Then what was the point of complaining, other than advance justification for the crappy tip he was probably going to leave her? She made nice for another moment, hoping to salvage something, and then moved on to the next table.

Her section was almost full, and most nights she would have been happy about the potentially full tip cup. But she was tired and out of sorts.

And the problem with getting pregnant on their first date was that she couldn't pinpoint the exact start date or cause of her irritability. Was it the baby...or the baby's father?

"Miss, can I get some more coffee?"

She poured and fetched and carried for another hour before it was time for her break. After filling a coffee mug three-quarters full of decaf for the baby and a splash of the real stuff for herself, she made her way to the small table shoved into the back corner of the noisy kitchen.

The granola bar tucked into her apron pocket would get her through to the end of her shift, and, if she took small bites and chewed slowly, she could almost convince herself it was satisfying. She'd only lived over the bar a few days, and the Jasper burgers were already going to her waist.

Julia joined her when she was chewing the last bite. Rumor had it the salt-and-pepper-haired woman had been waiting tables there since the restaurant opened in 1976. Beth didn't know if that was true, but it was remarkable if it was because Julia was a bit cantankerous for the business.

"What's wrong with you this week?" Julia asked by way of a greeting.

"Just a little tired. I moved and you know how it is trying to sleep in a new place."

"When's the baby due?"

It was a good thing Beth was done with her granola bar or she would have choked on it.

Julia gave a short, smoke-roughened laugh. "I've got three sisters and two daughters and they've all had kids. Sometimes you get a faraway look on your face and put your hand over your stomach. Probably think you have cramps if not for the dreamy expression."

She hadn't wanted anybody to know yet, and that went double for her coworkers. And their employer. Not until she had a backup plan in case they fired her.

They wouldn't fire her because of her condition, of course. They'd find another reason to let her go because, right or wrong, a lot of people weren't comfortable being waited on by a visibly pregnant woman. Made them feel guilty.

"June 28," she said when Julia made a *come-on* gesture. "Please don't tell anybody. I… It's bad luck."

"Hell, I won't tell anybody, honey. You make sure you eat right and take your prenatal vitamins or you ain't gonna get through the day."

"I will."

"By eat right, I mean more than a granola bar, by the way. But I better go out back and have my smoke. And, if you don't want anybody to know you've got a bun in the oven, keep your hands in your pockets."

Beth smiled, but it faded as soon as Julia walked away.

It weighed on her constantly—the question of what she would do if or when she couldn't do this job anymore, whether because of her pregnancy or because she'd been fired.

The idea of not having an income was so repulsive it made even the benign granola bar roll in her stomach. She wasn't used to being responsible for anybody but herself, and her needs were pretty simple. A baby's weren't.

But now she had Kevin, the mini devil on her shoulder whispered. Kevin wouldn't evict her, and he wouldn't let her go hungry or without medical care. The plus sign on the home pregnancy test had seriously rocked her boat, but she had Kevin now. Kevin, who was able and willing to steady the boat.

The problem with that, the overly cautious angel on the other shoulder argued, was that Kevin would not only steady the boat, but he'd grab the tiller and steer her boat wherever he wanted.

Then, if he decided to abandon ship, she'd be

even worse off. Not only would her boat be rocked again, but she'd be lost without him. Helpless.

No, Beth wasn't going to depend on Kevin. She was having enough trouble keeping him at arm's length—a decision her body in no way supported, judging by the way it tossed and turned every night, aching for him.

"You still sitting here?" Julia's voice jolted her out of her thoughts.

She glanced at her watch. Oops. "Just finishing up."

She drained the rest of her coffee and dropped the empty mug into a bus pan. Then she tossed the granola bar wrapper into the trash and hit the restroom.

Time to paste on a sunny smile and concentrate on making as much money as she could—while she could.

A GLASS SMASHED BEHIND KEVIN, and he didn't even have to look to know Paulie'd done the dropping. How did he know? Because that Sam Logan guy was sitting at a front table—eating a burger, drinking a beer and watching *SportsCenter* on one of the big-screen TVs, like he had almost every night for the last two weeks or so.

Kevin ducked as Paulie went by him with the

broom, muttering words he couldn't quite make out under her breath. "You need help with that?"

"No."

Tempting as it was to keep his nose out of her business, Kevin knew that Logan guy got to her for some reason, and those glasses weren't cheap. "You wanna tell me who he is yet?"

"You know who he is." She squatted down and swept the broken glass into the dustpan. "He's a suit from Boston, building a swank conference center. Staying at that fancy bed-and-breakfast place down the street."

"I heard that. What I haven't heard yet is how you two know each other or why you're afraid of him."

Paulie stood and poked him in the chest. "I am *not* afraid of him. We had a thing once, okay? The thing ended, never thought I'd see him again, but here he is. End of story."

It wasn't the end of the story he was interested in. He wanted to know the beginning—how a guy like Logan and a woman like Paulie even met, never mind how they came to have a thing. "The offer still stands. I'll throw him out if it'll make you stop breaking my glasses."

"You've got no grounds to throw him out. He hasn't started a fight and he's not a Yankees fan."

"My bar, my rules. I can throw him out if I want to."

"Forget it." She gave him her best pissed-off-Paulie look. "End of story."

He shrugged, but gave Sam Logan a look none-theless. Since the man was watching them instead of *SportsCenter,* he didn't miss it. He didn't cower, though. Just smiled and raised his glass before taking a swig of Michelob. Kevin was debating whether or not to have a chat with the guy when the door opened and Beth walked in.

His nephews were big into superheroes, and Kevin knew enough about them to know being a Wonder Woman fan was a big hit with the ladies, but he'd never stopped to ponder what it meant when Spider-Man's spider senses tingled.

Now he imagined Spider-Man felt a little like he did when Beth walked into a room, minus the imminent danger on Kevin's part, of course. There was definitely some tingling, and it was as though he was hyperaware of her presence.

And there was some frustration, too. She *hadn't* changed her mind in five minutes about having sex with him. And because their primary interaction in the week since she'd moved in had been him listening for her door to open and close, he wasn't hopeful she'd change her mind anytime soon.

She didn't sit at the bar but walked down to the quiet end and waited for him. "I just wanted to let you know I did some looking around and found a doctor I think is really good. I have an appointment with her in a few days. Nothing big, just a test to confirm the pregnancy and verify my due date."

"Do you want me to go?"

Judging by her expression, no, she didn't. "No, I just thought you should know because...you know."

Because he was paying. "We should run down to the bank and open a *joint* account. It'll make it eas—"

"No." She said it so fast she cut off the end of his sentence. "We're not doing the joint thing."

"You came to me so we could share in the financial responsibility, Beth. So you could have a good doctor."

"Yes, and as the bills come in, if there's some I can't pay, I'll ask you to chip in. I never intended for you to foot the entire bill."

Rather than argue with her, he leaned on the counter and smiled. "You're getting prickly again."

When her gaze dropped to his mouth, he knew she was remembering the last time he made mention of her being prickly. The night he'd kissed her in the moonlight and changed their lives forever.

She sighed. "Okay, maybe a joint checking account isn't a bad idea, but only for the medical bills and I'll give you photocopies of all of them."

It was tempting to say, "There, that wasn't so hard," but all he said was, "Let me know when you've got time and we'll go down to the bank."

"Okay. Right now I have to get ready for work."

"You just got home."

"I'm bartending another wedding tonight, so I've got just enough time to take a power nap, shower and eat before I go."

"Should you be working so much?" That seemed like an awful lot of time on her feet.

"I'm fine." She was gone before he could do something stupid like tell her she should quit her job. As stubborn and full of pride as she was, that would only piss her off.

"Aren't we a pair?" Paulie said as she reached past him for a glass.

"At least I'm not breaking all the glasses." Yet.

CHAPTER SEVEN

BETH WAITED UNTIL AFTER the doctor confirmed what the calendar and home pregnancy test had already told her before picking up the phone and dialing her mother's cell phone. She was armed with a dish of chocolate ice cream. A big dish.

"You moved again, didn't you?"

She would have laughed at her mother's exasperated tone if not for the jittery nerves. "Actually, I did."

"You owe me a new pair of shoes," she heard her mother say, presumably to her father. "I wish you'd call *before* you move. When you don't, there are times I don't even know where my own daughter is. Where to now?"

"Same city. Just a new apartment." She snuck a quick swallow of frozen chocolate courage. "I have some news, actually. I'm, uh…having a baby."

The silent seconds ticked by, then her mother's screech pierced her head. "Oh, my goodness, I'm going to be a *grandmother!*"

In the background there was an eruption of cheers and congratulations that made Beth groan. "Mom, where are you?"

"We're at the all-you-can-eat luau buffet. Did you buy some of that frozen sperm? Or canned... however they do it."

Beth almost choked on her ice cream. Hopefully her mom had at least moved away from the crowd. "No, I... There's a guy."

She'd spent so much time focusing on how her parents were going to react to her pregnancy, she hadn't really thought about how she was going to describe Kevin. He wasn't just some guy who'd come and gone. But she didn't want her parents getting their hopes up on the matrimonial front, either.

"Artie, she has a man!" Beth licked ice cream off her spoon while her parents jabbered. "What's the man's name, Beth? We want to know everything!"

"His name's Kevin Kowalski and, well...he owns a sports bar and has a big family."

"How long have you been seeing him?"

A lot longer than she'd intended to. "We're not exactly seeing each other."

More silence. More ice cream. "Did he break

up with you because you got pregnant? Somebody should tell that man it takes two to—"

"Mom!" She should have brought the entire half gallon to the coffee table with her. "He didn't break up with me. We… It's complicated."

She resigned herself to telling her mother the entire story, wondering how much it would change in the retelling to her father. In the game of parental telephone, her mother was the queen of judicious editing and embellishment.

When Beth was done talking, her mom sighed. "Why don't you come back to Florida, honey? We'll find you a nice apartment close by so you have family to help you."

It was tempting. If ever she'd wanted her mother close, it was now. But if she'd thought the smothering was bad when she was younger, she couldn't imagine what it would be like while she was carrying their grandchild. "I'm going to stay here, Mom."

She could imagine all too well the look on Kevin's face if he had to watch her get on a bus and take his baby away. Not that she intended to live in his back pocket, but she wouldn't make him miss the birth of his child by fifteen hundred miles.

"Ask her if she needs money," she heard her father say.

"I don't need money. And, before you ask, I don't want you jumping off the boat at the next port to fly up here."

The sniffles came through loud and clear. "I want to hug you."

Beth smiled and licked the last of the chocolate ice cream off her spoon. "Just hearing your voice is like a hug, Mom."

"We should come home for Christmas."

"No, you shouldn't. It's not like you can play with your grandchild yet, so enjoy your cruise and we'll get together sometime after you get back."

"I shouldn't be out in the middle of the ocean. What if you need me?"

Beth would have laughed, because she'd guessed right about the potential for hovering, but she remembered just in time the miscarriages her mother had suffered. "I'm okay, Mom. Kevin's apartment is right across the hall, and Paulie, his assistant manager, lives below me, so I'm not alone. And I'll call you if I have any problems. I promise."

They chatted a few more minutes—most of that her mother making a list of all the people she had to call because she was finally going to be a *grandmother!*—and then Beth hung up and collapsed against the back of the couch.

She closed her eyes as her new reality sank in. It

was official. At the end of June she'd be a mother. The doctor had confirmed it, and Beth had told her mother. It didn't get any more official than that.

No more stepping off a bus wherever the mood struck, with only one suitcase to her name. And no more walking away from lipstick-phone-number-collecting guys who were trouble, no matter how charming and good-looking they were.

It was going to take a bigger freezer to hold all the chocolate ice cream in her future.

PAULIE IGNORED THE NEW TEXT message reminder beep for as long as she could—less than two minutes. Then she flipped the phone open while muttering every bad word she knew. And she knew a lot of them.

Meet me out front at six.

Pompous prick. Why?

Because I'm taking you to dinner. Dress appropriately.

Bite me.

Six. Sharp. Or else…

Paulie didn't bother to respond. She'd either be out front or she wouldn't. And she didn't intend for him to know which it would be until exactly six o'clock.

At four she clocked out and went upstairs. A

quick shower and then it was decision time. To go or not to go…that was the question.

She should let her absence send him a screw-you message because she didn't live under any man's thumb—especially the thumb of a blackmailing bastard. If she started letting him boss her around now, where would it end?

But there was a part of her—a needy, aching, missing-him part—that wanted to sit across from him in a nice restaurant, making eye contact over the rims of their wineglasses.

Maybe, if the wine was good and the vibe was right, she'd bring him back to her place because Mr. Samuel Thomas Logan the Fourth was as good in the bedroom as the boardroom. If he wanted to play games with her, she should at least get an orgasm or two—or three—out of it.

To hell with it. She'd go. Either it would go badly and he'd leave her alone, or it would go well and she'd get some really good sex out of the deal.

Dress appropriately. From deep in the dark recesses of her closet, where she never had to look, she pulled a garment bag. She slid off the dustcover and laid the suit across her bed. It was five years out of date, but only somebody like her mother would notice it. It was a classically cut jacket and skirt in a sedate navy. Matching pumps sat in a box at the bottom of her closet.

It was all nothing more than a designer strait-jacket. For the hundredth time she reminded herself she didn't *have* to do this. She could tell her Jasper's family who her real family was—the Athertons. Old Boston money. It wasn't as if she'd lose her job or her home.

But they'd look at her differently. They'd wonder why a nice girl like her was tending bar. The other waitresses would resent every dollar bill she took in tips when she had millions of them in her trust funds. Word would get around, as it inevitably did, and even her customers would treat her differently. Men didn't laugh and joke with wealthy women, or ask them what they thought of the Bruins' chances for the Cup.

No, she'd go along with Sam's stupid black-mail scheme for now. To keep her secret, as well as taking care of a certain itch Sam was particularly good at scratching.

It was a pain in the ass, but to avoid catching hell from her regular patrons, she went out the back door and walked around the building at six. She wasn't surprised to find a limo double-parked on the street, with a chauffeur holding the door open. Not wasting any time in the hope nobody watching through the bar window would recognize her, Paulie slid onto the seat and pulled her legs in.

And bumped shoulders with Sam.

"Hello, beautiful," he said, just as the door closed, leaving them isolated in a dimly lit, expensive leather-scented cave.

"Hello, arrogant ass." She wasn't going to make this easy for him. "I'm ordering the most expensive thing on the menu, just so you know."

"Nice to know some things never change."

"You're a funny guy." She braced her feet so she wouldn't lean into him as the car turned a corner.

"You look nice tonight," he said after a few minutes of awkward silence.

"You mean I look like you think I should."

"Are you going to be like this all night?"

"Like what?"

"Antagonistic."

"If your question is whether or not I'm going to behave like a woman being blackmailed into doing something against her will, then, yes."

When he threw back his head and laughed, she had to fold her hands in her lap to keep from backhanding him in the gut.

"We both know," he said, "that you wouldn't be here if you didn't want to be and to hell with any threats I may or may not have made."

"Oh, you made them."

She braced herself for more wiseass banter, so she was really thrown off-kilter when he tucked a strand of hair behind her ear. "I've watched you while you work. You look really happy."

She was...mostly. Sure, she'd spent more than a few lonely hours lying awake, playing the what-if game. What if she hadn't bolted from the church? What if she'd vowed to love and cherish him until death did they part? They'd be five years married now and, no doubt, the parents of the golden child—Samuel Thomas Logan the Fifth.

She'd be pearl-necklace deep in managing households and nannies and the endowments that would ensure no door was ever closed to Sammy the Fifth. Serving on charity boards. Attending benefit dinners and balls.

Blowing out an exasperated breath, Paulie shifted herself away from Sam. How freaking unfair was it that the man of her dreams came wrapped up with the life of her nightmares?

"Are you happy?" he prompted.

"I was."

"Was?"

Yeah, or at least she'd thought she was. Until the only man who'd ever heard the *L*-word cross her lips had strolled back into her life. "Blackmail's a bit of a mood killer."

The restaurant was expensive and classy—just the kind of place Paulie went out of her way to avoid—but she had to admit the wine was good. And, so far, Sam had resisted the siren call of whatever latest and greatest smartphone he was using now, giving her his undivided attention.

"You haven't asked me about your parents," he said after they'd ordered their entrées.

The rosy glow she'd been nursing while gazing into his eyes over the flickering candle evaporated like a drop of water on a hot skillet. "I look them up on the internet occasionally. Same society pages, different year."

"Have you called them at all?"

"No." If he was trying to weasel his way back into her pants, he'd picked the wrong topic of conversation. "What are we doing here, Sam?"

He took a sip of his wine, then shrugged. "I don't know what you're doing, but I'm here to enjoy a good meal and the company of a beautiful woman."

"And then what?"

He smiled at her over his wineglass, just the way he used to when the evening was winding to a close and making love was on his mind. It wasn't a cocky look, exactly, and maybe she'd pondered an orgasm or two herself, but she didn't like the assumption. "What's your endgame? Payback?"

His smile faded. "I'd almost managed to make myself believe I was over you, but when I saw you again, I realized I'd been lying to myself."

She didn't want to hear that and had no idea what to say to it, so she sipped at her wine. It had hurt to leave Sam behind, but she'd had to for her own sanity, and she'd convinced herself he wouldn't care. That he was only marrying her because it was expected of him. If he'd really loved her…

"Can't stand an acquisition slipping through your fingers," she said, determined not to go there.

She saw the flash of hurt and anger cross his face before he forced the smile back. "I didn't bring you here to argue with you. Tell me about the people you work with."

They managed to get through the rest of the meal making benign small talk, but Paulie's stomach was so tied in knots she couldn't even have dessert. And when the limo pulled up outside Jasper's, she turned toward the door before Sam could even think about moving in for a good-night kiss.

"Thank you for dinner."

"Paulette, I—"

But she was on the sidewalk, closing the door behind her, before he could finish his sentence. If there was any chance at all she'd really hurt him by leaving the first time, she had to end whatever this was now because she'd just hurt him again.

"JOSEPH KOWALSKI, nobody wants to hear about your rear end while we're eating!"

Kevin tried to stifle a chuckle as his oldest brother drew their mother's wrath, but he must not have succeeded because she turned her maternal evil eye on him. "Come on, Ma. It's funny!"

"That's because you didn't have sand in the crack of your—"

"Joseph!"

"I was going to say bum."

"Sure you were." Mary Kowalski turned her attention to the kids' table and her only granddaughter. "You don't like my mashed potatoes anymore?"

Stephanie shrugged. "I'm on a diet."

"You don't need to diet. You're perfect. Plus, bathing suit season's over. Why do you think women live in New England and put up with the snow and the wind chill? Because sweaters and winter coats hide all sins, that's why. And we're supposed to gain weight in the winter. It's insulation."

Kevin managed to avoid pointing out his mother was well insulated from the summer heat, too, by shoving a forkful of pot roast in his mouth. Even though Thanksgiving was right around the corner, they were having a family dinner to celebrate Joe and Keri returning from their honeymoon on some tropical island where an amorous, sunset moment had apparently led to Joe getting sand where the sun didn't shine.

When there was a rare lull in the conversation, Kevin set down his fork and cleared his throat. "So Beth and I have some news."

"Who's Beth?" Keri asked.

"The bartender at your wedding."

"Oh, that's right. How could I forget when my husband almost got thrown out of our own reception for trying to hire her like a hooker or something."

"What's a hooker?" Bobby asked.

Keri's island tan flushed pink. "Oops."

"You put it on the end of a fishing pole, dummy," Brian explained.

Bobby frowned. "Uncle Joe tried to hire a worm?"

"No," Danny told his younger brothers. "Not *that* kind of hooker."

"Enough," Lisa yelled at her kids. "You'll understand when you're older."

"I'm going to be a genius when I get older," Brian mumbled at his plate.

"We're having a baby," Kevin said before his family could fly off on another tangent. "At the end of June."

The only time he'd ever heard his mother's dining room that silent was the night he'd stayed over during a nor'easter and snuck down to rummage through the fridge at two in the morning. Then, of course, everybody spoke at once.

One young voice stuck out. "Uncle Kevin's having a baby with a hooker?"

He slapped his forehead. Not good.

"I'll talk to them before they go back to school on Monday," Lisa promised.

"Thanks." He was having a hard enough time convincing Beth he was a decent guy without trying to explain why his nephew thought she was a prostitute…or fish bait.

As the questions flew at him, he realized how few answers he had. Other than the baby's due date and the fact Beth had moved across the hall from him because her apartment had lead paint—but no, they weren't living together—there wasn't much he could tell them.

"Why didn't you bring her with you?" Mike asked when the conversation had settled to a dull roar.

"She's probably working. I tried calling the apartment to invite her, but she didn't answer. And she doesn't have a cell phone."

His niece almost inhaled the mashed potatoes she was forcing down under her grandmother's watchful eye. "She doesn't have a cell? Seriously? How does she text people?"

"I think she actually talks to people, like they did in the old days." It was a good question, though. Not how she texted people, but how she'd reach out if she needed help. What if she had a problem and couldn't reach him? She needed a cell phone, dammit.

An hour later, Kevin left the family room in the direction of the bathroom but took a detour into the kitchen instead, hoping to sneak some of the leftover peach cobbler. He found Terry there already, with the plastic wrap peeled back and fork in hand.

"Busted."

She jumped, then grinned and put a finger to her lips. "Grab a fork."

He joined her over the cobbler and dropped an arm around her shoulders. "How you been, sis?"

"Better. The counseling helps."

Earlier in the year, Terry and Evan had hit a rough patch and separated and, though they'd reconciled, their marriage was very much a work in progress. "Glad to hear it. You know we're all pulling for you."

"Stop pulling the plastic back so much. She'll smell the peaches." She shoveled in another bite, then swallowed. "So, Doctor Tiffany, who's like twelve years old and twirls her hair, which makes me want to slap her hand, says I have control issues."

"You? No."

"Very funny. Don't put the fork in the sink, dumbass. Put it in the dishwasher or she'll know." Terry pulled the plastic wrap back over the cobbler, making sure it was on just so. "So…a baby, huh?"

"Yeah." Kevin leaned against the counter and folded his arms. "Just my luck. I finally start a family and it's with the one woman who walks into my bar and *doesn't* throw herself at me."

"I can give you Doctor Tiffany's number."

He laughed, then slapped his hand over his mouth. "Shit."

Too late. "You two better wrap that cobbler back up just the way I left it or it'll dry out."

"Yes, Ma," Kevin bellowed in the direction of the family room.

Terry rolled her eyes, then licked her thumb. "You've got a bit of cobbler. Hold still."

He ducked left and swiped his sleeve across his mouth. "Don't even think about spit-washing my face."

"Just wait. Couple years from now, you and Beth'll be running around spit-washing random people, too."

He snorted, but his mind had fast-forwarded a couple of years into the future. He'd have a walking, talking little guy or girl of his own. But he wasn't sure if he and Beth would be running around doing *anything* together.

Sometimes, late at night when he was staring at his ceiling instead of sleeping, he worried she'd take off. She was nomadic by nature. Her parents lived in Florida. She had no ties to New Hampshire other than the pregnancy. There was nothing to stop her from hitting the road, taking their child with her.

Nothing but him convincing her she wanted to stay.

The happy peach cobbler glow was fading, so he grabbed a clean fork and peeled back the plastic wrap. Just a few more bites.

CHAPTER EIGHT

BETH WAS PRETTY SURE Friday supper shifts were one of the circles of hell. She'd made some good tips, but it was hectic between the regulars and the tourists jumping off the highway for a bite to eat. And, since her conversation with Julia, she'd been concentrating on not resting her hand over the place where she'd soon have a baby bump, and that kind of self-awareness was exhausting.

Unable to summon the energy to be sociable, she let herself in the back door of Jasper's to avoid going through the bar. She'd already hit the up button on the elevator before she realized she should have taken the damn stairs. You could hear the elevator motor in the kitchen, and anybody at that end of the bar could feel the subtle vibration.

Sure enough, she hadn't even gotten her shoes off yet when there was a knock on her door. She let Kevin in and sank onto the couch.

"I only have a few minutes because it's insane downstairs," he told her, and she said a silent prayer of thanks for busy Friday nights at the bar. She wasn't in the mood for company. He pulled out a cell phone and a user's manual and handed them to her. "I got you something."

"What is this?"

"It's a…cell phone. I know you don't have one, but you have to have seen them on television, at least."

"Smart-ass. I know it's a cell phone, but what's it for?"

"Making phone calls."

"Oh, for the love of…" She tossed the phone on the coffee table and stood up. He was a royal pain in the ass, and she'd had her fill of those today. Pushing past him, she headed for the fridge. "Forget it."

"Okay, I'm sorry." He touched her arm, but she kept walking. "Beth, come on. It was funny!"

"I'm tired, Kevin."

"The phone's yours. I programmed my number in—it's the emergency contact, too—and my parents and my brothers and Terry and…oh, Paulie. Hell, everybody's programmed in there."

He'd bought her a cell phone. She jerked open the fridge door and stared at the contents, as much to cool her face as to find a snack. If she wanted a damn cell phone, she'd buy one. Sure, it wouldn't have any bells and whistles and it would be a pre-paid thing, but she could buy her own.

"You're mad."

Yes, she was mad. "It's not your job to buy me things."

"It was no big deal. I went to a family plan and added your line. Cheapest way to do it, so it made sense. They both have texting, too, if you want to try that sexting thing…"

Family plan. The word hit her like a punch to the face.

She'd made it clear they weren't a couple, and he'd gone and made them a family. With his cell phone in her pocket, the hovering would start. Where was she? What was she doing? When would she be home?

Beth slowly closed the fridge door—so she wouldn't slam it like she really wanted to—and turned to face him. "A family plan."

He shrugged. "That's just what they call it. Like I said, it's no big deal."

It was a very big deal, but she was starting to think having this conversation with Kevin was like beating her head against a good-looking, T-shirt-clad brick wall. "It is a big deal, and the fact you still don't get why it is tells me I was right about you."

"Right about what?"

"That you'd try to take over my life."

"Well, excuse the hell outta me for being a nice guy." He threw up his hands, and anger tightened his jaw. "What do you want me to do, Beth? Ignore you? Pretend you don't exist until it's time to send you a child support check every month?"

She could do angry, too. "So there's nothing between ignoring me and sharing a family plan?"

"You need a goddamn cell phone!"

"No, I don't. And if I did, I'd buy my own goddamn cell phone."

"What if you need help? What if you think something's wrong with the baby?"

She wasn't going to be manipulated into caving by his using her pregnancy against her. "Women gave birth in this country for almost four hundred years without cell phones."

He laughed, but it wasn't a happy sound. "That's a great argument, Beth. You plan to go squat in the woods when your water breaks, too?"

Before communications broke down any further, Beth turned and took a deep breath. She wanted to say something reasonable—if not quite conciliatory—but she couldn't think over the word *family* echoing through her mind.

And Kevin didn't give her a chance. "News

flash for you—that baby you're carrying is my responsibility even if you think you're not, so I need to know you can call for help no matter where you are or what time it is. So I bought you a damn cell phone."

He went to the door to let himself out but stopped to look over his shoulder. "I'll try to be more of an asshole from now on if that'll make you happy."

As if to prove his point, he pulled the door closed behind him so hard she felt it vibrate through the floor.

"Dammit." Beth returned to the couch, sinking onto the soft cushions with a weary sigh.

She hadn't meant to be such an irrational bitch. At least, she thought maybe she was. It's not as if he'd dictated what clothes she should wear. Or bought her a minivan. Or locked her in her apartment so she couldn't go anywhere.

He'd bought her a cell phone. Not to take over her life but because he worried about her and the baby, and knowing she had a phone would bring him some peace of mind. And he knew she didn't have a lot of money, so, instead of pushing her to get one, he'd added her to his plan.

His *family* plan.

And there was the word that had scared the

crap out of her, which, unfortunately for Kevin, manifested itself as an extreme fit of bitchiness he didn't deserve. He really was a nice guy, and the way he'd adjusted to a surprise pregnancy and impending fatherhood was nothing short of a miracle. So he'd bought her a phone. A simple thank-you would have sufficed.

She picked up the phone and started thumbing through the menus. Her apology would have to wait until he wasn't so busy—she'd already dumped enough on him—so in the meantime she'd get comfortable using it. There was Kevin's number, just as he'd said, and marked as her emergency contact.

Besides the numerous members of his family and Paulie, he'd put in the bar's number and the restaurant where she worked. The pharmacy. And he'd even put in her doctor's number. Every number she could possibly need, already programmed in. It must have taken him a while, too.

Tears blurred her eyes, so she leaned back against the couch and closed her eyes. She'd apologize in the morning and thank him for the gift.

And try not to dwell too much on the word *family*.

KEVIN WAS SHAVING the next morning when his phone announced a new text message with a cheerful doorbell tone. Good thing it was out of arm's reach or he might have smashed it.

Cheerful, he wasn't.

A few more swipes of the razor and then he rinsed his face. The phone had moved on to a much less cheerful reminder beep by the time he was done patting dry and he flipped the thing open with a curse.

It was from Beth. I'm sorry.

He'd been sorry, too, while trying to maintain his cool finishing off his shift last night. And while he'd stared at the ceiling instead of sleeping, trying to figure out how he'd managed to screw things up so badly. Not that he thought he was wrong to buy her a cell phone because he wasn't, but maybe he could have handled it better.

He knew, though, if he'd brought up the subject beforehand, she'd have told him no. She was proud, not that that was a bad thing, and she would have tried to convince him she didn't need a cell phone. If he'd talked her into admitting she did, she would have bought one herself, probably going without something else in order to afford it.

Smarter, easier and cheaper to add her to his plan. And it might have gone more smoothly if she hadn't been so tired and he hadn't been such a smart-ass.

Apology accepted. Hungry?

He pulled his shirt on, his mood already improving. In the future, he'd have to remember to walk more softly around Beth's pride, but they'd be okay. And she was using the phone, which was the most important thing. He wanted her to be able to reach him or anybody else if she ever needed help.

Sure. Fifteen minutes?

He smiled and hit Reply. I could serve you breakfast in bed.

Funny. In the hall, 15 mins.

He was ready, keys in hand, when she stepped out of her apartment, looking as tired as he felt. "Morning, sunshine."

"Morning." She closed her door, giving the knob a twist to make sure it was locked. "I'm ready."

"Where should we go?" he asked as they rode down in the elevator. She seemed awkward with him, but he couldn't tell if she was embarrassed or still pissed off. Either way, he'd tread lightly.

"Someplace quiet...or really loud, I guess. Where we can talk."

Uh-oh. That didn't sound good. "I know just the place."

He drove her to one of his favorite restaurants— a place he frequented often enough to request a quiet table away from the crowd. She waited until they had their coffee and had ordered before she got down to it.

"I like you, Kevin," she started, and the little *uh-oh* voice got louder. There was usually a *but* after an opening like that. "But it's like you're pretending we're a couple and we're not."

"We could be." No sense in denying he wanted it.

"I told you when I moved into your building the personal aspect of our relationship is over, and I thought I explained why, but you either don't understand or you don't respect what I was trying to say."

"You said I'm overwhelming and suffocating which, quite frankly, offends me. There's a big difference between taking over somebody's life and helping a friend—and my unborn child—move out of an unsafe apartment."

She looked miserable, but he felt pretty miserable, too. They needed to talk through this so they could move the hell on. And by moving on, he meant her accepting that the Kowalskis didn't go through anything alone or want for anything they needed, and she was close enough to a Kowalski to count. There were a whole bunch of people waiting for opportunities to give her gifts and do things to help her out.

After taking a sip of her coffee, she stared down into the mug. "It would be so easy to let you take care of me."

"Then let me."

"I can't."

He reached across the table and took her hand in his, rubbing his thumb across the back of her knuckles. "Why?"

"Because I liked you before we—" She looked around. "Before we slept together. But if I...if I start liking you more now, how do I know it's not just because I'm having your baby, which is scary, and it's easier to let you take care of me?"

Rather than open his mouth and say something stupid, Kevin kept it zipped while he tried to come up with the right thing. Thankfully the waitress bought him an extra few minutes by delivering their plates and promising to come right back with the coffeepot.

When she was gone, he talked while they fixed their coffees. "So you're afraid you're more attracted to having somebody to lean on than the person who's willing to be leaned on?"

"I guess you could put it that way. I'm just afraid if I get too used to leaning on you and you decide to walk away, I'll...fall over, I guess. And that scares me because the one thing I've never needed is somebody to depend on.

"And I'm afraid I'll hurt you, too. My parents… they're great, but they stifled me. So I move around and, when I reach the point in relationships people start keeping tabs on me and making decisions for me, I get on a bus to someplace new. But I can't do that this time."

The key to getting through this conversation, he figured, was making sure he kept food in his mouth so the chewing could keep buying him time to think. He'd had sticky making-up and/or breaking-up conversations with women before, but this was a first for him. This was the first relationship he'd ever had he couldn't make a clean break from and that made it sticky. No matter how badly they hurt each other or pissed each other off, they'd never be able to make a clean break. The baby bound them together forever, and that put a shit-load of pressure on the conversation at hand.

"Tell me you won't just disappear," he finally said. "If you decide to take off, at least call me first. I don't want to wake up someday to find you gone."

"I wouldn't do that to you, Kevin." Tears made her eyes sparkle for a moment, but she blinked them back. "Just staying here is a big adjustment for me, and being pregnant. I think a serious relationship might be too much on top of it, and I'm afraid if we hook up and it goes wrong, it'll be ugly, and that's not what I want for our child."

"When it comes to the baby, I won't ever walk away. Even if things go south between us, you will never have to worry about feeding that baby or buying it medicine or clothes or anything else it needs. I can promise you that."

He watched her chest rise and fall as she took a deep breath. "I believe that."

"As for us…I don't know, Beth. I can't promise I'm your Mr. Right. I like you and I'd definitely been thinking about a second date. I guess you probably weren't, since you snuck out in the middle of the night, but—"

"I liked you, too. And it was morning, not the middle of the night. But I got the impression you were done with me, so—"

"I explained that to you. I was half-asleep. Hell, more than half. I'd planned to take you out for breakfast and everything. But I've already told you that and apologized for it."

"I wasn't trying to accuse you again. Just explaining why I didn't think we were heading for a second date."

"Okay. But anyway, I wasn't trying to trample your personal boundaries by buying you a cell phone. I was just trying to make your life a little easier and buy myself some peace of mind. I swear, it wasn't some nefarious plot to become the evil overlord of your life."

She blushed, nibbling on a slice of toast in a way that made him think she was also using the food as delay tactic. "I overreacted to the cell phone. Badly. I panicked, hearing you say *family plan* because we're not. A family, I mean. We're neighbors having a baby."

He couldn't stop himself from reaching across the table to squeeze her hand. "I prefer *friends* having a baby. And I'm sorry I didn't consider you'd take it as anything other than a gift."

"You didn't do anything wrong. I had just had a really rough day and you didn't deserve to be my whipping boy."

Now was not even the time to crack a joke about her, a whip and his backside, so he used his free hand to shove a forkful of scrambled eggs into his mouth and chewed until the urge passed. "You need to understand that I think of you as family now. All the Kowalskis do, actually. If Lisa needed a new dryer, we'd make sure she got one. If Terry's car broke down, we'd chauffeur her around until it was fixed. And if you need a cell phone, we buy you one. No strings. Definitely no leash."

When the waitress returned with the coffeepot, he squeezed Beth's fingers before letting go of her hand. He would have preferred to keep holding it, coffee and breakfast be damned, but it was pretty obvious at this point he had to tread very, very lightly around Beth. If he got pushy, she'd shut him down totally.

"I'll try," she said when they were alone again. "To do better at understanding where you're coming from, I mean. Your family's so…devoted and generous, and I need to learn how to appreciate that."

"Good." Then a very, very horrible thought popped into his head. "But, um…when I say we think of you as family, I don't mean you're like my sister or anything."

"That would be pretty weird, considering the whole baby thing."

"The baby thing, sure, but also the fact I'm still thinking about that second date."

"Oh." He loved the way she blushed. "I haven't changed my mind about having that kind of relationship with you. Since I'm pregnant, it's not a good idea."

"I haven't changed my mind, either." He grinned

at her over the top of his coffee cup. "And I'm a pretty patient guy."

She laughed and rolled her eyes, but deep inside, he didn't find it quite as funny as she did. If she really didn't want to be involved with him while she was pregnant, it was going to be a long wait.

Eight months. Eight months of cold showers, tossing and turning and walking slightly bow-legged. Oh, and then another two months, at least, before she'd even think about feeling sexy again, based on what Mikey and Evan had said about their wives.

Holy shit, that was a long time. If thinking about box scores was a good way to keep your mind off sex, he was going to be the freaking Rainman of baseball statistics before the ten months—almost a whole damn year—was over.

Then she smiled at him—a real smile that made her dark eyes crinkle—across the table and every ERA and RBI stat he'd ever known flew out of his head.

If she didn't change her mind about letting him back in her bed, there was a damn good chance the kid she was carrying would be his only one because his balls were going to explode.

CHAPTER NINE

KEVIN WAITED UNTIL THE BAR traffic slowed before telling Paulie he was taking a break and heading upstairs. He knocked on Beth's door and had to quickly stifle a grin when she pulled it open. Sweats, crazy hair and chocolate smears in the corners of her mouth only six weeks in? Between his sister and his sister-in-law, he'd witnessed five pregnancies, and he knew it only went downhill from there.

"I wasn't really expecting company," she said, but she stepped back and let him in. "I would have brushed my hair, at least."

"Isn't that tousled bed-head thing the style these days?"

"Only if you do it on purpose."

The chocolate was killing him. He wanted to kiss her. Run his tongue over her lip and lick the chocolate away. "I…uh…oh, I came to invite you over for Thanksgiving."

"You can roast a turkey?"

"No. But my mom cooks a mean Thanksgiving dinner, which is why we all go there every year."

She didn't look exactly thrilled with the invitation. "I told you we're not seeing each other anymore. There's no relationship, which means no taking me home for the holidays."

He wasn't about to give up that easily. "The baby wants to come home with me for Thanksgiving."

"She does, does she?"

"Yes, he does." She rolled her eyes, but a smile tugged at the corners of her mouth, so he kept going. "Ma makes this stuff with yams and marshmallows. It's delicious and I'm pretty sure the baby wants to try some."

"Yams and marshmallows?"

"Yeah. Oh, and a green-bean casserole thing with soup and these French-fried onions things on top. Wicked good."

She pressed a hand over her stomach. "Yams, marshmallows, green beans, French-fried onions… and you think the baby will like that?"

Good point. So far so good in the morning-sickness department, but marshmallows and French-fried onions might be pushing it. "You don't have to try anything you don't want. Just come and eat what you do like and hang out with the family."

"I'm not sure I'm up to that."

"Eating?"

"Very funny." But she didn't even smile this time. "I'm not sure I'm up to pretending I'm a part of your big, happy family."

Apparently it was going to take a pneumatic sledge hammer to drive the fact she *was* family, whether she liked it or not, into her head. "It's not that big a deal. We'll eat turkey and marshmallow yam stuff and pie. That's about it."

"I don't know, Kevin."

"What else are you going to do? Sit here alone all day?"

She shrugged. "I'm used to being alone, and the truth is your family intimidates me. There are so many of you and you're pretty loud, you know."

"Just one of our many charms. And, speaking of the truth, you and my family are going to be entwined forever. You're going to be the mother of my child for the rest of your life. The mother of my parents' grandchild. The mother of my sister and brothers' nephew—"

"Niece."

"—forever. So I think some bonding over sticky

yams and green-bean casserole is just the thing to jump-start a long and loud entwining."

"We're not supposed to be entwining." She poked a finger at his chest. "Remember?"

"I remember you said you and I couldn't do any more personal entwining between the sheets." Which was tragic. "But you're already entwined with the Kowalskis."

"Forever," she muttered. "So you said."

"You told me you were going to try to do better at doing the whole family thing."

"I remember."

"So you'll come?"

"I don't know, Kevin."

Time to bring out the big guns—aka, his mother. "If my mother finds out you're spending Thanksgiving alone, she'll whack me upside the head so hard with that wooden spoon of hers, when I wake up my clothes will be out of style. Then she'll pack up all the food in those Tupperware things she's got a closet of and drag the whole family over here. You don't want that."

She blew out a breath and shook her head. "Fine! I give up. I'll bring the baby to your mom's for Thanksgiving."

He wisely limited his victory dance to a mental celebration and walked to the door. Paulie needed a break before it got busy again. "Great. We can ride over together, about eight-thirty."

"In the morning?"

"Sure. Ma does a breakfast buffet and then we watch the parade. After that it's football and more food. We have the first round of pies midafternoon. Come early evening Ma lets us pick at the leftovers and make turkey sandwiches. Then there's more football in the den or *It's a Wonderful Life* in the living room and we get more pie."

Beth looked shell-shocked. "That's not Thanksgiving dinner. That's a marathon."

"Yeah, but we don't do it often. Thanksgiving, Christmas, Easter and the Fourth of July, usually. That's not too much to take. Although, once that little guy pops out, you'll have a Kowalski 24/7."

He was still laughing when she shoved him out into the hall and slammed the door in his face.

PAULIE WAS ON THE VERGE of a nervous breakdown, and when she checked herself into the mental hospital she was putting the words *Sam* and *Logan* in the "why" box of the intake form.

He'd made a steady habit of dropping in for at least a drink, if not dinner, after his workday was over. Unfortunately, his being there watching her made her jittery, so his presence and her reaction to it weren't going unnoticed by her coworkers. Hard to fly under the radar when she turned into a totally self-conscious klutz whenever he was in the bar. She'd broken more glasses in the past few weeks than she had in the past five years.

He hadn't asked her out on—or blackmailed her into—another date since their last one, but she knew he wasn't done toying with her. He was just dragging it out, hoping to build the anticipation, and it was working, dammit. She was hyper-aware of his staring at her ass while she walked and… his just staring in general. It made her aware of her movements and body language in a way that kept her in a constant state of sexual tension.

Even now he was watching her as she tried to work the bar with Kevin—who, judging by the looks he kept giving her and Sam—was more aware of what was going on than she would have liked. Not surprising, though. Her boss had seen her tired and cranky and pissed off and upbeat and happy, but he'd never seen her flustered by a man's interest.

When Sam winked at her and she turned away too quickly, knocking an empty shot glass off the edge of the bar, she knew the jig was up. Kevin signaled for Randy to clean up the broken glass, took her by the elbow and very firmly guided her into his office. She sighed and sank into a chair while he closed the door and went to sit behind his desk.

"What's the deal with Sam Logan?"

She knew her boss and best friend pretty well, and she knew she didn't have a chance in hell of putting him off this time, but that didn't mean she wouldn't try. "Old business. My business."

"And now it's my business."

"Yeah, I broke a few glasses. Dock my pay."

"Cut the shit, Paulie."

Defeat slumped her shoulders, and she let it out with a shuddering sigh. "Five years ago I changed my name—legally and for reasons that aren't illegal. My real name is Paulette Atherton."

His expression didn't change. "So?"

"My father is Richard Atherton."

She watched understanding dawn in his eyes. "The gazillionaire from Boston Richard Atherton?"

"Yup."

"No shit." He leaned back in his chair and crossed his arms over his chest. "No offense, doll, but what the hell are you doing tending bar?"

"Being myself. Being happy."

She waited for him to accuse her of slumming for kicks. For taking a job from a person who actually needed the money. She waited for him to look at her differently. Any or all of the reactions she'd imagined over the weeks. But he didn't.

"How does Sam Logan figure into this?"

"We were supposed to get married—be the darling power couple of the country club set. Wedding of the decade...until I got halfway up the aisle and bolted like a spooked horse."

"No shit," he said again. "I remember hearing something about that. Don't usually read the society pages, but Terry and Lisa talked about it. You must have looked different."

"I did. My hair was dyed because my natural red is unseemly, and always straightened because wild curls are unseemly. I was a lot more seemly then than I am now. Probably why nobody ever made the connection."

"So you left him at the altar? Bet that didn't go over well."

"I don't know. I went home long enough to grab some clothes, cash and the few things I cared about, but, by the time my parents got home, I was on a bus out of Boston. Threw my cell phone in the lobby trash can."

"So you left with nothing?"

It was tempting to let him believe that, but now that she was confessing, she'd cough it all up. "I didn't have a lot of cash when I left, but I have trust funds set up in such a way my father couldn't cut them off. I choose to live week to week on my pay-checks, but I have access to millions."

"Damn." He didn't say anything for at least a minute, and she started to sweat. "Paulie, you're shaking."

She was, and she couldn't seem to stop. But this man was her best friend in the world, and she'd just told him everything he believed about her was a lie. She didn't want to lose him or Jasper's or the life she'd been living quite happily for five years. "I'm sorry."

He looked perplexed. "Sorry about what?"

"I haven't been honest with you. Not that I've really lied, but I'm not who you thought I was and I'm sorry."

"Bullshit." He sat forward in his chair again. "I thought you were a hot redheaded bartender with a sassy mouth who not only manages my bar like a pro, but is one of the best friends I've ever had. Isn't that who you are?"

"It is. It really is."

His grin was such a relief to see, she couldn't help but smile back. "Okay, then."

"Okay."

"So this Logan guy, is he giving you a hard time about the wedding?"

"He's blackmailing me."

Kevin jumped to his feet so fast, she sat back in her chair. "He's a dead man. I'm going to kick his ass so bad he won't even be able to cry for his mommy. Gonna fold him up like a napkin."

His loyalty warmed her heart, even as embarrassment warmed her cheeks. "It's...not what you're thinking."

"I'm thinking by the time I'm done pounding on his face, even dogs will be afraid of him." He was pacing in a tight pattern, something he only did when he was spectacularly pissed off.

"He's making me put up with him being here—and I had to go on a date with him—or he'll tell you who I really am."

The anger on Kevin's face didn't ease. If anything, his hands fisted tighter. "Well, now I know so he can get his sorry, blackmailing and soon to be black-and-blue ass on the next bus back to Boston."

Paulie looked down at her feet. "I don't want him to know I told you."

The pacing stopped, with his toes facing her, but she didn't look up. "I don't get it."

"I want him to think I'm still seeing him so he won't out me."

"Now I really don't get it."

"I loved him." She looked up again when Kevin plopped back onto his chair, the fight gone out of him. "I didn't run from him. I ran from...I don't know. The life I was going to be stuck living until death did we part."

"Just because you've reinvented yourself doesn't mean he has. When he's done with the hotel job, he'll go back to Boston and the country club set."

She knew that. She thought about it a lot, actually, during the hours she was supposed to be sleeping but wasn't because of Sam. "I know that. I'm just..."

"Just what? When he's around you're so damn nerved up I'm going to have to start serving booze in paper cups, so either you're scared of him or you're still in love with him."

Or maybe it was a little of both. "No in between, huh? Fear or love?"

"Nothing that would make you as jumpy as a long-tailed cat in a room full of rocking chairs."

She wasn't going to admit to either one, so she shook her head and stood up. "He's leaving, anyway. He's going back to Boston for the holidays and to finish up some work. He's making at least one trip to Europe. It'll be a while before we see him again."

"Absence makes the heart grow fonder."

She snorted. She didn't know about that, though she did know five years hadn't made the heart any *less* fond. "I need to get back out there. Bad enough Randy had to clean up my mess, but he should have gone on break two minutes ago."

"You let me know if you change your mind about Sam Logan needing his ass kicked."

Paulie nodded on her way out the door, but it wasn't likely. After five years it seemed her mind hadn't been changed about Sam. And neither had her heart.

WITHIN FIVE MINUTES of walking through the Kowalskis' front door, Beth knew her parents would fit right in. They were huggers. Every damn one of them—and there were a *lot* of Kowalskis. Apparently Kevin hadn't been exaggerating about how her carrying his child gave her some kind of instant family status, and they didn't hold back on the touchy-feely.

And Kevin was just as bad as the rest of them. He kept draping his arm over her shoulders or taking her arm to guide her or resting his hand on her back. It seemed the only time he stopped touching her was to let a member of his family hug her.

There was a blur of introductions. She'd already

met his father, Leo, who had a voice that com-
manded the room, and his mother, who gave her
a warm hug and a speculative look that made her
wonder what Kevin had told them about her ap-
pearing at their family dinner.

The rest of the horde she'd only seen from a
distance, as the nameless bartender handing out
drinks at the wedding. Joe and Keri had been the
bride and groom. Then there was his sister, and
Joe's twin, Terry. She and her husband, Evan, had
a thirteen-year-old daughter named Stephanie. His
brother Mike had four sons with his wife, Lisa.
Joey was fifteen, Danny was twelve, Brian, nine,
and Bobby, seven.

"Don't worry," he whispered, his breath tickling
her ear. "There's no quiz later."

It was a little overwhelming, even though they
were a very likable bunch of people. Like agreeing
to learn the doggy paddle and being shoved off the
high-dive board. And to keep things interesting,
somebody told Bobby, Kevin's youngest nephew,
the baby could hear stuff, and he was determined
to make his new cousin his BFF *in utero.* It was a
bit disconcerting having a kid randomly tell bad
jokes to her stomach. Like now.

"Why did the weasel cross the road?" he yelled
at her belly button. "To prove it wasn't a chicken!"

Then he laughed so hard he almost fell over. He was a cute kid, she thought, and then it hit her—a little over seven years from now, she might have one just like him. Some faceless, nameless boy with too much energy and the knees almost worn out of his jeans, telling jokes to crack himself up. Maybe, if they were lucky, he'd look like his daddy, dimples and all.

Bobby stopped laughing and craned his head to look up at her. "I hope it's a boy."

"So does your Uncle Kevin."

"I'm sick of being the smallest boy. We need another one so I have somebody to pick on, too."

"Oh…great." It was scary to think her baby was going to be the low man on the totem pole of trickle-down family dynamics.

The home-baked cinnamon rolls made her a fan of Mary Kowalski for life, though having to pass by the gigantic urn of coffee almost killed her. She was trying to go caffeine-free, so she made do with instant decaf even though she could have used the high-test to keep up with the Kowalskis.

Friendly, warm, numerous and—holy hell— loud. They ate and laughed and ate and argued and ate and laughed some more. The green-bean casserole was wicked good, and the baked yams with melted marshmallows were absolutely to die for, just as Kevin had promised. As the day wore on, the background noise changed from the parade to football, but the family cacophony never dimmed. It was so different from the quiet meals she'd shared with her parents in the past, she spent most of the day reeling from something akin to culture shock.

When the opportunity arose, she ducked through the sliding doors onto a spacious back deck. Fortunately, it was a mild day for late November, and, even without her coat, she wasn't too chilly.

Folding her arms across her chest, she looked out over the sprawling backyard. It was chaotic, just like the family. Immaculately tended gardens. Sports debris strewn from one edge of the lawn to the other. A sagging volleyball net.

It was a *home*.

The realization her child was going to belong to this insanity brought tears to her eyes. He or she would run amok in this backyard with cousins. Play and laugh and argue and then laugh some more.

The mixed feelings made the corners of her lips tilt up even as a tear ran over her cheek. She wanted her baby to have this—the loud and loving family. Would she pale by comparison, though?

Just boring old mom who sucked at sports and couldn't bake cinnamon buns or name all the balloons in the Macy's Thanksgiving Day Parade. What kind of kid would want to hang out with her when the Kowalskis had all of this?

"Hiding?"

She whirled around to find Kevin's sister-in-law, Lisa, behind her. "Oh, I didn't hear you come out."

"I was being quiet so nobody would know I escaped. Here, move to the left and we can't be seen from inside."

Beth shifted to the left as instructed, though she wondered if she should go back inside and let Lisa have a few minutes of peace. They'd spoken a few times over the course of the day, but she didn't know her very well.

"I'm impressed you haven't run screaming into the street yet."

Beth laughed. "I tried. Came out the wrong door."

"We can be a bit...much."

"No, you've all been really wonderful. Especially considering...the circumstances."

"The baby? Please. We're all thrilled about the baby. And so is Kevin."

He really was, and that was part of what worried her about him. Beth didn't have a lot of experience with failed birth control, thank goodness, but she'd somehow gotten the impression men didn't usually react so well to discovering they'd been caught up in an accidental pregnancy. Kevin, on the other hand, had taken to it—and to her—as if they were a real couple, and making a baby had been the reason they'd fallen into bed in the first place.

"I think you guys are doing the right thing," Lisa said. "Not rushing into anything because of the baby, I mean. Mike and I got married because I got pregnant with Joey."

"Do you ever…" She let the words die away, unsure how to intrude on Lisa's marriage without being rude or hurtful.

"Every marriage hits rough spots, but it's hard when you know your husband proposed because you got knocked up, not because he loved you. With Bobby starting first grade, I had a rough summer. Even thought about having another baby because I thought he'd leave me once the little guy was old enough to handle it."

Beth couldn't imagine living like that. "So you spent all those years not trusting your marriage?"

Lisa shrugged. "It came and went, depending on how things were going. But he proposed to me again a few months ago and in January we're going on a cruise—just the two of us. We're going to get married again in a sunset ceremony."

Beth smiled and congratulated her, but inside her stomach was twisting into a knot. That's what she was afraid of—why deep down she knew insisting they not have a *real* relationship was the right thing to do. Not only imagining herself in one place with one person, but wondering for the rest of her life, especially during the rough patches, if they were just pretending for the sake of the child. Not something she was eager to sign up for.

Lisa laughed. "Can you imagine us with another baby? Especially another boy. God. How about you? Hoping for a girl?"

"Maybe. Bobby wants a boy so he can finally have somebody to pick on."

Lisa laughed and shook her head. "Girl or boy, your baby's going to be short kid on the Kowalski totem pole. But don't worry—kids toughen up pretty damn quick around here."

Both women turned when the slider whooshed across the runner, and Kevin stepped onto the deck. He closed the slider and immediately moved to the left.

Beth chuckled. "Not much of a hiding spot."

"It won't stop anybody from finding us," Kevin

said. "But it'll slow them down for a few minutes. Thought maybe you ran off and left me."

"Like I told Lisa, I tried but I went out the wrong door."

He laughed and hooked his arm around her waist as if it was the most natural thing in the world. The entire day he'd been waging a constant campaign of subtle looks and slight touches, but she didn't want to kick up a fuss in front of his family. And then there was the troublesome possibility she might like it. No doubt he was attentive. And sweet. And so damn hot she'd swear her skin sizzled everywhere he touched her.

"Lisa," somebody bellowed from inside the house, and she sighed.

"Time to go." On her way by, she punched Kevin in the arm. "Behave yourself out here."

"I'll try, but no guarantees." Beth shivered when he turned his piercing blue gaze on her.

After Lisa closed the door behind her, Beth stepped out of the circle of Kevin's arm. With Lisa's words fresh in her mind, she needed to reestablish some boundaries. "We talked about this over and over and—"

"It's time for pie."

He had to be joking. "You're going to eat again?

And stop trying to change the subject. You're not getting—"

"Chocolate cream pie. Homemade, even the whipped cream."

"I'm not going to let you distract me."

"Six. Inches. Deep."

Well, hell. She supposed she could tolerate the sexiest man in the world touching her in exchange for a slab of homemade chocolate cream pie.

CHAPTER TEN

THERE WAS NOTHING SWEETER than watching the Patriots kick some Jets ass on a cold December Monday night in Foxboro. With a brother on each side of him, Kevin watched Brady in the shotgun, looking for Wes Welker. Another first down and the crowd went wild.

"So Beth seems nice," Mike said during a lull in the action.

"Yup." He'd known, since this was the first time he'd been alone with Mike and Joe since Thanksgiving, she'd come up in the conversation. "And she didn't run away screaming, so that was good."

"No offense," Joe said, "but it looked like maybe you were a little more into her than she was into you."

No offense, his ass. "She'll come around."

"You've got women practically lined up in the bar looking for a date, and you're chasing the one playing hard to get?"

"I don't recall Keri exactly throwing herself at

your feet. If you gave up the first time she didn't run into your arms, she'd be in L.A. and you'd still be in a monogamous relationship with your right hand."

Mike laughed, but Joe just shrugged. "She snuck out on you and—"

"That was a misunderstanding."

"—then you didn't hear from her again until she found out she was pregnant."

Kevin watched the Pats line up in the red zone to buy himself a minute to think. He knew Joe was just looking out for him, but he didn't really want to hear it. It was complicated—Beth was complicated—and maybe she was trying to keep him at a distance, but that didn't mean he was going to abandon ship.

She just needed some time to recover from having her life turned upside down, and he was going to give her the time she needed because he liked her—a lot—and he thought maybe they could make a go of it. She was smart and funny and stubborn and independent, and even now when he was doing one of his favorite things, he counted the minutes until he'd see her again.

After the Patriots walked the ball into the end zone and the cheering died down, Mike elbowed him. "Women can be...unstable, emotionally, during the first part of a pregnancy, just so you know. Stick it out if you really think she's special."

She was special. He wasn't sure how special yet, because it was hard to separate how he felt about her from the fact she was having his baby, but he did know he'd be devastated if she ever pulled another Cinderella act on him. "I'm not going anywhere."

"So you really like her, then?" Joe asked.

"I really do."

Joe, being Joe, probably had more to say, but the Patriots intercepted the ball, and the brothers rose to their feet, cheering with the crowd, as the cornerback engaged in a rowdy foot race with the Jets offense.

As the clock ticked down on the third quarter, the conversation moved on to draft-pick progress, injury reports and whether the blonde two rows down had real breasts or not, but Kevin had only one foot mentally in the game.

When the crowd erupted into an angry roar and Kevin had no idea why, Mike sadly shook his head. "Man, you got it bad."

Yeah, he was beginning to think he really did.

PAULIE SLID INTO A BOOTH at her favorite greasy-spoon diner, careful not to catch her jeans on the duct tape covering a split in the vinyl. She'd caved when Sam returned after Thanksgiving weekend in Boston and *threatened* her into another dinner date, but he'd been stupid enough to leave the reservations to her.

This place didn't take reservations, and there was never a wait. And she had a nice view of Samuel Thomas Logan the Fourth's face as he walked through the door. His expression was pretty similar to her mother's the day six-year-old Paulie accidentally dripped chocolate ice cream on her dress. She'd been restricted to bland, non-staining vanilla until she turned sixteen and could drive her shiny new BMW to the ice cream parlor herself.

Sam grimaced as he slid into the booth. "Do they print the menus on the back of the condemned signs they rip off the door?"

"Snob." Besides the meat loaf special, she'd brought him there for a reason—the diner perfectly illustrated how different her world was from his.

"It's called standards." He pulled a menu out of the rack behind the condiments and sugar dish. "How long did it take you to find a place you thought might scare me off?"

"Paulie!" Cassie, who not only waited the tables but owned the place, rushed over. "The flowers you sent Mom were beautiful! It was the biggest bouquet in the entire wing and everybody was jealous."

She smiled, noting Sam's incredulous stare in her peripheral vision. "I'm glad she liked them. How's her new hip?"

"Good. The doctor says she'll be good as new in no time. You both want coffee?"

When they nodded, Cassie left them, and Sam nudged Paulie's ankle with his toe. "You actually eat here? On a regular basis?"

"Yes, I do, so do you get it now? Your life and my life have nothing in common."

"You're telling me we don't have a future together because you've got a fondness for one-star food?"

As if the critics would get close enough to give the diner one star. She didn't have to answer him, though, because Cassie came back with their coffees. After they'd both ordered the meat loaf special, Sam leaned back in the booth and sipped his coffee.

"Not bad," he admitted.

"This is my idea of a date. Not some fancy restaurant with a maître d' who'll only seat you if your family's listed in *The Social Register*. I'd rather come here or go to a game and eat hot dogs from a street vendor."

"I can do that."

"Sure, right now. Once or twice, maybe. Not as a lifestyle."

"Why are you being so stubborn about this?"

Only the fact she needed the caffeine kept her from whacking him upside the head with her coffee mug. "Sam, you know this isn't going to work. I don't know if it's a game to you or—"

"It's not a game."

"If I thought we'd be happy together, I would have met you at the end of the aisle the first time."

"That was then. Now I know how you feel, which you never bothered to tell me before."

"And what's knowing going to change?"

He managed to capture her free hand in his before she could snatch it away. "No matter how much I told myself I didn't, every day for the last five years I've missed you. And this time I'm going to fight for you."

"Even if you have to fight dirty," she muttered.

"You know I'm not going to tell anybody who you are. That was... You're so damn stubborn I knew that was the only way I'd get you to go out with me."

"I already told Kevin, anyway."

He smiled, squeezing her fingers. "So you're not here because you were afraid I'd tell him, which means—"

"It means I wanted to tell you in person that you should find yourself some scion's daughter to marry you and have Sammy the Fifth because you and I aren't going anywhere."

He should have been mad, but she saw amusement in his eyes. "You named our son?"

Dammit. "Not our son. *Your* son. Doesn't take a genius to figure out what's going on the kid's birth certificate."

Cassie showed up with their meat loaf, then refilled their coffees, buying Paulie a few minutes of silence. Why wouldn't the man give up? She couldn't really make it any more plain.

After taking a bite of his dinner, he actually moaned. "I take back my crack about the condemned signs. This is the best meat loaf I've ever had."

She could do without the sexy sound effects, thank you very much. It was hard enough keeping her mind on all the things wrong with their relationship without being reminded how good the sex had been.

"I'm never going back to Boston," she said

abruptly, just to remind him—and herself—where they stood.

"I didn't ask you to."

"You're going back to Boston."

He nodded. "I told you that. I'm leaving straight from here and I'll be gone…a couple of months, I guess. Christmas season and then a trip to Europe for business. I need to wrap up some loose ends so when I come back here I can concentrate on this job. And you."

His gaze met and held hers, and she knew he meant it. He wanted her back, despite her objections it wouldn't end well. "Maybe I'll be gone when you get back."

"This time, if you run, I'll come after you."

Would she have stayed and married him if he'd come after her? She didn't know if it would have made a difference or not. It was her parents and Boston and the life she'd had to lead she was running from, not Sam.

"I'm going to call you while I'm gone," he said.

"Texts are better," she said. "Easier to deal with when I'm working."

"Then I'll text you."

She should have told him she wasn't interested in hearing from him at all. If she pushed hard enough, his pride would keep him from groveling, and he'd walk away. But even though she wouldn't say it out loud, she was going to miss him, too. A text or two probably wouldn't hurt.

As she walked through the front door of Jasper's Bar & Grille after a long lunch and dinner shift at the restaurant, Beth heaved a sigh of relief. She was home.

It surprised her how, after just shy of six weeks, this was home in a way her former apartment would never have been, and if she wasn't careful she might actually start liking the word. Besides the obvious lack of stale cat urine, there were the people. Paulie, who was fast becoming a very good friend. And Kevin. Despite the almost constant barrage of charm and sex appeal, she enjoyed their relationship a lot, too.

The rest of Jasper's staff were warm and welcoming. She wasn't sure what they'd been told about her. With no obvious signs of pregnancy showing, they might just think of her as a new tenant. Or who knew what Kevin might have told them?

Beth climbed onto her usual stool at the end of the bar and waited for Paulie to finish up with a customer. On her way over to say hello, Paulie grabbed one of the cans of cranberry-lime seltzer they'd started stocking for her.

Beth cracked it open and took a long drink. "Thanks."

"No problem. You gonna eat something?"

She was going to be good and have a salad. "A side salad, with light dressing and...oh, hell, a side of bacon cheeseburger, please."

Paulie laughed and went to give the order to the kitchen, leaving Beth with her seltzer and some kind of sports recap show on the television. Sports wasn't really her thing, but her attention was caught when the show went to commercial— a blitz of Christmas sales.

Her comfortable mood dimmed as she wondered—for the umpteenth time—what she was going to buy Kevin for Christmas. Business at the restaurant had picked up as promised, so she'd been able to set aside some Christmas money as well as putting away money for future prenatal checkups, but it wasn't a lot.

She needed to find the perfect gift on a tight budget. Something special because he really did deserve it after stepping up to the parenting plate and being there for her in so many ways. But not so special he might mistake her intentions.

A few minutes later, Paulie arrived with her food. "You look a little stressed out."

"Christmas is coming. Two weeks."

"Ah." Paulie set her plate down and leaned against the counter. "Nothing makes you crave the Pepto Bismol and Xanax like decking the halls."

"Do you and Kevin exchange gifts?"

"Sure. What are you getting him this year?"

"I guess there's no chance I can get out of this." Paulie's look pretty much confirmed it. "He's going to go nuts, isn't he?"

"If, by nuts, you mean him using the occasion as an excuse to give you all the things you won't let him buy you, then probably."

"And that's why I'm stressed out."

"Better for your blood pressure to accept now you're going to get smothered in presents and you're not expected to smother back."

"I hate that."

"And they know that about you, so hopefully they'll make some kind of attempt at self-control."

"They?" This conversation was *not* making her feel better.

"All of them. The whole Kowalski clan."

She'd been so focused on Kevin, she hadn't even thought about the rest of them. Why did there have to be so many? "Great."

Paulie laughed. "Don't even try to get out of the Christmas Eve party. Even I have to go and I don't have a Kowalski tadpole swimming in my pond."

When a guy at the other end of the bar bellowed for Paulie, Beth dove into her cheeseburger, letting the explosion of cheese, bacon and Jasper's special seasoning blast at her anxiety. She'd find something for Kevin and Paulie and then worry about the rest of them. Or maybe just token gifts for the kids. She could only do what she could do.

Paulie was gone a while, but eventually she wandered back and dumped Beth's dishes into a bus pan. "You want another seltzer?"

"No, thanks. I've still got some and I'm going to explode as it is." She didn't even want to think about buying new clothes as her waistline expanded. "So I haven't seen that guy around lately."

Paulie's cheeks turned pink. "What guy?"

"You know what guy. Did you drive him off?"

"He had to go home for the holidays, plus he had some business to do in Europe." She shrugged. "He's a bad penny. He'll turn up again."

"Has he called?"

"I hate phones. We've exchanged a few emails. Some text messages."

It wasn't like Paulie to clam up, and Beth wasn't

sure she knew her well enough to know how hard to push. "So he'll be back, then?"

"Probably not for a couple more months. There's not much he can do on site here, so he's trying to finish up a bunch of other stuff, so once he's needed back here, he can focus on the job."

Regardless of the lack of enthusiasm her words conveyed, her voice and the puppy dog look gave away just how much she was missing him. "And focus on you."

Paulie snorted. "Lucky me. Now back to Christmas shopping—"

"Ugh. I don't even know where to start."

"I know this great artisan gallery with home-made gifts for a wicked great price. Because I like you, I'll even give you my list. There was a scarf I thought Steph might like and a wooden pop gun for Bobby and…some other stuff. Oh, a hand-pressed journal for Danny because he wants to be a writer. You could get something small for each kid and maybe a hostess thing for Mr. and Mrs. Kowalski for about fifty bucks."

Fifty dollars was a lot, but she could do it. A little more scrimping would be worth it if it meant not feeling awkward about joining in the family's holiday. "I have Wednesday off this week. I could get the directions from you if you're sure you don't mind giving up your ideas."

Paulie waved a hand at her. "I'll get them all Nerf guns and call it good. And if you go in the morning, I can go with you. I'll drive and treat you to lunch after as long as I'm back by two."

The warm glow Beth had felt walking through the door returned with a vengeance. "I'd like that."

"Nine o'clock, then." She rolled her eyes as somebody bellowed for her again. "I swear I'm going to change my name. I'll talk to you later."

After Paulie walked away, Beth stood up and dug in her pocket for a couple of ones, which she dropped on the counter to cover the tip. They refused to let her pay for her meals, and she'd stopped arguing the point. Kevin was happy and she was able to save that money, but she wouldn't let his employees wait on her for nothing. Feeling more optimistic about the impending holiday, she headed for the elevator.

All she needed to do now was figure out the perfect gift for Kevin.

CHAPTER ELEVEN

IF THERE WAS ONE THING about his parents, Kevin thought as he helped Beth and then Paulie out of the Jeep, they seriously knew how to deck the halls. And they didn't go for boughs of holly, either. His parents' house was ablaze in flashing, multicolored lights that illuminated every inflatable reindeer and snowman known to man.

"Wow."

He looked down at Beth, her awestruck expression bathed in twinkling lights. "My mom's favorite holiday."

"I can see that."

As they walked up a path lined with gigantic plastic candy canes, Kevin hummed a merry holiday tune under his breath. It had been a while since he'd felt so jolly about spending Christmas Eve at his parents' house. Vicky had never really warmed up to his family, and they'd usually argued about it on the drive up from Boston.

After the divorce, he'd usually spent the evening

in the corner trading barbs with Joe—the other single guy in the crowd—watching the family make merry. But this year Joe had Keri, and he kind of had Beth, and they had a baby on the way. A few trips to the enormous buffet table and it just might be the best Christmas ever.

Once the hugs and kisses were over, Kevin made the multiple trips to the Jeep to carry in the gifts. The kids hovered as he added the presents to the mound already surrounding the nine-foot Fraser fir, trying to spot their names on the gift tags, and they protested loudly when Kevin placed them all upside down.

He found Beth in the corner of the dining room, where she stood with a heaping plate of food. She laughed when she saw him, showing him the assortment of goodies.

"Your mother made it pretty clear eating isn't optional."

"I think it's how she keeps us all under control. You don't move fast when you're in a food stupor."

"Paulie wasn't kidding about the nutcrackers."

Kevin laughed, looking around the room and trying to see it from Beth's point of view. His mother collected wooden nutcracker soldiers, and they covered pretty much every flat surface downstairs. If something didn't have food set on it, there was a soldier there.

"When we were kids, Terry got it in her head they should all be lined up in order of height. Ma likes them random. The battle went on forever until Terry superglued them down. That was an interesting Christmas."

Beth was laughing at his story when Bobby ran up to her. She lifted her plate out of harm's way and smiled at Kevin over his nephew's head as the boy put a hand on either side of her waist.

"Hey, cuz!" Bobby yelled at her stomach. "What does a snowman eat for breakfast? Snowflakes!"

Then he laughed like a loon and ran off in another direction. Kevin chuckled as he reached for a plate. "Sorry about that."

"Don't be. It's sweet and I like being here with your family, knowing that the baby's going to be a part of all this."

As if the constant aching need for her wasn't enough, Kevin lost another chunk of his heart. While he wouldn't call himself a mama's boy, his family was everything to him, and he'd struggled with being torn in two before. He wouldn't do it again.

Even before his captain had started banging Kevin's wife, putting the final nail in the coffins of his relationship and his career, his marriage had been shaky. Vicky had never really warmed up to the Kowalskis. Not that she strongly disliked them, but she was always trying to maneuver Kevin in a different direction. She'd wanted to go to Cancún over Thanksgiving or stay in Boston for the Fourth of July.

He'd tried to compromise. She'd been his wife, after all, and that meant something to him. But rather than appreciating his meeting her halfway, she'd pushed for a skiing trip to Colorado over Christmas. His flat-out refusal had caused drama that would have put Shakespeare to shame.

"Presents!" The joyous shout from the living room echoed through the house.

"Brace yourself," he warned Beth. "Picture a tornado tearing through a wrapping-paper factory."

The chaos lasted nearly an hour, even with the men passing out the gifts while the women shoved paper into garbage bags as fast as the kids could strip it. He noted the thoughtful gifts she'd brought for the kids and the hand-carved nutcracker she gave his parents, as well as the fact his family had respected his request they not make Beth uncomfortable by spoiling her with presents. A gift card to the bookstore, a stuffed bear for the baby. A few things like that, and she was glowing with happiness.

The chaos came to an abrupt halt as everybody held their breath when Brian pulled the trigger on one of the Nerf guns Paulie had brought and accidentally shot Beth in the forehead.

"Brian," Lisa shouted at her third son.

Beth blinked in surprise, then carefully set her gifts to one side and rose from her chair. Kevin stood, too, in case she was going to try to lock herself in the bathroom or make a break for the front door.

She did neither. Grabbing a gun from under the tree, she very calmly started loading darts into the clip, and then she smiled at Brian and cocked it. "You are so gonna get it."

Brian screamed and took off toward the dining room, Beth on his heels. Bobby grabbed his gun with a whoop and took after them as the sounds of running headed toward the kitchen. Joey and Danny, being older and wiser, headed in the other direction with stealth, readying to cut the others off.

"Epic Nerf Gun Battle of Doom!" Keri shouted, and all the adults laughed. Joe's new bride had already suffered through the Tandem Cannonballs of Doom and the Annual Kowalski Volleyball Death

Match Tournament of Doom over the summer, but she wrestled Stephanie's gun away from her and took after the crowd.

A minute later they heard Brian's screech and Beth's triumphant shout. Then Bobby yelped, and all the footsteps started pounding in a new direction.

Kevin felt his mother's arm slide around his waist, and he kissed the top of her head. "I like this girl, Kevin."

"I do, too, Ma." A lot.

HER CELL PHONE CHIRPING out a rather tinny and way-too-cheerful-for-the-hour Christmas song woke Beth the next morning. She fumbled for it and managed to answer it before it went to voice mail. "Hello?"

"Merry Christmas!"

Kevin's voice was as cheerful as the ring tone, and she winced. "What time is it?"

"Nine o'clock, which is way too late to be in bed on Christmas morning. I've been crossing the hall and listening at your door since seven, but you won't get up."

She stretched and looked at the clock. Nine o'clock. "That's kinda creepy, you know."

"Maybe a little."

"I should get to sleep late after the Epic Nerf Gun Battle of Doom."

"Ma gave me a batch of homemade cinnamon rolls. All I have to do is pop them in the microwave for a few seconds."

Throwing back the covers, Beth sat up straight. "Your place or mine?"

"I've got coffee made."

"Yours. I need a few minutes to get dressed."

She heard him snort over the line. "You don't get dressed on Christmas morning. Everybody knows that. I'm putting the sugar in your coffee cup as we speak."

"Two minutes," she said and snapped the phone closed.

She brushed her teeth and hair and washed her face in record time, then grabbed Kevin's gifts and went across the hall. His door was standing open, and he grinned when she walked in. "Merry Christmas!"

The pajama rule obviously applied to him, as well, since he was wearing nothing but a well-worn pair of drawstring flannel sleep pants, riding low on his hips.

Merry Christmas, indeed. She repeated it back to him and eyed his table, where two steaming mugs of coffee and a plate of Mary's cinnamon buns were waiting. But first she went to the small, artificial Christmas tree in the corner of the living room and set her gifts down next to a gigantic box with her name on it. While the size of the box intrigued her, she was thankful it appeared he'd held himself in check rather than burying her in an avalanche of presents she couldn't reciprocate.

"Presents first?" he called, and she laughed. Christmas mornings at the Kowalski house must have been insane when Kevin and the others were kids.

"Coffee first. Always."

"It's decaf, because—"

"Shh! Don't say the *D*-word out loud. It destroys the pretense."

They sat at his table and drank coffee and plowed through the warm, sticky cinnamon buns while Beth tried hard not to stare at Kevin's naked chest. It was impossible to avoid it entirely, but she tried not to let her gaze linger. They were in a good place, relationship-wise, and she didn't want to give him any ideas.

The second she'd licked the last crumbs from her fingers, Kevin jumped out of his chair. "Presents!"

Their baby was going to have the best Christmases.

The thought blindsided her, and her eyes teared up as she imagined Kevin and a small child shouting and laughing as they rushed to the tree and tore into wrapping paper. She blinked away the unshed tears and joined Kevin in sitting cross-legged in front of the tree. In a few months, she wouldn't be able to sit like that anymore.

"You first." Kevin picked up the big box and set it in her lap.

She took a few seconds to savor the moment and look at the present. Either Kevin had unexpected skills or he'd paid somebody—or coerced a friend or family member—to wrap it for him.

"Come on," Kevin urged. "Rip it open."

Usually she took her time unwrapping a gift, picking at the tape and carefully unfolding the paper, but Kevin's enthusiasm was contagious. She tore into the paper and lifted the lid off the box.

Folded up under a layer of tissue paper was a beautiful, warm—and expensive-looking—winter coat. She pulled it out of the box, already in love with the weight of it and the sumptuous feel of the dark green fabric. And it was plenty roomy enough for a growing belly. It was the kind of coat that went right past winter necessity to luxury item. The kind of coat she'd probably never buy for herself, which he knew.

"It's beautiful," she whispered. "Thank you."

"Are you sure? There's a gift receipt if you want to change it."

"I love it." She buried her face in it, as much to hide the few tears threatening to escape as feel the warm fabric against her cheeks.

"Okay, I get to open one of mine now, and then you have another."

She didn't argue that it was too much. That the coat was so much more than enough she couldn't possibly accept another gift. He got too much joy out of the giving, and she wasn't going to put a damper on it. "The smaller one first."

He ripped apart the paper with the same gusto the kids had the night before and groaned when he found a white shirt box underneath. "Uh-oh. Clothes."

"You got me clothes."

"A coat's not clothes. And you're not a little boy on the inside."

She laughed as he struggled with the tape holding the box closed and then held her breath as he rummaged through the tissue paper. His grin broadened to full dimple phase as he held up first one T-shirt and then another. One was big and man-sized, the other a miniature version. Both were emblazoned with the Jasper's Bar & Grille logo.

"Awesome!" He laid the big shirt flat on the floor and put the toddler-size version on top. "Me and the little guy will look cool in these."

She laughed and shook her head. "Notice the gender-neutral red."

"Thanks, Beth."

His gaze was warm and the smile genuine, killing the last of the reserve she'd felt about the gift. She'd thought maybe it was cheesy or not enough. And, deep down, she'd been afraid, too. It was too soon to buy things for the baby. If something happened...

Shoving down hard on that thought, she returned his smile. She'd live in this moment, and this moment was a happy one.

"Okay," he said, "right front pocket of your coat."

She fished around until her fingers closed over the small box. Her heart stuttered for a few terrifying seconds when she recognized the wrapping paper of a well-known local jeweler, but calmed when she realized the box was longer and flatter than a ring box. She'd learned not to put anything past Kevin, but that would have been too much.

This time she took her time unwrapping it while he squirmed with impatience. Nestled inside was a simple yet elegant sterling silver mother-and-child pendant on a delicate chain.

"Oh." She ran her fingertip over the beautiful symbol. "This is..."

"Worth a kiss?"

The laughter kept her from dissolving into a puddle of tears. "You're shameless."

"I am. But I can't sit here next to a present with my name on it, so a rain check on the kiss until after I open it."

She hadn't actually agreed to the kiss, never mind issued a rain check, but he was already ripping the paper of his second present.

It was a huge collage frame—the kind with cutouts for a dozen small pictures—she'd filled with photos from Joe's wedding. She'd spent hours looking at the pictures Keri's photographer had taken and then copying the ones she wanted onto a disc to have made into prints.

She'd skipped over posed photos, choosing instead from the many candid shots as she tried to capture the essence of his family. There was one of his parents dancing, gazing into each other's eyes as if they were the newlyweds. One of Kevin dancing with his niece, Stephanie. The three brothers standing together, laughing as though at a private joke. Joe and Keri, in all their finery, leading a laughing Conga line around the room. His nephews all sitting in a row, making a variety of goofy faces at the camera.

Her favorite was a photo obviously taken during the formal bridal party shots. Only it wasn't very formal. Kevin had the groom in a headlock, while Mike noogied him and Evan made rabbit ears behind Joe's head.

Kevin didn't have to tell her he liked the gift. She watched the smile playing across his mouth as he touched a fingertip to each of the photos in turn. "This is amazing."

"I'm glad you like it."

"I love it. Seriously. This is so cool, Beth. Thank you." He ran his finger over one of the pictures again. "Look at my parents in this one. You can see how much they love each other, even after all this time."

She wasn't even aware he moved, but suddenly he was right next to her. He tipped her chin toward him and kissed her.

It was a warm kiss that tugged at her insides and heated her skin, but a quick one. He didn't push it. "Thank you, Beth."

"Merry Christmas. And thank you right back."

He stroked the side of her face, then dropped his hand. "You really get me."

"Thank you for keeping this sweet and simple."

"You mean rather than buying you everything in the mall like I wanted to?" He winked, flashing his dimples at her. "I must get you, too."

He did. "So what's next on the Kowalski list of Christmas Day traditions?"

"Sex with the neighbor."

Laughing, she pushed herself to her feet. "Nice try."

"Cheesy action movies and more food."

His hand was warm in hers as she made a pretense of helping him up. "That's my kind of holiday."

Explosions, laughter, car chases and more cinnamon buns. It was one of the best days she'd ever had and leaving that night—rather than succumbing to his charm and falling into his bed—was one of the hardest walks she'd ever taken.

CHAPTER TWELVE

February

THE BABY WANTED a bacon cheeseburger. Sure, Beth knew it was still too early to really be playing the baby-cravings card, but she wanted a bacon cheeseburger, and she didn't intend to feel guilty about it. Screw the salads.

At this time of day—about an hour before people starting come in for a beer and *SportsCenter*—her favorite end of the bar would be deserted.

She'd grab a stool, inhale a heaping plate of too many calories—what was a bacon cheeseburger without fries, after all—then retreat back to her apartment where she'd spend the rest of the night hiding from the harsh February weather.

She was surprised to find Kevin already keeping one of the stools warm, his nose in a book. As always, the small jolt of desire mingled with regret caught in her chest when she looked at him.

He was such a good guy. She was pretty sure if

she made a list of all the good things about Kevin and a list of qualities she was looking for in a man, there'd be a lot of overlap. If she was honest with herself, the list would probably be a close enough match to win a game show.

The problem was just what she'd feared, though. At the top of the list of the ways he made her feel was safe. Safe and taken care of and not alone while going through a pretty major life upheaval. And it was because of that she couldn't trust her emotions where Kevin Kowalski was concerned. Nor could she trust his—he wanted a child and she was giving him one. That might be enough in his mind, but not hers.

But she couldn't stand around staring at the back of his head, so she pasted on a friendly smile and walked over. "Whatcha reading?"

His head jerked up and he slapped the book closed before laying it facedown on the bar and resting his hands across the back cover. "Nothing."

"Come on. I love books." She craned her neck and could make out the distinctive cover pattern. She should. She saw it on her bedside table every night. "You're reading *What to Expect When You're Expecting?*"

His cheeks turned as red as the Patriots T-shirt he wore. "So?"

"So...I think it's sweet."

"How sweet?" He leaned close, his dimples framing the naughty grin he flashed at her.

"Not that sweet." She shoved him upright again before giving her order to Randy. When the guy not only didn't write it down but barely paid attention, she realized it might be time to cut back on the Jasper burgers.

Kevin tapped the cover of the book. "So when they take the baby's tabloid picture, do we want to find out if it's blue or pink?"

"Tabloid picture?"

"Yeah, you know—the fuzzy black-and-white picture of what looks like an alien head?"

"You mean the ultrasound."

He shrugged. "Yeah, that. According to the book it's almost time for one. Isn't that how they tell the sex of the baby?"

"My appointment's Tuesday, but a lot of time it's too early or the baby's not in a good position."

"Tuesday as in three days from now?" She nodded and popped open the can of seltzer Randy set in front of her. "When were you going to tell me? What time's the appointment? I need to know so I can make sure I'm covered."

"You want to go with me?"

His look went beyond annoyed and well into seriously offended. "Of course I want to go."

She should have guessed he'd want to go, and not just because his name was also on the checks made payable to her doctor. He'd want to go because he wasn't the kind of guy who'd miss his baby's first picture.

There hadn't been a conscious decision on her part not to ask him. It just seemed so...intimate, which was ridiculous, of course. They'd made love, which was a lot more intimate than his sitting next to her while a woman ran an ultrasound wand over her naked stomach.

"I'm sorry," she said and meant it. "It's an early appointment, at eight-thirty, which means leaving at eight, so the bar shouldn't be a problem."

"I'll be waiting in the hall. So, if it's not too early and the baby *is* in a good position, do you want to know?"

She hadn't really thought about it yet. "Do you?"

"I don't know."

"I don't, either. What if it's wrong? Sometimes they are, and then you're all set on a name and you buy a bunch of pink or blue and then...surprise! It's all wrong."

"Have you thought about names?"

She shook her head. "It's too soon to choose

names. Bad luck. But maybe if we find out the sex and it's a girl, knowing ahead of time would give you time to come to terms with it."

He looked offended again and swiveled on his stool so he was fully facing her. "What's that supposed to mean?"

"If it's a girl, I'd rather you get over the disappointment now."

"I don't care if it's a boy or a girl. As long as it's healthy, I'll be over the moon."

"But you're always saying him and his and calling it the little guy. It's pretty obvious you want a son, Kevin."

He leaned in close and smiled. "I only say that because it flusters you. You roll your eyes and smile at me and it's very cute."

She pushed him back upright again as Randy set her burger down in front of her. "I think I want it to be a surprise."

"Then we'll tell the doc we don't want to know." He snuck one of her fries. "You might want to avoid the bar tomorrow, by the way. I can have the kitchen send up a burger for dinner, but it'll be rowdy as hell down here. And packed."

She slapped his hand when he went for another fry. "Why? What's going on tomorrow?"

The look he gave her was a cross between horror

and disbelief. "Seriously? It's Super Bowl Sunday. Only the single most important day in football."

"Are the Patriots playing?"

"No, they got knocked out. But it's still the Super Bowl, and people still want to watch it with other sports fans, so it's a banner day for Jasper's."

When he went for yet another fry, she slid her plate to the right. He should be ashamed of himself, trying to steal fries from a pregnant woman like that. "Thanks for the warning. I'll probably stay in and read."

"There's something else, too. We usually do this thing—Pop and Evan and my brothers and me—where we go up north for a long weekend of snowmobiling. Just the guys. We're planning to leave not this coming Thursday, but the next. Leave Thursday, come home Monday."

"Okay."

"So...are you okay with that?"

She swallowed the bite of burger she'd taken and washed it down with some seltzer. "Why wouldn't I be?"

"I don't know." He shrugged. "There's no cell phone reception up there, so you won't be able to reach me."

"Then I'll call Paulie. Or one of the many other numbers you programmed into my phone. I swear, the only number you didn't put in is the National Guard's."

"Okay." Was he pouting? It looked as if he was pouting. "Just wasn't sure how you'd feel about me being gone that long."

"Kevin, if you wanted a woman who's helpless if she doesn't have your strong shoulders to lean on, you should have slept with the redhead at your brother's wedding."

"There was a redhead there?" He gave her the look that never failed to make her feel all warm and squirmy inside. "Promise me you'll call Paulie or Ma if you need something."

She promised, then made a point of eating her cheeseburger so maybe the conversation could be over.

A four-day break would probably be good for them. He needed a vacation from hovering and she needed a vacation from being hovered over. And she could use a break from the tension that came from her body not being totally on the same page as her mind when it came to not sleeping with him.

"Will you miss me?" he asked, probably hoping to distract her from another French fry grab.

"Hey! You're stealing food from your baby. You realize that, right?"

He laughed so loud he drowned out the television for a few seconds. "Honey, that baby's not starving. At the rate you're going through Jasper burgers, his—or her—first word will probably be 'moo.'"

She picked up the hefty pregnancy book and whacked him in the arm with it. "Smart-ass. Just for that—no, I'm not going to miss you."

"Oh, I bet you'll think about me once or twice."

She shook her head, but when he winked and started walking his fingers toward her plate again, she thought he was probably right.

PAULIE WAS WORKING an excruciatingly slow Tuesday lunch shift when Kevin and Beth walked through the front door. Finally. She tossed her towel on the bar and beckoned them over. "Well?"

Beth beamed. "The ultrasound went really well. Everything's perfect."

"I'm happy to hear that." She folded her arms and glared at Kevin. "Not that I worried a lot when you left for a test at eight in the morning and here it is one o'clock and I'd heard nothing. It's not like I was afraid something had gone wrong or anything."

The bastard flashed his dimples at her, as if he'd forgotten she was totally immune to them. "Sorry. We went out for breakfast after and then went to look at cribs and stuff and then it was almost time for lunch so—"

"Whatever. So did you find out what you're having?"

Beth shook her head. "We want it to be a surprise."

"Prepare to be overwhelmed with mint-green stuff, then. Or even worse, yellow. Oh, Kev, you've got that brewery rep coming in a half hour to go over his new product line."

"I hope he's bringing samples because I could use a beer. Who knew there were so many different kinds of cribs? And don't even get me started on car seats and strollers. I'm going to need a spreadsheet. Or a pie chart."

"It's not that bad," Beth said. "And I have to get ready for work. I had to switch to get this morning off, so I'm working the supper shift tonight, until closing."

"I'll pick you up."

"I can walk, Kevin. It's good for me. If the weather turns bad, I'll take a cab."

"At nine o'clock? I'll pick you up."

They were still arguing as they walked away, and Paulie shook her head. Cute couple, even if they were trying to pretend they weren't one.

While she understood where Beth was coming

from, as far as not getting married because of the kid, it was clear to everybody in a hundred-foot radius they had some serious chemistry going on. Instead of fighting it, she should just go with it.

She was making a list of which supplies needed replenishing after the Super Bowl bash when her cell phone beeped to let her know she had a new text message. As hard as she tried to stop it, she felt herself smiling when she saw it was from Sam.

Miss me?

Like she was going to give him the satisfaction. Speaking of fighting chemistry... Not really.

I miss you. What are you wearing?

Nothing. I'm naked. Bob says hi, btw.

The phone rang almost immediately, Sam's name flashing in the caller ID window. "Hello."

"By Bob, you better mean that stupid Battery Operated Boyfriend acronym."

"Hi, Sam."

"Tell me you're not in bed with some guy."

"Okay. I'm not in bed with some guy."

She could practically feel his anger buzzing through the phone. "Dammit, Paulie, I'm in Germany and I'm supposed to be meeting a few very important investors for drinks in a few minutes. Don't screw with me."

"I'm working, dumbass. Who has time for a

roll in the sheets at one in the afternoon?" She
leaned her hip against the bar, trying not to dwell
on how much she'd missed hearing his voice over
the past couple of months. Email and text messag-
ing weren't the same.

"I've got a few more days in Europe and then
probably a week to ten days closing some deals
in Boston and making some arrangements to be
away for a while. I probably won't be back in New
Hampshire for a couple of weeks."

"Take your time." He needed to make arrangements to be away for a while. How long was he
planning to be around? "No need to rush on my
account."

His low chuckle seemed to vibrate from the
phone, through her hand and to parts of her body
that felt sorely neglected of late. "I'll see you soon,
Paulie."

"Yeah, whenever," she forced herself to say, and
then she snapped the phone closed.

It annoyed her the way her pulse seemed to
quicken when she thought about Sam Logan. Sure,
he'd been great in bed five years ago. And sure,
she'd come within about twenty feet of rose-petal-
strewn aisle of marrying him, but that was a long
time ago.

And the underlying problem—her discontent

with being Paulette Lillian Atherton—remained.
She wasn't going back to being that person, even
for Sam. And Kevin had been right about the situation. While it was fun hanging out here in her
world, Sam hadn't left her parents' world. Eventually, if she let him in, he was going to want to take
her back there.

There was no way in hell that was going to
happen.

THE ANNUAL Guys-Only Sledding Trip—of Doom,
of course—was usually a highlight of the year for
Kevin, but this time he couldn't get his head in
the game.

He usually lost himself in the feeling of skim-
ming over the packed snow. The wind rushing past
his windshield. The sheer adrenaline rush of flying
over a frozen lake. The smell of two-stroke ex-
haust. But all he could think about was Beth.

He should have kissed her goodbye.

She'd played it so cool, telling him to have a
good time and bidding him goodbye with a cheerful wave as if he was a casual acquaintance she
was wishing *bon voyage.* He should have gone
back and kissed her until she wrapped her arms
around his neck and begged him not to go.

Instead, he'd let her act as if it was no big deal.

Just a bunch of guys flying through woods at seventy miles per hour—or more if nobody was looking—in the snow. Icy corners. Fallen trees. Thin ice. Assholes coming around corners on the wrong side of the trail. There were a hundred ways he could get hurt, and she hadn't even seemed concerned he'd come back in one piece.

He slowed down for a notoriously sharp and icy corner he normally would have slid through sideways and heard a machine creeping up behind him. If he could hear Pop, he was too damn close. It was dangerous to be right up on his ass like that.

When he hit the straightaway, he saw Mike and Evan had pulled off onto the side of the trail, so he fell in behind them. After killing his engine, he unplugged the cord to his face shield and got off the machine. With his visor flipped up, he unbuckled his helmet and took it off, then dragged the balaclava off.

Mike slapped him on the shoulder. "You leave your balls in your other jeans or what? We go any slower and we'll have to draw straws to see which one of us gets roasted and eaten first because we sure as hell won't ever make it back to town in time for supper."

"And what happens to Beth and my kid if I wrap myself around a tree?" He tossed his helmet onto his seat. Watched it bounce off. "I shouldn't have left her alone."

"Alone? She'll be lucky if she's had a moment's peace with everybody checking on her all the time. Lisa said you wanted to write out a schedule of who was calling her when."

"I don't have a will. I should have done that before I left." When his brother laughed at him, Kevin resisted the urge to punch him in the mouth. "Yeah, wanting to make sure my kid's taken care of if I die's all kinds of funny."

"Who's dying?" Pop joined in the conversation.

Joe was right on his heels. "Me, if we don't pick up the pace."

"Kev's afraid he's going to hit a tree," Mike said, "and we'll abandon Beth and the baby and leave them to fend for themselves in squalor on the streets."

"That's not what I said."

"Hit a tree?" Joe snorted. "You may as well, 'cause at the rate you're going, the kid's going to be in middle school before we get back anyway."

"Screw you. I'm not going *that* slow. And you—" He pointed at Mike. "You've got four kids at home. You shouldn't be tearing up the trails, either."

"Unlike you, I guess, I try to have fun when I

can. Don't make me beat that old dead *could get hit by a bus* horse."

"Lot better chance of hitting a tree than getting hit by a bus," he muttered. "Gonna go take a leak."

Maybe it was easier for Mike, he fumed, while watering a nearby tree. If something happened to Mike, Lisa would be smothered by all the support she'd get from the family. Beth had nobody. Without Kevin, she'd be alone.

Not that he believed for a second the Kowalskis would turn away from her. But she was proud and used to going it alone. Since it was like pulling teeth to get her to accept help from him, he couldn't see her turning to his family for aid. Paulie would watch out for her, but it wasn't the same. She'd probably get on a bus back to Florida and that would be that. He owed it to her, the baby and his family to get home in one piece.

"When are you and Keri gonna add to the family tree?" Mike was asking Joe when Kevin rejoined the group.

"Working on it. A lot. As often as I can talk her into trying."

Since his moderate pace was causing his manhood to be called into question, Kevin felt justified in saying, "Only took me once, big brother."

"Bragging about the fact you can't even use a rubber the right way? Sounds like you."

"Not my fault they don't make one that can hold me."

"All right," Leo said. "Let's hit the trail before you boys start giving each other noogies and Indian burns."

When they geared up and pulled back onto the trail, he wasn't surprised when Joe pulled out of line to cut in front of him. Pop stayed behind him, though, so he wouldn't be alone when his brothers and Evan left him in their snow dust.

To hell with it. He hit the throttle hard, hoping the loud *braaaap* of the engine would snap him out of his funk. As he ate up the distance between him and Joe, he tried to force all thoughts of Beth out of his mind.

And the fuzzy, tiny black-and-white alien with the steady heartbeat and the cute bump of a nose that had totally stolen his breath. And his heart.

Joe started pulling away again, and Kevin gave it some more throttle. After all, he didn't want his kid sitting around the family gatherings listening to the story of the trip when Daddy rode like a girl.

CHAPTER THIRTEEN

TWO KEVIN-FREE DAYS DOWN, two to go.

Beth sighed and tossed the parenting magazine she hadn't really been reading onto the coffee table. It was pathetic, really, how out of sorts she was without Kevin across the hall.

She should be enjoying the alone time—enjoying a few days free of his overwhelming energy. Instead, the third floor felt so empty she was afraid her voice would echo if she got so lonely she started talking to herself. And she was worried about him.

When he'd left, it had taken every ounce of her willpower not to throw her arms around his neck and beg him not to go. The only thing that stopped her was knowing he would have stayed. If he thought for a minute his being gone might cause her anxiety, he would have watched the guys leave without him, just for her. And that was just the kind of codependency she was trying to avoid.

She'd spent an hour on the phone with her mom.

They'd planned to fly up, but her father had caught some kind of lingering crud on the cruise, and the last thing they wanted to do was expose her and the baby to his germs. So she'd emailed them a picture of her belly, and her father had emailed back a picture of her mother, crying and laughing at the same time.

After cleaning her already spotless apartment for the third time since Kevin had left, a knock on the door was a welcome relief. Especially since Paulie was on the other side.

"Screw it," the redhead said by way of hello. "The place is dead. I left Randy in charge and figured I'd see how you're coping with Kevin not being around."

"I'm bored, actually. I didn't realize how much space he fills up in my day until he wasn't filling it."

"At least he'll be back Monday."

Something about the way she said it made Beth take a closer look. "When's Sam coming back?"

"A couple of weeks, he said. Not that it's a big deal. There's nothing really going on there, anyway."

"But there was once. Seems like he's interested in rekindling the flame." Too late she realized what she'd said.

Paulie pounced on it. "Kevin told you, didn't he?"

Beth hesitated, but there was no sense in lying. "Yes, but I swore I wouldn't tell anybody."

"That bastard," she said, but without any true heat in her words. "Since you guys are still pretending you're not a couple, he doesn't get the significant-other pass."

"We're not pretending. We're really not a couple. Just two neighbors and friends who happen to be having a baby together."

"Sure. You keep telling yourself that, sweetheart."

"Speaking of pretending you're not a couple, what are you going to do when Sam comes back?"

Paulie flopped on the couch and put her feet up on the coffee table. "I don't know. There's no sense in pretending we can make it work, but I can't quite bring myself to toss him out of my life again."

"Why can't you make it work?" Beth sat down in the chair, wincing as her pants seemed to cut off the circulation at her waist, even unbuttoned with her shirt pulled out to hide it.

"He's still necktie-deep in Boston society and I can't go back there. It was a total hell. Social status determined by what shoes you were wearing, and God forbid you should be seen looking at the sale rack, even if there was the cutest red sweater there. Seriously, Beth, you have no idea."

No, she didn't. Her childhood had been comfortable, but it was still hard to identify with a woman who'd never had to look at a price tag. "I still don't see why you can't make it work. Thousands of people commute from here to Boston. So could he."

"He has to attend hundreds of fancy functions every year—the kind of functions you bring your wife to, all dolled up. And his wife would be expected to serve on charitable foundations and play tennis at the country club. That's just not my thing. You got anything to drink?"

"Sure." She stood, then had to pause to give her pants a hike. Not being able to button or zip them comfortably, she'd left them undone, but since her butt wasn't getting any bigger yet, they wouldn't stay up.

"Time to hit the maternity racks." Of course Paulie had to notice.

Beth knew it was time to hit the maternity racks, but her bank account thought she should try to squeeze out a few more weeks—literally. She'd been determined to keep the medical bills at a fair fifty-fifty split and the bill for that ultrasound would be expensive.

Even if she went to the Goodwill store, springing for a new wardrobe would hurt. Then again, her pants falling down while she was carrying a tray of plates at work wouldn't feel so good, either.

Paulie stood, excitement lighting up her face. "Let's go shopping!"

"I'll probably go next week and pick up a few things."

"When? I'll go with you."

The idea of taking Paulie of the trust funds to the Goodwill store with her was so ludicrous she didn't know whether to laugh or cry. "I...don't know exactly when I'll be able to go."

"Let's go right now. Randy can handle the place for a while."

She really didn't want to tell her she couldn't afford any maternity clothes yet, but Paulie wasn't going to give up. "I need to save up a couple more weeks first."

"Oh." Paulie looked disappointed, but then she perked up again. "My treat. Consider it my baby shower gift to you."

"Oh." She hadn't really thought about a shower yet. There were a few women at work she was friendly enough with, but she wasn't sure they were the kind of friends who threw baby showers. Kevin's mom, sister and sisters-in-law. Her mom would fly up, of course. "If I have a shower, it'll just be a small one."

Paulie threw back her head and laughed. "Are you kidding me? I heard Mrs. Kowalski made Mr. Kowalski move his stuff out of the closet because she's running out of space for all the stuff she's already bought the baby."

Beth's cheeks grew hot again, and she covered them with her hands. "Tell me you're joking."

"Nope. Trust me, by the time those women are done shopping, that kid won't even need shoes until third grade. Which is why you should let me give you your shower gift early—something just for you."

She couldn't do it. Paulie was turning into a good friend, but it wouldn't be right for her to be buying her stuff.

"Listen," Paulie said, the laughter gone from her eyes. "Here's how it is. I get along well with Kevin's family and the other women who work here, but I haven't had a girlfriend in forever. I miss that. And you know my history, so you know I can go out and blow some money without having to explain how I got it. I'm in the mood for a good shopping binge and I've barely used my credit card lately."

"I don't know." It didn't seem right.

"There's no classy way to say this, so I'll just say it straight out. I could buy you one of everything in the mall—including the new cars they put on display in the center court—and barely dent the interest on one of my trust funds."

Beth couldn't even begin to wrap her mind around that kind of money. To buy anything that captured your fancy without even glancing at the price tag? Totally unreal.

Paulie clasped her hands together, begging. "Come on, Beth. Let's splurge. Spend some of my grandmother's money."

She was caving. Although she wanted to be responsible and politely decline, she couldn't stop the rush of excitement. She hadn't had a girlfriend in a long time, either.

"Just a couple pairs of pants, maybe," she finally said. "And if the Kowalskis do throw me a baby shower, you can't give me another gift."

"Okay." Paulie managed an innocent look but not an ounce of sincerity in her voice.

"I mean it. Just some pants. Two pairs."

"Okay."

DESPITE KEVIN'S INABILITY to bring himself to ride balls to the wall like he usually did, the guys did make it back into town in time for supper. There was a pub they liked—one that catered to snow-mobilers and didn't mind coats and bibs draped everywhere—and they each ordered the steak. It wasn't some chain restaurant girly steak, either. It was a *steak*.

Beth would be at work, he thought, staring morosely down into his beer. On her feet all night, carrying trays of food and running laps with the coffeepot. And since she didn't look pregnant yet, they wouldn't know to cut her some slack.

"Kevin." He looked up at his father's tone, embarrassed to be caught moping. "What the hell is wrong with you?"

"I've got a delicate situation with a woman."

Mike snorted. "You mean other than the fact you knocked one up you barely knew?"

"You're a funny guy." He took a long pull off his beer. "I'm serious."

"You should talk to your mother," Leo said, slapping his shoulder. "She's good at delicate woman situations."

"Ma's not here. You guys are. And you did ask."

"Then, shoot." Joe leaned back in his chair and crossed his arms. "But don't blame us if the advice sucks."

"We're going to need more beer." Evan waved to the waitress and ordered another round. "I've been married to your sister so long I'm the master of delicate."

Mike snorted. "Terry? Delicate?"

"Not that *she's* delicate. I meant that I have some experience with delicate situations—walking on eggshells, if you know what I mean."

When they all had a fresh Sam Adams—and a Coke for Joe—Kevin picked at the corner of the label and tried to figure out where to start.

"So...Beth can be a little prickly."

They all laughed, and Mike said, "Dude, you think she's prickly now? Wait until she can't see her feet."

Kevin threw a balled-up napkin at his brother. "Shut up, asshole."

"Boys." When Leo spoke, they all quieted down. "Okay. Out with it, Kevin, or we'll be too drunk to find our rooms by the time you're done."

"Beth is touchy when it comes to accepting help. She's very independent and hung up on boundaries, so it's a total battle to get her to accept the smallest thing from me."

"That's not necessarily a bad thing," Evan said. "A lot of women would be sucking you dry. Probably even with the court system's assistance."

"Maybe the court system could assist me in convincing Beth to become a kept woman."

Not surprisingly, that brought on another bout of laughter, but this one went on and on, long enough for him to drain a third of his beer.

Then his dad started coughing until Mike and Joe thumped him on the back a few times. "You trying to kill me, Kevin? Kept woman? Welcome to the twenty-first century, son."

"What else would you call it? She can't be on her feet all day, waiting tables. I want her to quit her job and let me take care of her financially, but it was freakin' World War Three when I bought her a cell phone."

"Women work right up to their due dates," Mike pointed out. "Even waitresses. Then it's maternity leave, unpaid for her, then back to work."

He didn't want her to work that hard for that long. She was already displaying signs of tiring easily, and she wasn't even showing yet. Throw in her mother's history of miscarriages, and he wanted her off her feet.

"If she worked in an office or something, maybe. But she doesn't even get to sit down, except on her break."

"Has she mentioned not wanting to work?" Joe asked.

"No. Beth doesn't… She takes care of herself. It wouldn't even occur to her not to work."

Evan slapped him on the back again. "You sure got it rough, Kowalski. A woman who had sex with you, but doesn't want gifts and won't take your money?"

"Whether she likes it or not, it's on me to make sure she's taken care of."

"You really like her that much?" Joe asked.

"Of course I like her. She's having my baby."

Leo shook his head. "That makes the baby yours. Not the mother. If she doesn't want help from you, that's her business."

That didn't make any sense, even after downing some more beer. Why wouldn't she let him help her? What was good for her was good for the baby. Being bounced around half of every day while his mother ran around delivering cheeseburgers couldn't be good for him. Therefore, for the baby's sake, she should stop waitressing.

"You know what you need to do?" Mike asked.

"If I did, do you think I would have asked you idiots for advice? Well, not you, Pop. These other idiots."

"Whatever." Mike leaned forward, as though

he was about to give up the key to understanding women. "You need to offer her a job yourself."

"Waiting tables at Jasper's every night would be different than what she's doing, how?"

"Not waiting tables. Office stuff. Inventory shit. She went to college for business management. Didn't get her degree, but she knows the stuff."

He didn't know that. "How the hell do you know what she went to school for?"

"Lisa told me."

"How did Lisa know?"

"Fucked if I know. I assume Beth told her. Or Beth told Paulie who told Terry who told Ma who told Lisa. You know how it is."

He considered Mike's plan for a few minutes, but he didn't think it would work. "She knows I've been managing the place two years with no problems. If she thinks I'm just trying to get her off her feet, she'll refuse."

"You need to make her think you need the help. Screw some stuff up. Lose some papers. Run out of something. Shit like that."

Evan was nodding. "You gotta be sneaky. Trust me, I know. There isn't a woman on the planet more stubborn than Terry."

"She gets it from her mother," Leo said. "They're

right. Nothing makes a woman happier than thinking a man can't function without her."

"Are you sure you want to do that?" Joe asked, and they all groaned. As the oldest brother, he usually felt a need to be the voice of reason. Not a quality his younger brothers or brother-in-law appreciated the way they probably should. "You're already giving her a place to live. Now you want to give her a semifake job. Making her totally dependent on you is a pretty big deal."

It was a big deal, and she would absolutely hate hearing Joe sum up the situation like that, but Kevin was convinced it was the best thing to do. For the baby's sake, of course. Not just because he couldn't think of anything he'd like more than working side by side with Beth every day.

The waitress brought their steaks, but Joe had to take a final shot at him. "Families aren't sea monkeys, Kev. You can't just add water and watch them magically appear. The fact you made a baby together doesn't mean she's the one for you. Or that you're the one for her."

"I know that." He shoved a hunk of steak into his mouth so he wouldn't have to say more.

He did know that. But he also knew how much time he spent thinking about her. Wanting to kiss her when she was with him and counting the minutes until she returned when she wasn't. The hours he spent tossing and turning at night, imagining what it would be like to wake up every morning to her in his bed. That couldn't all be just because she was carrying his baby.

He was almost sure of it.

FOUR HOURS AND SEVEN elevator trips later, Paulie collapsed next to Beth on the couch and waved a hand at the mountain of shopping bags. "Did we even remember to get some pants?"

"I think so." Beth looked as exhausted but happy as she felt. "I still can't believe I let you talk me into all this. It's too much."

She didn't think so. A few grand was a small price to pay for the afternoon she'd had. "I loved every second of it."

Uh-oh. Beth's eyes had that welling-up-again look. Damn pregnancy hormones. "Thank you, Paulie. I... Thank you just sounds so lame."

"You're welcome. And happy early baby shower." Paulie stood before the waterworks could start. "I should get downstairs and see how Randy's doing. This is the first time he's run the show alone. Plus, there's no way in hell I'm sticking around here to cut the tags off all that."

She managed to get out of Beth's apartment without triggering another pregnancy-related crying jag and stopped by her own place for a yogurt before heading down to the bar. Not too busy, but a steady crowd of mostly regulars. Nothing Randy couldn't handle. She gave him a wave, chatted up a couple of regulars for a few minutes, then went back upstairs. When it picked up around suppertime, she'd head back down but in the meantime, maybe a movie.

First she fired up her laptop, disgusted to find herself holding her breath as she checked her email account.

And there it was, the email with the sender listed as S. T. Logan.

She shouldn't be so ridiculously happy to see it. It was a dead-end relationship, after all. Not even a relationship. It was a flirtation destined to go absolutely nowhere because the reason she'd run was still between them. But she couldn't stop the pleasant thrill of anticipation as she clicked to open the message.

Do you remember the day we blew off that luncheon and drove the convertible up to the mountains in New Hampshire to see the fall foliage? In the sunshine, laughing, and trying to keep your hair out of your face, you were the most beautiful woman I'd ever seen. You still are.

How could she forget that day? They'd played hooky—running from their social calendars and responsibilities—and cruised up the Kancamagus Highway until they found a pull-off overlooking a panoramic blaze of autumnal color. He'd kissed her senseless as the sun had slowly dropped behind the mountains, and she remembered wishing they could keep driving north and leave it all behind.

But, as always with Sam, business and duty had beckoned, and the idyllic day had faded into a fond memory. When she'd suggested they do it again, he was too busy. She'd pushed and got the lecture— he couldn't just drop everything on a whim, especially her whim. He had *responsibilities*.

Her hand hovered over the touch pad, ready to hit Reply, but she didn't know what to say. Was there any sense in encouraging him? If she let him continue laying on the charm, she was going to end up in his bed. And if she ended up in his bed, he was going to push for more. It was in his nature.

Her cell phone rang, the bar's main number showing in the window. "Hello?"

"Hey, Paulie." It was Darcy. "We've got a table

getting rowdy, and they're not all that impressed by Randy's stern looks."

"I'll be right down." She closed the lid on her laptop, grateful for the reprieve. She'd deal with Sam later.

CHAPTER FOURTEEN

KEVIN WOULD BE HOME SOON. That, and thoughts of a Jasper burger, were all that kept Beth going through a long seven hours on her feet.

One of the other waitresses had a sick kid at home, so she'd agreed to work the early shift on her scheduled day off. Opening at six in the morning was tough enough, and now it was the tail end of the lunch rush. Her tip cup was full, but her back and feet ached.

To make matters worse, the manager had made a few snide remarks about priorities and single mothers being unreliable because it was the second shift in a month the other waitress had missed. Then there were a few sideways glances at the burgeoning bump under Beth's apron and she was getting nervous. Now that she was feeling a lot more pregnant, she was more aware of what a maternity-unfriendly place she worked for.

Which meant if she didn't keep her aches and pains to herself and a smile pasted on her face, she could find herself out of a job. But dwelling on the possibility of financial ruin wasn't conducive to the fake smile, so she'd shoved it out of her mind.

Kevin had told her he'd be home in the evening but probably not early enough for supper. That left her time to enjoy a long, hot shower and a cheeseburger before she saw him. With her spirits bolstered, maybe he wouldn't be able to tell she'd spent the day exhausted and stressed out.

When the time finally came to punch out, she wrapped herself in her warm winter coat and made the walk back to Jasper's. She let herself in the back door so she wouldn't get sucked into a conversation with Paulie or Darcy or even Randy, if he was feeling chatty.

The shower revived her, as did slipping into one of her new maternity outfits—a soft, pink dress with a white sweater to throw on over it. The fabric felt like heaven against her skin, and the color cheered her up immensely. All she needed was a bacon cheeseburger and Kevin and she'd be one hundred percent.

Not that she needed Kevin to feel complete. It would just be nice to have him home so she could stop worrying about him. He was her baby's daddy after all. It was natural for her to be concerned about him getting in an accident.

Or so she told herself as she rode down in the elevator. It couldn't be a simple matter of her missing the sound of his voice or his touch or the way he looked at her, because that would mean she was falling for him.

There were people in the hallway when the elevator landed, and it took her a second to realize it was Terry, Lisa and Keri, in the middle of a rousing debate on whether or not the elevator would hold all three of them.

Keri spotted her first. "Hey! We were just going up so we could drag you down here for dinner, but there was some question about plummeting to our deaths."

"I don't think you can plummet to your death in a three-story building," Terry said. "Fall, yes. Plummet? No."

Since she rode in the elevator several times a day, those weren't semantics Beth cared to dwell on. "So you're all going to dinner?"

"No, *we* are all going to dinner," Keri corrected her. "A quick last hurrah before our men come home. We called ahead and Paulie held us a table. We'd go somewhere else but we heard you're in a pretty monogamous relationship with Jasper burgers."

The women's laughter was comfortable and

easy, and she found herself joining in. On the surface she would have thought they had nothing in common. Keri, with her blond hair and lingering big-city chic. Lisa, a short but feisty mother of four. And Terry, who had the same blue eyes and dimples as her brothers but wasn't quite as rowdy as the men in the family. An unlikely trio who seemed more than happy to make her their fourth.

It was nice, having Paulie and the Kowalski women in her life. She hadn't realized how her nomadic lifestyle had robbed her of close friends until she made some. Not that they were the kind of friends she could spill her man troubles to because, if there was a his and hers column, they were definitely in Kevin's. But it was nice, nonetheless.

They all ordered burgers with fries, and Darcy brought them a pitcher of soda and frosted glasses. They talked about movies, most of which she hadn't seen, and Mike and Lisa's wedding cruise. Then the kids and whether or not they'd all survive a week off from school since winter break had begun that day. All the while, Beth kept sneaking glances at the clock, wishing Kevin had given her a better idea of when he'd be home.

"Look at these two," Terry said to Lisa, waving

her hand in Beth and Keri's direction. "Watching every minute tick off the clock."

Beth blushed, but Keri just laughed. "Damn straight. Joe and I are looking to make some babies and that's not going to happen while he's two hours away. I've got an itch and he needs to get his ass home and scratch it."

Thankful the other woman had drawn the attention to herself, Beth took a drink, hoping her face would cool off. She had an itch, too, and it was hard sometimes to remember why she couldn't let Kevin scratch it.

Terry shook her head. "Trust me, in a few years you'll look forward to him being gone a few days so you can sit around in sweatpants and read. Although it's a lot easier when your kids are old enough to leave you alone for a few minutes at a time, at least. Eventually, though, you guys will be packing their bags for them. Trust me."

It was on the tip of Beth's tongue to point out it was different for her because they were talking about their husbands going away for a long weekend. In her case, it was her neighbor who was away. And, of course, when the baby was older, he or she would miss him while he was gone. But it wasn't the same.

But she couldn't say it. One, because she wasn't

sure exactly what Kevin had told his family about the status of their relationship. And, two, because deep down she wasn't sure it was true. She could try to tell herself anything she wanted, but the truth remained Kevin was more than her friend and neighbor. He was more, even, than the man who'd fathered her child.

She craved him, the way a dieter craved a thick slab of chocolate cake. With ice cream. And whipped cream. And maybe a drizzle of hot fudge sauce.

But like any dieter, she knew that, although chocolate cake might be delicious and sinful and make her feel so very, very good, that didn't make it a good choice. And if there was one thing Beth had in spades, it was willpower.

No chocolate cake—or Kevin—for her.

KEVIN RUSHED AS MUCH as he could without attracting the ridicule of his brothers and brother-in-law, anxious to get home to Beth. Or anxious to get home across the hall from Beth, really, since she was stubborn and wouldn't even sleep with him. Chances of her agreeing to move in with him were pretty slim.

Because he didn't have a garage at Jasper's, he left his snowmobile in its enclosed trailer behind his dad's and jumped back on the highway. Twenty minutes later he was fresh out of the shower and knocking on Beth's door.

She was smiling when she opened it, and the warmth in her eyes was all the welcome home he needed. "Hi."

"Hi," he said back as his gaze wandered down her body. She was wearing a long pink dress with a sweater unbuttoned over it that looked new.

And there was a bump. A little round bump where her taut stomach used to be.

It was beautiful. "Holy shit. It's a baby."

She put her hand on the bump, a shy smile warming her face. "The maternity clothes make it look bigger than it really is. Paulie took me shopping. As an early shower gift."

In the recesses of his mind, a not-very-happy voice wanted to know why she'd accept stuff from Paulie but not from him. He ignored it, though, for now, because all that mattered was the sweet curve under her hand.

A baby. Not an *idea* of a baby that brought to mind memories of his niece and his nephews when they were small, but his baby—real enough and big enough to be seen…sort of.

Beth stepped back to let him in, forcing him to

look away from the baby bump. "I heard you come home. Was wondering if you'd stop in."

"I grabbed a quick shower. Smelled like two-stroke and sweat."

She closed the door behind him. "Did you have fun?"

"Yeah. Missed you, though. Everything go okay?"

"Fine." Pink tinted her cheeks. "I missed you, too."

Interesting. "I thought you'd be glad to be rid of me for a few days."

"I thought I would be, too. But I was worried about you being crazy up there, which made me think of you in general, which made me miss you, I guess."

It was a big risk—huge—but he lowered his head and kissed her. She stiffened for a second, but then her mouth turned soft and welcoming under his. He shifted his body closer, and when he dipped his tongue between her lips, she slid her arms around his waist so her hands pressed against his back.

Afraid the mood would be broken along with the kiss, he made it last as long as he could, until her body melted against his and her fingernails dug into his back and she made a whimpering sound deep in her throat. His body tightened in response, and he pulled her hips against his so she could feel exactly how much he'd missed her. How much he wanted her.

"Chocolate cake," she whispered against his mouth.

"Okay." He blazed a trail of kisses down her jawline, trying not to lose the moment. "Is this one of those food cravings pregnant women get, because…really? Right now? I mean, I'll go, but it might take a while because I'll be walking funny."

"No, you're my chocolate cake." When he moved on to her neck, she tilted her head. "It's like being on a diet and you're my chocolate cake. I really, really want a slice."

That's when it hit Kevin, and all the blood north of his waist rushed south. She was pregnant. It's not like she could get *more* pregnant.

He'd never in his life had sex without a condom. Vicky hadn't wanted kids yet, which turned out to be a blessing, and she couldn't take the Pill, so even as a married man he'd had to make regular trips to the drugstore. But Beth was pregnant, and she was clean and he was clean and…if she made him stop now he was going to spontaneously combust.

"The problem with you," she said as she threw

back her head to bare her throat for him, "is that I've already had a taste. You're not just any old slice of chocolate cake. You're really, *really* good chocolate cake with whipped cream and a swirl of hot fudge."

He slid his hands under the open sweater to cup her breasts through the soft fabric of her dress. "One slice wouldn't hurt."

"One slice," she agreed. He pushed the sweater down her shoulders, ready to find out if the dress had a zipper or not, but she took his jaw and forced him to look at her face. "Just one."

He knew what she was saying—this wasn't going to change anything between them—but he didn't let it discourage him. One slice, then another. Sooner or later you had yourself an entire chocolate cake.

Grinning, he pulled his T-shirt off over his head and tugged her toward the bedroom. "If we're only having one slice, let's enjoy the hell out of it."

He savored her like she was the last bit of chocolate cake he'd ever have—taking his sweet time licking her, tasting her, nibbling at her until her back arched off the bed, and she pounded a fist on his shoulder.

"I can't take anymore."

At least that's what he thought she said. She

was panting pretty hard, so it was more gasping than talking. He lifted his mouth from the nipple he'd been enjoying, though he kept his hand right where it was, between her thighs. "I'm going to make damn sure you don't ever eat a slice of *actual* chocolate cake again without thinking of me."

"It's bad enough you've ruined me for other men, but now you have to ruin dessert for me, too?"

Hearing that—that he'd ruined for her other men—almost sent him straight over the edge, but, just to be sure, he kept a tight leash on his control and made her whimper his name a couple more times before he surrendered and gave her what she wanted. What they both wanted.

Sliding into her uncovered, just flesh against flesh, was by far the most amazing feeling Kevin had ever experienced. So amazing, in fact, he had to stop moving and just hover over her, his weight rested on his forearms.

Unfortunately, he must have teased Beth too much because she wasn't messing around. Digging her fingers into his hips, she tried to force them to move. He resisted, determined to get himself under control before sliding another fraction of an inch into her.

He saw Beth smile a second before she raised

her own hips, taking all of him, and that was all she wrote. A few hard thrusts. A few seconds of hot, unfettered friction, and he was a goner, and he took her with him.

Gasping for air, he took pity on his trembling muscles and collapsed, sliding slightly to one side so his weight didn't crush her stomach. "Holy... wow."

"Mmm."

"Good cake?"

"Mmm-hmm."

He rolled onto his side, and she spooned against him, both of them still trying to catch their breath. There was more he wanted to say, but she was so soft and pliant against him, he didn't dare open his mouth for fear all of his feelings would come falling out, and she'd run screaming.

For now it was enough just to hold her.

BETH SPOONED AGAINST Kevin's warm and naked body, determined not to let the first pangs of regret ruin the *oh, yeah, I needed that* afterglow.

And when he draped his arm across her waist so he could rest his hand on the small bump of baby, she closed her eyes and smiled. Whether they should have gotten naked together or not—and it was definitely a not, even if her willpower had evaporated the second she opened the door—she was going to let herself enjoy this moment.

He nuzzled her hair. "If I go snowmobiling tomorrow, can we do this again tomorrow night?"

She didn't want to talk about tomorrow night—or any other night—because her arguments against their sleeping together were still valid, if temporarily forgotten. Making a noncommittal noise, she avoided answering the question.

He was quiet long enough she would have thought he was asleep if not for the fact she already knew he snored. And he was lightly stroking her belly, too, in a distracted way that made her think he was lost in thought. Maybe thinking about the baby or maybe about the fact they'd just had sex despite her best intentions to stay out of his bed. Or her bed.

"I can practically hear the wheels turning in your head," he mumbled against her hair. "How long do I have before you throw me out?"

"A few minutes." She rolled under his arm until she was facing him. "I'm trying to enjoy the moment before I remind you—and myself—of all the reasons we can't do this."

He looked too serious, which could lead to the same old discussion she didn't want to have yet, so she ran her finger down the bump in his nose. He smiled and said, "Go ahead. Ask me how I broke it."

"I'm sure it was some kind of fun Kowalski family activity."

"Family, yes. Fun…not so much. Joe used to have a pretty bad drinking problem, and one day I caught him trying to go for a joyride in his car, drunk off his ass. He busted my nose, but he didn't get his keys back."

"I can't imagine Joe acting like that. He seems so…not like that." She knew they could get boisterous, but that was serious stuff. Not playing. "Must have taken you a while to get past that."

"Not really. That was the rock-bottom moment that made him quit drinking, so it was worth it. Plus, it adds that ruggedly handsome element that keeps me from being too pretty."

As close as his family was, she imagined it had been a lot more painful than he let on, but she let it go. "Heaven forbid you should be too pretty. Imagine all the napkins the bar would go through, then."

"There's only one napkin I want. The one with your lips imprinted on it and a message asking me to do unbelievably naughty things to you."

She laughed and pushed at his shoulder. "I told you, it's never gonna happen."

"A man can hope."

She was about to reiterate how futile that hope was when the baby kicked. Not just the little flutter that was more of a fleeting tickle, but a real kick. Without thinking, she grabbed Kevin's hand and laid it flat over the spot, pressing down gently.

He froze, and a few long moments later, she saw the amazement light up Kevin's face at the same time she felt the baby kick again. Sporadic and faint, there were several more jabs before the baby seemed to settle in.

Kevin smiled and kissed her forehead. "He's feeling feisty tonight."

"She sure is."

They were quiet for a few more minutes, and she was content to lay with her head on his arm and her face against his chest as his hand rested on her stomach. But then she felt his muscles start relaxing as his breathing slowed, and she pulled out of his embrace. No matter how much she wanted to, they couldn't fall asleep like that.

"Time to go."

He groaned and stretched out on his back. "Are you serious?"

"Very." She pulled at the blanket and tucked it firmly under her arms. "I had a long day at work and I need to sleep."

The muscles in his jaw flexed, but he kept his tone light as he climbed out of bed. "I can't believe you're sending me on the walk of shame."

"It's only the walk of shame if you sleep and then go home in the same clothes you were wearing. I'm actually *saving* you from the walk of shame."

"Gee, thanks. This is so much better than holding you in that nice comfy bed."

As inviting as that sounded, she knew falling asleep in his arms and waking up next to him the next morning would make it so much harder, if not impossible, to rein the relationship in. She'd had her chocolate cake, and that was bad enough. But waking up with the whole damn dessert cart next to her wasn't the way to get back on the wagon.

Not that she didn't feel a few pangs of regret as he put his clothes back on. Or when he looked at the empty spot next to her and heaved a dramatic sigh. But she knew the decision she'd originally made for them to just be friends was the right one, so she didn't cave.

He offered her one last moment of temptation. "You're sure? I could be naked again in ten seconds or less."

No, she wasn't sure at all. "I'm sure."

He shrugged as if to say it was her loss, but

there was a sadness around his eyes she hated seeing. "Good night, then."

"Good night. Oh, and Kevin? Make sure you lock the door when you leave."

He was laughing when he walked out her door, which made her feel a bit better, but as exhausted as she was, it still took her a very long time to fall asleep.

CHAPTER FIFTEEN

NOTHING LIKE A BIG Friday-night game to attract a crowd, Kevin thought with satisfaction as he drew another beer off the tap. The place was hopping, the mood was good and the money flowed like liquid gold.

And Sam Logan was back, sitting at his usual table. He wasn't sure if that fell into the good or the bad column, but it might snap Paulie out of the mood she'd been wallowing in. He was willing to replace a few more broken glasses if it meant she'd stop moping around.

They couldn't both mope at the same time, and Kevin wasn't done with his turn yet. Beth was firmly back in friends mode. And not friends with benefits, either. No, they were right back to neighbors who just happened to be having a baby together.

When he'd tried to talk to her before she left for work, she'd offered him a very fake smile and a brisk excuse about how she was running late but maybe she'd run into him later. With the conversation put off, he'd had all day to dwell on it.

Now that there was some time and distance between him and the Machiavellian men in his family, he was starting to think concocting an elaborate scheme to trick Beth into working at Jasper's wasn't the way to go. He wasn't a very good liar, and, if she saw through it, he'd be in trouble.

Better to respect her intelligence and straight-up tell her about the job. It was a solid offer for a solid reason, so what about it could possibly offend her?

Well, the timing sucked, for one thing. Since she had some kind of hang-up about him suffocating her, trying to become her boss on top of already being her landlord and the father of her child, and only a few days after they had sex, probably wasn't going to be a big hit.

But he wanted her off her feet all day, dammit, so he'd just have to present his case in a rational manner and hope she didn't jump to all sorts of irrational conclusions.

Darcy picked up the tray of drinks he set up for her. "Heads up on twelve, boss."

He glanced over at the table in question and raised an eyebrow. A patron was getting grabby with Paulie, and she wasn't taking his head off his shoulders. Odd. Maybe she wasn't as snapped out of her funk as he thought she was.

Then he looked over at Sam's table. The guy's eyes were practically glued to table twelve and his hands were curled into fists. He might have been born with a silver spoon in his mouth, but Logan had the look of a scrapper.

Not good. Not good at all. He caught Paulie's attention and gestured her back to the bar.

"Sam's not a big fan of that guy's hand on your ass."

"He can join the not-a-big-fan club, then. That guy may be a big spender, but if he puts his hands on me again, he's getting a lapful of Budweiser."

"If he puts his hands on you again, I think we'll be bailing Sam out of jail tomorrow morning."

She glanced over at Sam, then back again. It was a quick look, but he saw the way her jaw tightened. "None of Sam's business whose hand is on my ass."

"I'm guessing he'd beg to differ."

She just rolled her eyes and walked away. He went back to tending the bar alongside Randy, but he kept an eye on the situation. The crowd was a happy one, but he could tell by the vibe, if a punch was thrown the place was going to get really rowdy, really fast.

Sure enough, fifteen minutes later, the big spender at table twelve put his arm around Paulie's hips and tried to pull her onto his lap. When he got the slushy ice from the bottom of his not-quite-empty pitcher of beer instead, he launched out of his chair with a roar of anger.

Kevin was only halfway across the bar, Louisville slugger in hand, when the asshole put his hands on Paulie's shoulders and shoved. She had to backpedal, but she didn't go down.

It didn't matter. Jasper's erupted in outrage. Besides the basic fact a man didn't put his hands on a woman in anger, Paulie was a particular favorite with the regulars.

Unfortunately for Twelve, Sam reached him before Kevin did. Kevin might be the one with the bat, but he was a lot less likely to swing. Sam, on the other hand, spun the guy around and plowed his fist into the fellow's face.

Twelve folded like a napkin, but his buddies were on their feet, ready to jump in. A trio of local college boys came in swinging, and the table collapsed with a crash under the weight of two brawlers. Kevin shouted, but anybody who actually heard him over the melee ignored him.

Paulie, being a smart woman, had taken refuge behind a couple of cement workers who looked as if they could change a flat tire on their truck without a jack. Over in the corner a smaller brawl broke out for no apparent reason other than *what the hell, why not?*

Twelve was back on his feet, and, because Sam was looking around for Paulie, he managed to land one hell of a sucker punch. Sam stayed on his feet, but he'd had his bell rung, and only the fact Twelve got bumped from behind kept him from throwing the knockout punch. Sam regrouped enough to throw a mean right hook, and Twelve staggered.

When he saw one of the frat boys lifting a chair as a weapon, Kevin decided enough was enough. He put two fingers in his mouth and let loose a whistle that probably made every dog within a ten-mile radius whine. Everybody froze. "No cops if it ends right now."

Twelve wasn't too steady on his feet, but that didn't stop him from running his mouth, though the swelling lip didn't help. "What's this guy's problem?"

Kevin pointed the Louisville slugger at him. "You get the hell out of my bar. If I ever see you in here again, I'll bust your kneecaps up so bad you'll need a new couch 'cause your legs'll bend the wrong way."

Twelve and his buddies, who hadn't fared well

at the hands of the college boys, made a big show of grumbling, but they headed out the door. Without dropping any cash on the table first, of course. Jasper's would be eating that bill, along with the table and busted glasses.

As he relocated some of his patrons to a more intact section of the bar so he and Darcy could start cleaning up, he saw Paulie practically dragging Sam toward the door to the back hall. No doubt she'd been snapped out of her funk now, as the poor guy was probably about to discover.

With the excitement over and everybody resettled, Kevin got a couple of buckets and exchanged the baseball bat for a broom and dustpan. The mindless cleanup would be good for him. Give him time to dwell on how he was going to convince Beth she wanted to work for him.

PAULIE SLAMMED HER APARTMENT door behind Sam and shoved him toward her couch. "You're an idiot."

"I missed you, too."

"What the hell were you trying to prove down there?"

He leaned back against the couch, watching her as she went to rummage through her freezer. She should have grabbed some ice from the bar, but she was so focused on getting him upstairs before he did anything else stupid, she didn't think of it. She had a bag of frozen French fries, though, for days when she wanted something even worse for her than the hand-cut fries served downstairs.

She walked over and slapped it in his hand. "Use this."

He very gingerly pressed the bag to his face, wincing. "It did hurt, you know."

"I'm sure it did. The entire right side of your face is turning black-and-blue."

"No, not that. Well, yes, that hurt. But I mean when you left. You said if you thought I'd have been more hurt than embarrassed you never would have run in the first place. It hurt."

"Your pride maybe," she muttered because she'd rather pick a fight than go near a conversation that dug down into how they really felt.

It was one thing when his blackmail scheme was a game. Maybe they'd hang out, hit the sheets a few times. The fact she might still have some feelings for him was an unpleasant surprise. Him still having feelings for her would be downright worst-case scenario.

He grimaced as he shifted the bag. "More than hurt, actually. I was wrecked."

"Give my French fries back." She tried to snatch

them away. "Go downstairs and beg somebody who cares for some ice."

He tossed the fries to the side and grabbed her wrists. Before she could even think about reacting, he had her flat on her back on the couch with his body pinning hers down. "Is that your bitchy way of saying you don't care about me?"

"If I cared about you, I probably wouldn't have dumped your ass at the altar, would I?"

"Ouch." He shifted on top of her, and she forced herself to ignore how parts of him were rubbing against parts of her. Or tried to, anyway. "You panicked and you ran and I've spent the last five years hating myself for standing there and watching you go. I could have caught you before you hit the main doors."

"Bullshit."

"In those heels you were wearing? It would have been like sacking a third-string rookie quarterback."

"A third-string rookie quarterback wouldn't drive a three-inch heel through your—"

He shut her up with his mouth. She stiffened and jerked her wrists out of his hands so she could put them on his shoulders. The intention was to push him off, hopefully onto the floor, but her hands felt those familiar muscles and slid around to his back, holding him close. All the tension left her body as five years of longing burned through the kiss.

"I should have gone after you," he said against her lips.

"It wouldn't have changed anything."

"It would have changed everything." He lifted his head so he could see her eyes. "You loved me."

"Don't go there, Sam. What was it you said? You're just a businessman from Boston and I'm the saucy serving wench who struck your fancy. That's all we've got going on here."

He kissed her neck, just below and behind her earlobe in the spot he'd long ago discovered drove her wild. "You're lying."

She gritted her teeth, trying to ignore the delicious shivers playing with her spine. "Nothing. Has. Changed."

"Everything's changed." He licked at the spot, then blew gently on the moist skin. "I know what you want now."

"I want this life, not yours."

"I'm not trying to take you away from your life. I'm asking for a chance to be a part of it."

She wanted so desperately to believe that. But the real problem, which he seemed to be ignoring, was not whether or not Sam Logan fit into Paulie Reed's life. It was whether or not Paulie Reed fit into the life of Samuel Thomas Logan the Fourth. No matter how hard he pushed, Paulette Atherton wasn't coming back.

He kissed her again, a soft and gentle kiss that made her heart tumble, and then he looked down at her. "Just give me a chance, Paulie. We can make this work."

What the hell, she thought as she pulled him back down for another kiss. She'd left him once and survived. If things hadn't changed as much as he claimed, she could do it again.

He slid one of his hands between them and tried to tug up her shirt, but she grabbed his wrist. "Doesn't your face hurt?"

"Not as much as my body aches for you."

There was no resisting that, so she yanked the hem of her T-shirt out of her jeans. "Let me help you with that."

NO MATTER HOW BETH CRUNCHED the numbers, she couldn't justify anything short of working right up until the minute her water broke. She'd been diligent about saving every spare penny, but being pregnant was expensive, even with only half the medical bills.

Prenatal vitamins and additions here and there to her wardrobe, though Paulie's *gift* had definitely helped out there. She was trying to eat better, which cost a lot more than eating junk—and she had to lay off Jasper burgers or she was going to be pretty damn sad when she finally had the baby and the excess weight didn't magically fall off. Then there was the adorable stuffed lamb she'd had to buy even though it wasn't on sale.

A knock on the door made her jump, but the flush she felt heating her cheeks had less to do with being startled than it did with the probability it was Kevin in the hallway.

She didn't know if it was the hormones or the excess cheeseburgers in her diet or what, but she'd been having some steamy dreams lately. Steamy and explicit and relentlessly hot. All starring the guy next door—or across the hall, actually.

After scooping up her bank statements and bills and shoving them back in the drawer, she did her best to stifle her raging libido and opened the door.

Why did he have to be so damn good-looking? And why did she have to go and sleep with him? Twice. Abstinence was a hell of a lot harder when you knew what you were missing.

"You okay?" he asked. "You look a little flustered."

Hopefully not as flustered as she felt. "Sure. I

was just looking at my finances and thinking about work."

And, dammit, she hadn't meant to tell him that, because if he thought there was a problem he'd get all wound up trying to fix it for her. It just seemed better than confessing she'd been thinking about last night's dream—the one with the hot shower and the scented, slippery body wash.

"Funny you should mention that. Can I come in?"

"Oh. Sure." She let him in and sat on one end of the couch, hoping he'd sit in the chair across from her. Out of arm's reach. "Why is it funny I should mention work?"

Being Kevin, of course, he plopped himself on the couch, too. Well within arm's reach. "Okay, so we had this whole elaborate plan worked out—"

"We?"

"Huh? Oh, it was mostly Mike's plan, though Evan helped, I think. There was also beer involved."

"One of *those* plans."

"Yup. Anyway, the plan was to be really sneaky and trick you into doing something I want you to do."

Wow. She crossed her arms and narrowed her

eyes at him. "You thought tricking me was a good plan?"

"Beer," he reminded her. "More than one."

"What, exactly, did you guys hope to trick me into doing?"

He leaned back against the cushions and gave her his best *you can't be mad at me because I'm so damn cute* grin. "Just remember, for the record, I dumped the elaborate plan to trick you because I respect you."

"Thank you. And so noted."

"And I trust you to be reasonable and hear me out without getting offended."

Meaning whatever it was, it probably wasn't going to be good. "Maybe. Just tell me what it is, already."

"I was thinking maybe you could come to work for me. At Jasper's, I mean."

Wow. Speechless, she just stared at him, trying to make some sense of it in her mind. He wanted her to work at Jasper's? She was dead on her feet after a shift at a low-key family restaurant. But a fast-paced, thriving sports bar? She'd be lucky if she didn't drop halfway through her first shift.

"Not waiting tables, though," he continued. "I was thinking you could work in the office. Do the books and stuff, which I hate like you wouldn't believe. We could get you a cushy chair with one of those lumbar pillow things and everything. Rumor has it you went to college for business management."

"Community college. And I didn't get my degree."

"No, but you know the stuff. And, to be honest, if I hired somebody from the outside, it would probably only be a part-time job. But if you learn how to do some inventory and stuff, we can stretch it out so you get the hours you want. And you'll be off your feet most of the time."

It sounded wonderful. Off her feet, in a cushy office chair with lower-back support. Nobody complaining when the staff couldn't read their minds. No more smiling and kissing ass in the hopes of filling the tip cup.

But working for Kevin? She already rented from him. It was shaky enough having a roof put over her head by the man she'd had two sort of one-night stands with. Having her paycheck come from him, too, was a whole new level of vulnerability.

His grin faded. "You're not saying anything."

"I'm thinking." It was so tempting, but the consequences if it didn't work out could be catastrophic. Nobody was going to hire a visibly pregnant woman.

"See, this is why I was going to trick you."

"That wasn't a very good plan." She sighed, so conflicted she didn't know where to begin. "But making up a job so—"

"Whoa. It's not made up. I hate doing the books, and the only reason I haven't already hired somebody to do it is the fact advertising and interviewing and hiring somebody's even more of a pain in the ass than accounting. It's a legit job. Promise."

It sounded not only legit, but perfect. Or almost perfect, because the risk in giving up the job she already had to work for the man whose baby she was carrying and apartment she was renting wasn't inconsiderable.

She chanced looking into his eyes, expecting to find sincerity warming the usually playful glint. And there it was, practically pleading with her to give him a chance. To give the job a chance.

With no crystal ball, she had no idea how things would turn out—not with the baby and not with their relationship. But she didn't need a fortune-telling device to know that, no matter how they were getting along a month from now, in three months or three years, Kevin wouldn't walk away from her. No matter how pissed off or tired of her he got, he'd do right by her and the baby.

"I'll do it," she said before she could talk herself out of it.

His dimples flashed as he slapped a hand over his heart in mock surprise. "Just like that?"

"Did you want me to argue with you first?"

"Hell, no, but I had pictured this conversation going somewhat differently. You'd get all offended I didn't think you could do your job and then you'd get all pissed off and accuse me of trying to be the boss of you and then..."

"And then?"

"And then I had kinda pictured us having make-up sex. And then christening-the-new-office-chair sex. And maybe christening-the-old-office-desk sex because, as far as I know, it was never christened. And—"

"Stop!" She held up her hand, laughing at his overly innocent expression. "How did you get from me being offended and pissed off to having sex?"

He shrugged. "It's like that six-degrees-of-Kevin-Bacon game, only I have a lot fewer degrees. Pissed off? Make-up sex. New office furniture? Christening sex. Grocery shopping? Whipped cream sex."

"Scrubbing the toilet?"

"Sneaking up and bending you over the vanity sex."

Or shower sex. Steamy, scented, slippery shower sex. "Okay, here's a hard one—pregnant lady."

"Oh, that's an easy one." He reached over and tucked a strand of hair behind her ear, making her shiver. "I think about that one a lot. Maybe a back rub that turns into slow, sweet sex. Me, flat on my back and you riding me so the baby doesn't get squashed."

As heat wound through her body, causing some tingling and aching, she cursed herself for giving him the opening. "Sorry. I have a rule about sleeping with my boss."

"Damn." He actually looked disappointed. "Hoist with my own petard."

"Do you even know what that means?"

"No. I don't think anybody does, but Joe says it."

"Regret offering me a job now, boss?"

"No." He heaved a dramatic sigh. "I still think we could make it work. Locked-in-the-beer-cooler-and-have-to-get-naked-to-warm-each-other-and-stay-alive sex."

"Nice try. I'm sure one of the many women who kiss napkins for you would be happy to get locked in with you, though."

"I haven't had sex with anybody but you since the night we met."

She'd suspected as much, but she worked some nights and he had women throwing themselves at him and…she'd hoped he hadn't. "You've only had sex twice since the beginning of October?"

"Yup. Same as you."

While a part of her went all warm and fuzzy at the fact he hadn't hopped from her bed to some other woman's, the other part of her was anxious. She didn't want him waiting around for something she couldn't give him. "We're not in a relationship, Kevin, which means you can sleep with somebody else."

"You told me before we can't have a relationship, and then we had sex. Kinda hoping we stay true to pattern here."

"That was… We agreed that wouldn't happen again."

"No, you said it wouldn't happen again and I didn't argue with you—out loud, anyway—because you can get prickly pretty damn fast."

Prickly? He should try feeling like the least sexy woman on the planet by day and suffering through porn dreams by night. He'd be pretty damn prickly, too.

Prickly…five o'clock shadow…the rasp of his prickly jaw over her breasts…

Crap, now she was doing it, too.

"When should I give my notice?" she asked, desperate to change the subject.

For a few seconds, she didn't think he was going to let it go, but then he shrugged. "Tomorrow. With the economy the way it is, they've probably got a file full of applications, so tell them you're done as soon as they hire a replacement."

Even as she nodded, Beth wondered if she was making a huge mistake. Not because she was worried about being without a job if things went south with Kevin, but because of Kevin himself. Now she not only lived across the hall, but she'd be working with him every day.

That was a lot of Kevin to resist, and she was barely managing now. A few more dreams like the ones tormenting her recently, and she might stop resisting him at all.

CHAPTER SIXTEEN

April

KEVIN SET A FROSTY MUG in front of his brother, almost dumping it in Mike's lap when Beth waddled by.

Countless women had walked through his bar. Walked. Sashayed. Danced. Staggered. He'd even had a few try to climb up onto the bar and strip. Who knew he'd be turned on by the one who waddled?

With only two months left until her due date, Beth had hit the basketball belly, walk-like-a-duck phase of impending motherhood. Funny, but when his sister and sister-in-law had gone through it, he hadn't found it nearly so attractive.

Could be he'd find Beth attractive no matter what she looked like. Or it could be the fact he'd only had sex twice in the past six and a half months, and the last time had been back in February. But if it was just a matter of neglected libido, things probably would have perked up a bit below the belt when he read some of the napkin offers.

Even *I'd ride you longer than eight seconds, cowboy* hadn't tempted him.

But the sight of Beth waddling from the kitchen to the office, time cards in hand, tempted him. Tempted him a lot. And when she paused to give him a smile over her shoulder, things definitely perked up.

Unfortunately, she was still all about being friends. Over the months, they'd proven themselves good at that, as long as he didn't get too pushy, but he was really starting to hate the neighbors who just happened to be having a baby together routine. He wanted more.

Kevin leaned on the bar so he could keep his voice down. "Tell me something, Mikey. Would you have married Lisa if she didn't get pregnant?"

Mike did a double take at the change in subject, since they'd been talking about Red Sox spring training, but a long swallow of beer helped him get over it. He shrugged. "There's really no way to answer that since she *did* get knocked up, but I'd like to think so."

Because, if not, it meant their entire marriage was based on an accidental pregnancy, not love. "Do you ever—"

"No. Whatever it is, no."

Fair enough. Kevin didn't think he'd want to go through his entire life second-guessing his marriage, either.

He mentally slapped his forehead. Which was Beth's whole point. She didn't want to spend her life wondering if Kevin would have stayed interested in her if not for the baby. He'd watched his sister-in-law have a meltdown just last year because of that, so why had he thought Beth wouldn't have the same doubts?

"You wanna know what I think?" Mike asked.

"Sure." At this point he needed all the help he could get.

"I think you should wait. Lisa and I had been seeing each other for a while, and it was still hard. You got Beth pregnant on your first date. That's not even enough time to know if you like her, never mind the 'til death do you part hookup."

Not entirely true. Call him crazy, but he'd known he liked her the day he'd broken her ex-boss's nose. He'd known he really liked her before Joe's reception had even been over. And since…

He loved the idea of having a baby with Beth. He loved the idea of being a father. He loved the idea of seeing Beth every day.

But did he love Beth?

How the hell was he supposed to know for sure? It's not as if there was a quiz he could take. Or a checklist or a Ouija board or a pie chart or any other damn definitive way to tell.

He picked up the bottled water he stuck to while working and, after taking a slug, picked at the label. "Wait for what, though?"

"Wait until the baby's a screaming, shitting ball of constant hunger and Beth hasn't had a decent night's sleep in months and she hasn't had time for a shower in three days, and no matter what you say, she takes your head clean off your shoulders. Then, if you still think she's the most beautiful woman in the world and there's nowhere else you'd rather be, then maybe it's the real deal."

It sounded real and horrible and wonderful. "Is that how you felt?"

"Hell, Kev, I was a lot younger than you. Young and stupid. Took me a long time to get my head straight, but there was never a day I actually would have walked out the door."

"I can't imagine walking out the door on Beth."

Mike tipped his beer mug at him. "It hasn't been hard yet."

"We've hit a couple of bumps."

"You ain't seen nothing yet. Trust me."

Kevin wasn't stupid. He knew having a newborn

was going to be the hardest thing they'd ever been through.

But she'd have him to lean on when she was tired. She'd get a decent night's sleep because he'd take his turn feeding and changing the screaming, shitting ball of constant hunger. Maybe he could handle breakfast duty so she could shower.

Hard to do with a hallway between them though. It would be so much easier if—

"Look at you, all starry eyed." Mike laughed. "Sucker. Trust me, whatever way it is, you're thinking your infant experience is going to be easier than my infant experience? You are *so* wrong."

He and Beth weren't scared shitless kids, for one thing. They were adults, with life experience and common sense under their belts. They made a good team. "We'll make out okay."

"Sure you will." Mike held up his mug for a refill. "Enough with the girl talk. I came here to watch the game."

PAULIE RAN HER FINGERS over Sam's bare chest, ignoring the crappy Western that had caused him to pause in his incessant channel surfing. They'd fallen into bed too early, so, after a rousing bout of mind-blowing sex and enough cuddling to keep him out of trouble, he'd clicked on the TV.

She closed her eyes and ignored the high-noon showdown going on. Sam wouldn't be getting up and going home, so she was free to drift off to sleep in his arms tonight. She'd wake up the same way in the morning, just as she had the morning before and the morning before that. It was a comfortable pattern, and he hadn't spent a night at the bed-and-breakfast for several weeks, at least.

She was almost asleep when he popped her bubble. She should have known it was coming by the way his body stayed tense rather than relaxing into a languid postlovemaking state. And the way he kept clearing his throat as if he was going to talk, then not saying anything.

"So Marsha's Spring Fling fundraiser is next week," he finally said in a very casual tone that set off alarm bells in her head. "I was hoping maybe you'd come with me."

She'd known it would come up eventually, but she'd been hoping eventually would be a long time coming. "I have to work."

"I bet you could switch shifts if it was important to you."

"It's not important to me." She rolled back to her

side of the bed and stared up at the ceiling. "That's the point."

She thought maybe that was the end of it, but then he sighed and turned off the television. Through the corner of her eye she saw him roll over to face her, but she kept her gaze on the ceiling.

"Is that so much to ask? One fundraiser?"

Of course it was too much to ask because if she went, he'd ask her again. And again and again and again. Before she knew it, she'd be Paulette Atherton again, broiling under the intense spotlight of her parents' disapproval.

"I told you I'm not that person anymore." She kept her voice level, but inside she was screaming. How could she have been so stupid as to think there was a chance in hell this would work? That was his world. Of course he was going to go back to it. And try to drag her with him.

"Putting on a nice dress and attending a function with me doesn't change who you are. And it's just one evening. What could it hurt?"

It could hurt her, that's what. Maybe it was different being the only son of parents who actually seemed like nice people, because he'd obviously never felt inadequate under a parent's censuring glare.

When she didn't say anything, he nudged her with his knee. "Okay, so you're not ready yet. Don't get all bent out of shape about it."

"If you're going to hang out and wait until I'm ready to go back to Boston, you might want to get really, really comfortable."

He moved closer to her and propped himself up on his elbow so he was looking down at her, which pretty effectively blocked her view of the ceiling and gave her no choice but to look at him. "Paulie, don't make a bigger deal out of this than it is."

"It *is* a big deal because it means you haven't been listening to me."

"I listen. It's one of the more fun and casual events on the social calendar, so I invited you. You don't want to go. No big deal." He leaned down and nuzzled below her ear. "It's not the first time you've rejected me, you know."

"Probably won't be the last, either." She turned her head to give him better access to her neck.

He skimmed over her neck and headed straight for her breasts. "I'll risk it."

BETH KNEW SOMETHING WAS UP when Paulie showed up wearing a black sweater and flats with her jeans rather than her usual sports jersey and sneakers. It also looked as if she'd gone easy on the eyeliner.

"You're awfully dressed up just to go to lunch."

Paulie looked down at herself. "I'm hardly dressed up. And I'm, uh…meeting Sam after for…something."

She was such a bad liar. "If we were going somewhere somebody might take pictures or something, you'd tell me, right? Because you're my best friend."

"I'm not telling you anything because Mrs. Kowalski is *fierce*. But a dab of lip gloss might not hurt."

"Give me five minutes."

"Not too much," Paulie called after her, "or people might wonder why you got all dolled up just to go to lunch with me."

Ten minutes later, Beth managed to lower herself into Paulie's Miata. "You're going to need a crane to get me out."

"Yeah, thought about switching vehicles with Kev, but we'd need a crane to get you up into his Jeep. Either way, not gonna be pretty." She got in herself and fired up the ignition. "You know, you're the only person I know who doesn't own a car."

"It's only a matter of time before I'm fishing week-old Cheerios out of my minivan seats. Enjoying my freedom while I still can."

A few minutes later they pulled up in front of a beautiful restaurant known for its function room, and Beth managed to hoist herself out of the tiny car without making too much of a spectacle of herself.

"You better look surprised," Paulie hissed before they went in, "or Mrs. K will tear me a new one."

She didn't have to pretend. Even though she'd suspected it was baby shower day from the minute Paulie had walked into her apartment, she hadn't expected it to be so…much. Balloons and streamers and banners.

And her parents. Seeing the happy tears in her mother's eyes, Beth came totally undone and was sobbing by the time she got her arms around her. She'd missed her mom, and she hadn't realized just how much until she saw her.

"Look at that belly," Shelly exclaimed, and Beth laughed through the tears.

Eventually her mother let go of her and let her dad have a turn. Then came all the Kowalskis. She realized with a start all the guys were there—Kevin's brothers and his dad and brother-in-law—and not just the women. Even his nephews.

After Stephanie hugged her, she had to lean forward so the girl could slip a tiara on her head. Then

Kevin was next to her, slipping his arm around her very substantial waistline.

"Surprise!" He grinned and kissed her cheek.

She spotted Darcy, Randy and a couple of the cooks over by the punch bowl. "Who's tending the bar?"

He shrugged. "We're opening late today. Our friends want to celebrate our baby, so, what the hell, right?"

"What the hell," she agreed. She saw Bobby practically running across the room toward her and laughed. "Here he comes."

The temporarily youngest Kowalski put his hands right on her belly. "Hey, cuz! Why do you have a baby shower? So the baby doesn't stink!"

They all laughed, and then she was guided to a chair decorated with pink and blue streamers and inflatable baby bottles. She felt incredibly special on her throne, wearing a tiara, and she didn't have to fake her smiles as the camera flashes blinded her.

Then the parade of gifts began. Big gifts. Small gifts. Everything in-between gifts. From socks to a top-of-the-line stroller and diapers to a car seat, the pile of things she wouldn't have to buy for the baby grew almost as tall as Kevin. And one thing her child would never want for? Sports T-shirts and onesies. Red Sox, Celtics, Bruins, Patriots and the Revolution—there was some kind of garment for every team. There was more red, white, blue, green, black and gold than mint-green.

The celebration continued in true Kowalski fashion—food and laughter and more food. And, even though she wouldn't have believed it, Artie and Shelly Hansen seemed to fit right in. Whatever stories Leo and her dad were exchanging had them laughing together, and her mother was more than happy to fuss through the pile of baby gifts with Kevin's mom.

When the waitstaff wheeled out a three-layer cake capped off by a cute pair of baby booties, Kevin leaned so close to Beth his lips were practically brushing her ear. "I specifically requested chocolate cake because I know how much you like it."

Even though the temperature in the function room skyrocketed, a deliciously slow shiver tickled her spine.

"It's been a while since you've had a slice." He rested his hand on the small of her back. "You must be craving a lick of that sweet, sticky frosting."

Oh, she was, with an aching intensity that almost took her breath away. So when the cake was set up and their family and friends were turning to see her reaction, she did the only thing she could to save herself the humiliation of throwing herself in his arms.

She elbowed him in the gut.

"Oomph." He took a step back.

The cake was delicious, but with every burst of chocolate on her tongue, her gaze was drawn to Kevin, who was making a big production of licking the frosting off his fork. With each swirl and flick of his tongue, the throbbing knot of need deep inside her seemed to tighten, but reality in the form of their friends and family kept her from doing something stupid, like straddling his lap and licking the frosting off his lips. Well, that and the fact she wasn't sure she *could* straddle his lap anymore.

But their mothers were watching. And the last thing she wanted was for them to start getting ideas about her relationship with Kevin. *Platonic.* That was the word she wanted cemented in their minds, not *wedding* or *bride.*

When the guys got together to start loading the gifts into Kevin's Jeep and whatever other large vehicles were handy, the knot eased up, so, as the mother-to-be, she helped herself to a second slice of cake.

Paulie plopped down in the chair next to her.

"You're going to be sorry when the sugar rush hits the baby and it starts kicking the shit out of your bladder."

Beth licked the buttercream frosting off her fork. "I don't care."

Paulie snagged a plate with a half-eaten slice abandoned by one of the kids. "I don't either."

"You kept your promise. Don't think I didn't notice."

Paulie shrugged. "I promised you I wouldn't give you anything else for a baby shower gift. I didn't, however, promise not to give the baby a gift."

She couldn't remember seeing a gift for the baby with Paulie's name on the tag. Whatever it was, though, it was too much after all the money she'd spent on maternity clothes.

"I've got some paperwork for you in my apartment. I set up a college fund for the little munchkin." The amount she said made Beth gasp.

She opened her mouth to protest, but Paulie shushed her. "I know it's a lot, but you and Kev? You're my family. That kid's my family and I like knowing that, no matter what happens, he or she's going to get a solid start on life."

Beth threw her arms around Paulie's neck and tried not to cry. "Thank you so much."

"You're welcome." She pulled away and swiped at what might have been a tear of her own. "Enough sappy stuff."

"Okay. So, how are things with you and Sam?"

"All right, I guess. We've been spending a lot of time together. Having fun. He's practically staying at my place now."

"That's really great, Paulie."

She shrugged. "For now. We'll see what happens when this job is over and it's time for him to go back to Boston. He asked me to go back, to a fundraiser thing. I said no. Things have been a little awkward since."

"But he's still here."

"Well, the sex is good."

Beth groaned. "I need another piece of cake."

"Don't tell me you're substituting sweets for sex when you've got a guy like Kevin watching you the way he's watching you now."

She didn't let herself turn around and look for him. "We're just friends."

"Uh-huh. Looks like they're passing out the baby shower bingo cards. Get ready to find out how cutthroat this family is when it comes to games."

"I know they're all pretty good at getting their way."

"Kevin hasn't yet."

Beth shrugged and swallowed past the lump in her throat. "Sure he has. He wants a baby. He's getting one."

"He wants you."

"Sure, because it's a package deal. Instant family."

Paulie shook her head and put a hand on her arm. "Tell me you don't really think that."

She was going to tell her she wasn't sure what she thought, but Stephanie was there, giving them each a bingo card, and then the games started. The moment for conversation was over.

But the thought remained, festering in the back of her mind as usual.

CHAPTER SEVENTEEN

"IT'S DEAD TONIGHT," Paulie said. "I'm taking a couple hours off."

Kevin looked at the clock and shrugged. "Go for it. If we get slammed, I'll call you, but I don't think that's going to be a problem. Oh, are you sure you don't mind covering my shift Wednesday night?"

"Are you kidding me? Working the bar, imagining you sitting through a childbirth class? Gonna be the best night of my life."

She was gone before he could ask her what was really wrong because she didn't usually split when it was slow. More often than not, she'd pull up a seat and chat up whatever regulars were in the place.

He figured it out a mere five minutes later when Sam Logan walked in and sat in his usual spot. Paulie was avoiding the guy for some reason, and Kevin wanted to know why. After drawing him a Michelob, he walked over himself instead of handing the brew off to Darcy.

"How's it going?" Sam asked casually.

"Can't complain. And nobody'd listen if I did." He set the beer down, then pulled out a chair for himself.

Sam cocked an eyebrow, but didn't say anything. They'd exchanged some small talk, of course. Sports and the weather and topics along those lines, but they weren't exactly friends.

May as well skip the song and dance. "What's going on between you and Paulie?"

"Guessing if it was any of your business, you wouldn't have to ask."

Fair enough. "Paulie's like a sister to me and—"

"And I love her."

"Oh." Well, that killed the *what are your intentions* question. "Is that why she's avoiding you?"

"I'd guess she's avoiding me because I asked her to go to some stupid party with me."

"In Boston?"

"Yeah, a charity event."

Kevin leaned back in his chair, trying to figure out where the hell he'd go from there. It wasn't as if the guy was mistreating her by inviting her to a party. And yet, he'd made her unhappy, and Paulie was as apt to throw Sam out of her life as try to work through it. He didn't think that would make her happy, either.

There was a fine line between looking out for a friend and sticking his nose where it didn't belong. "Did you know her mother started having Paulie's hair dyed when she was four, because it was too red?"

"I know the Athertons personally, so that doesn't surprise me." Sam took a sip of his beer, then wrapped both hands around the frosted mug. "I wasn't asking her to quit her job and go be a Stepford wife. I invited her to the most fun, casual event on the calendar. And I didn't push when she said no."

Kevin accepted the water bottle Darcy handed him with thanks, then started picking at the label. "She doesn't want to go back there."

"Didn't ask her to move. Just one night." Sam slouched in his chair, looking less like an arrogant trust-fund baby and more like a regular schmuck having his heart broken. "I can't let her walk away from me again."

It was on the tip of his tongue to tell the guy to be patient, but he couldn't spit out the words. He had enough experience with trying to be patient and it sucked. Royally. And, as far as he could tell, it didn't get a guy anywhere but frustrated.

He'd seen the effect his teasing about the choco-late cake had had on Beth at the baby shower, but, as usual, she'd resisted caving to what he knew she felt as badly as he did. And they were back to square one. Neighbors having a baby while one of them slowly died inside.

Sam scowled at his beer. "I think this is where you give me some lame shit about being patient, and, if it's meant to be, she'll come around. And I say, right back atcha."

Kevin laughed and twisted the top off his water. "How 'bout them Red Sox?"

"Beckett looked damn good the other night. And Papelbon's in good form."

"Keeping us in first. Yankees coming up. Should be a helluva game."

Like real men did, they spent the next hour talking sports, both pretending they weren't upset by the fact they had no clue how to make their women happy.

AIRPORT CHAIRS WEREN'T the most comfortable seats for pregnant women, but Beth wanted to spend every last minute she could with her parents before they got on a plane back to Florida. They'd be flying back when the baby was born, but she was going to miss them in the meantime.

When her father went off in search of coffee, her mother's expression turned serious and she rested her hand on Beth's knee. "Honey, Kevin seems like a very nice young man."

And here it came. "He is nice. One of the nicest guys I've ever met, actually."

"Mary told me he wants to have a relationship with you, but that you're insisting you only want to be friends."

"It's complicated."

"Love usually is."

The word hit her like a wrecking ball, and, going to miss her mother or not, she was tempted to get up and walk away. "There's no love, Mom. We had a one-night stand. He collects women's numbers on cocktail napkins, for goodness' sake. And I would never have seen him again if I hadn't gotten pregnant.

"We were done with each other, and a defective condom doesn't change that. We had no future together before, so therefore any future we have now is only due to the baby, and I don't want to spend the rest of my life knowing that."

Her mother squeezed her hand but didn't say anything. She probably knew Beth well enough to know there was more.

And there was. "I was going to Albuquerque. That's where I was going to go next, but then I met Kevin and I was stupid enough to sleep with him and now everything's different. My entire life is different and upside down, and I'm tied to him forever because he's going to be a great dad.

"He overwhelms me and I'm already so overwhelmed I don't know what to do. I can't think straight when I'm around him, but what we do will have such a huge effect on the baby's life. And I just don't want to spend my life wondering if Kevin really wanted me, or if I was just the first woman to give him a child."

Pouring her guts out was exhausting, and when her mother pulled Beth's head to her shoulder and stroked her hair, she didn't resist. For once she didn't feel smothered. Just comforted. "You've always been independent. And stubborn about it. You were only four years old when you told me you didn't need me to tuck you in anymore and you could do it yourself. I could never make you understand it wasn't whether or not you could do it. It was about sharing those last few minutes of your day with you. You have a way of not letting people in."

"If I let him in any more than I have, I'm going to fall in love with him, and there's no going back from there."

"I think you've both fallen in love a little already."

Beth closed her eyes to will the tears away. "We're okay right now. We're friends, and, as long as it stays the way it is now, we'll stay friends. But if we think we're in love and get married, what if someday he realizes he was more in love with the idea of a family than with me? Or what if I realize I only thought I loved him because he's such a great guy and I'm not sure I could go through this without him?"

"At least you'll have tried."

"And if we fail, it'll be ugly. Love doesn't end amicably, and I don't want us to hate each other. I don't want that for the baby. I want her—or his—parents to be friends."

When she opened her eyes, she could see her father coming, trying to balance two paper cups of coffee and a bottle of water. A waiter, he wasn't. Straightening, she swiped at her face, not wanting to look upset.

"Take it slow if you need to," her mother said. "Just don't close yourself off to him completely."

"I can't," she muttered. "He won't let me."

Her dad handed out the beverages, and Beth took a long drink of water, hoping to knock the last of the lump out of her throat. She was tired and uncomfortable in the chair. Plus, she hadn't slept worth a damn since Kevin, the rotten bastard, had

whispered naughty things in her ear about chocolate cake and licking sticky frosting. He'd done that
on purpose, hoping she'd get so wound up she'd
fall back into bed with him.

Instead, she was just wound up with no intention of falling back into bed with him, which meant
staying wound up. Payback was a bitch, though,
and, since he'd insisted on being her birthing
partner, she was going to have the satisfaction of
watching him suffer through childbirth classes.
If anything would kill the mood, that would. She
hoped.

Much too soon, it was time for her parents to
go through security, and they each wrapped her
in long, lingering hugs. She kept the tears back by
sheer willpower, but it wasn't easy.

"We'll be back when it's time for the baby," her
mother told her. "But if you have any problems at
all, just call. We'll come as soon as we can."

"I'll be fine, Mom. You met Kevin's family.
Even if I wanted to be left alone, I wouldn't stand
a chance."

"Take care of my grandbaby," her father said
gruffly, and then he wisely pulled his wife away
before both women could dissolve in puddles of
hysterical sobbing.

When she couldn't see them anymore, Beth

turned, and, after a trip to the ladies' room for a pit stop and quick cry, she walked out the front entrance of Manchester's busy airport.

Kevin was there, down the curb a bit, leaning against the Jeep. He smiled when she saw him, and she shook her head. "I don't think you're allowed to park here."

"Yeah." He opened the door for her. "The guy started to tell me that, but he got distracted by Red Sox tickets. Seems his son's sixteenth birthday happens to fall on a night we're playing the Yankees."

"Do you just carry sports tickets around with you?"

"Only if I think I might need them." He closed her door and walked around the front of the Jeep.

Once they were out of the parking lot, he looked over at her. "I thought it might be hard, your parents leaving. Didn't want you stuck being emotional with some strange cab driver."

"Why do you have to be such a nice guy?"

He flashed his dimples at her. "You've met my mother. Too scared not to be."

It made it so much harder to resist him, though. "Thank you."

"You know what would cheer you up?"

Licking frosting off his stomach before having hot and sweaty and sticky sex?

"Ice cream," he said.

"Strawberry?" Not nearly as good, but better for her in the long run.

His grin was on the wrong side of naughty. "Not chocolate?"

"No chocolate. Strawberry."

"With hot fudge? And whipped cream?"

She couldn't help laughing. "No. Just plain old strawberry ice cream."

He looked as if he was going to say something else, but then he just smiled. "I know just the place."

KEVIN WAS RUINED. No way in hell was he going to have a normal relationship with a woman's vagina ever again.

Shit. He was even using the word *vagina*. He was totally, irretrievably ruined as a man.

Even if his balls should ever relax and leave the shelter of his body, he was pretty sure they'd beat a fast retreat next time he encountered a...vagina. He needed to scrub that word—and the instructor's chipper voice—out of his mind. Or drown it out with a beer. Or tequila shots. Hell, he'd take the whole bottle.

"Are you okay?" It didn't sound as if Beth was even *trying* to hide her amusement.

"No." The instructor's voice bounced around in his mind like a rabid, chatty chipmunk. Vagina. Dilation. Effacement. *Mucous plug,* for chrissake.

"Do you want me to drive?"

He shook his head and forced himself to loosen his grip on the steering wheel. Having to drive was the only thing keeping him from curling up in the fetal position.

Fetal. Baby. *Vagina.* Dammit.

And Beth was laughing at him. "You're the one who bullied your way into being my birthing partner."

"I'm the baby's father," he said through clenched teeth. "I have to be there."

"I was going to ask your mom, actually."

It was on the tip of his tongue to bail. His mom being her birthing partner was the best idea he'd heard in a long time. She was a woman. She'd given birth to four kids of her own, raised one daughter and had five grandchildren. Certainly she couldn't be a stranger to the workings of the… female body part that couldn't be named.

That would be a huge step for Beth, too, as far as accepting she was a part of his family. Who was he to stand in the way of progress?

"No," he heard himself respond. "I want to be there for you. I just hope, when the time comes, I'm closer to your head than your feet."

She laughed, long enough and hard enough that he started keeping an eye out for places with public restrooms. Hopefully she'd make it home, but the woman had to pee more often than a toddler on a road trip.

"That was just a movie. How are you going to survive the live event?"

"Drunk?" Like he wished he currently was. "Let's change the subject."

"Okay. Have you thought about names?"

"You told me it was bad luck to pick a name."

"That was before. So if it's a girl, what would you think about naming her after Paulie? You're so close and she's been such a good friend to me."

"She hates Paulette, but Paulie Kowalski? Sounds weird, and I'm not sure I can handle two Paulies in my life."

"She told me her middle name is Lillian, and she kept it when she changed her name because it was her grandmother's name. It means something to her."

"Lillian's a bit old-fashioned, isn't it?"

"I was thinking Lily."

Lily. He liked that. "Lily Ann, instead of Lillian?"

"Lily Ann Kowalski. I like it. What if it's a boy?"

Since he'd been wondering for the past few weeks how to broach the subject of the baby's last name, it was a huge relief to hear her say it straight out. He wasn't sure if she'd want the baby to have her last name because they weren't married, or if she'd want to hyphenate it. Hansen-Kowalski didn't really work for him. "How about Carl Yastrzemski?"

"Carl Yastrzemski Kowalski? What the hell kind of name is that?"

"I can't believe I even let you in my bar." How did he end up with a woman who knew absolutely nothing about sports? "Yaz was only the greatest left fielder ever. A Red Sox icon."

"I'm not naming my child after a sports person. No Tom Brady Kowalski. No Derek Jeter or whatever Kowalski."

"Jesus, Beth." He almost ran off the road. "Jeter's a freakin' Yankee. I wouldn't even name an ugly, three-legged, one-eyed, rabid and mangy dog I hated Jeter, never mind my own son. Whatever you do, don't ever talk sports with anybody at Jasper's."

"I was making a point."

"Okay, fine, if your point was that you don't

know shit about sports. There's our dads. We could name him after them."

"Leo and Arthur?"

"Yeah, probably not. What's your dad's middle name?"

"Merton."

Crap. "How about Ray? Ray Bourque Kowalski. Gotta nice ring to it."

Through the corner of his eye he saw the disgusted look she threw his way. "Even I've heard of Ray Bourque, Kevin."

"I had to try. He's a Bruins legend."

"I hope you realize I'm going to have to run a Google search on every name you suggest now. Or at least run it by Paulie."

"We've gotta come up with something. In keeping with the Paulie theme, there's Paul." He turned his head just in time to see her wrinkle her nose. "Or not."

"We don't have to decide today."

"Just so you know, the kids offered up a couple of suggestions." When she groaned, he laughed. "Taking any and all sports figures off the table, the consensus from the boys would be Scooter."

"Scooter Kowalski?" Her giggles went a long way toward cleansing his soul of the horror movie—birthing documentary, rather—he'd been forced to endure.

"And Stephanie has requested Jacob Edward if it's a boy and Bella Stephanie if it's a girl. Something to do with some sparkly vampire werewolf books she's into, according to her mother."

"Let's just stick with To Be Determined for now."

He shrugged. "I kinda like Scooter."

"You would." She sighed and shifted in her seat. "I'm hungry. And I need to pee. Again."

He laughed and shook his head. She should have a T-shirt that said that. "We're five minutes from the bar."

"Wings. Yummy." She'd moved from Jasper burgers to wings a few weeks ago, and her appetite for them was insatiable.

Of course, watching her lick the sauce from her fingers was hell on his insatiable appetite, too, but chicken wasn't going to fulfill his craving.

Her craved her. Not just in his bed—though that was a big part of it—but just in general. He wanted to share his life with her. The last time he'd hedged around the subject, she'd laughed at him. They worked together and spent most of their free time together and lived five feet from each other. How much more sharing did he want?

He wanted it all. He wanted the five feet to go away. But after her amusement had faded, she'd gotten touchy and he'd dropped it. The last thing he wanted was for her to be uncomfortable with their current arrangement.

His worst fear was that, if she thought he was being too pushy, she'd bolt. Get on a bus to Florida or somewhere else and leave him behind.

So for now he kept his hands to himself and played the buddy-slash-neighbor who just happened to have fathered her child. It was hard, though, and getting harder every day.

CHAPTER EIGHTEEN

June

PAULIE STOOD IN THE BATHROOM of her fancy Boston hotel bathroom, staring into the mirror. Paulette Atherton stared back.

She hated her. Hated her hair sedately pinned up. Hated the subtle, tastefully applied makeup. The delicate straps of the slip waiting to be covered by the summery, yet elegant, dress perfect for a June brunch at the country club.

Her parents would be there. Sam had informed her they'd be sharing a table because it was long past time for reconciliation. What he didn't seem to understand was the utter lack of possibility she could reconcile who she was with who they wanted her to be.

After four months of getting along pretty damn well in her world, the time had come to take a tentative step back into his world. He'd been making some noise about it for a while, and then a fairly low-key charity brunch had come up, and he'd caught her during a soft moment and...here she was. Paulette Atherton.

She loathed everything about it. And she wasn't stupid. He'd talk her into accompanying him more and more often. When the job in New Hampshire was done, it wouldn't make any sense for him to commute. He'd try to talk her into moving to Boston. Eventually she'd grow to hate him as much as she did the image of herself in the mirror.

Screw him. Screw all of them.

She may as well shoot it all down in a big ball of flames now rather than wait until they were any more invested than they already were. It would still hurt, but it would hurt even more once the *love* word entered the equation. Out loud, anyway.

After dumping her hair-product bag on the vanity, Paulie unpinned her hair and did it up her way—red and as big as an '80s cheerleader's. Then she moved on to the rest of her. Heavy on the eyeliner. Her favorite faded jeans and broken-in sneakers. Black tank top with an oversize, fraying-at-the-cuffs Boston Bruins jersey.

This was the real Paulie, and if Sam didn't like it, he could just kiss her ass.

Okay, probably not a visual she needed in her head at the moment, she mused, slipping on big gold hoop earrings. Then she dumped the contents of the fancy purse and did what she always did— slid her license and her credit card into the back pocket of her jeans and stuck her keys in the front pocket, just as the front desk called to notify her the car service had arrived.

The country club dining room fell silent when Paulie walked in, but she'd been ready for that. She was also ready for the silent outrage robbing the color from her mother's face and the way her father's lips thinned. No joy at being reunited with the daughter they hadn't seen in almost six years. Just the same old judgment and disappointment.

What surprised her was the look on Sam's face. Amusement tugged at the corners of his mouth and crinkled his eyes. And the way he looked at her as she walked to the table was anything but disapproving.

"Paulette Lillian Atherton, what do you think you're doing?" her mother seethed when she sat down in the empty chair.

"It's Paulie Reed now, Mother." She sat in the chair Sam pulled out for her, though she didn't expect to be in it long. "This is me. It's who I am, and you're free to take it or leave it."

"Everybody's staring."

"So?"

Her father leaned across the table so he could keep his voice low. "How could you do this to Sam? Embarrass him in front of his friends and colleagues like this?"

"Actually, Richard," Sam broke in, "I'm not embarrassed by Paulie at all. I'm sorry you think I should be."

Paulie was as stunned as her parents. Her father wasn't lying. The place was full of people who were important to Sam either professionally or personally, but he didn't look the least bit upset his date had shown up looking like a late-'80s sports groupie.

"Look at her," her mother argued. "Quite frankly, I'm surprised they even let her through the door."

That had taken some fast talking actually, in the form of a half-ass lie about a luggage issue and needing her father's credit card to buy herself some new clothes. Only the Atherton last name and the fact they were used to seeing young women in desperate need of Daddy's plastic got her inside.

A foot nudged hers, and Paulie looked at Sam. He winked and rubbed his ankle against hers. "It could be worse. Could be a Canadiens jersey."

"You're a disgrace," her father told her. Sadly, not for the first time.

Sam pushed back his chair and stood, holding

out his hand to Paulie. "Richard, Mrs. Atherton, if you'll excuse us, we'll be leaving now."

Her parents started sputtering and were heading toward scraping and bowing, but Sam put his hand on Paulie's back and steered her out the door and down the walk, where he handed the valet his ticket.

"I'm sorry," she whispered after a few minutes. "I shouldn't have done that."

"They should have at least pretended to be happy to see you."

"If I'd worn what I put on first, they might have made the effort." His car pulled up to the curb and he stepped off to open her door. She waited until he'd gotten in and pulled away from the curb. "I didn't stop to think how this would affect you. I should have."

"It won't affect me. I'm a Logan and nobody wants to risk alienating my family. Or the trust funds, as the case may be."

He said it without arrogance, but rather as a statement of fact. Which it was. He didn't say anything else, so she sat back and watched the scenery go by. When he pulled up in front of her hotel, she assumed he'd tell her he'd call her sometime and show her the door.

Instead, he handed his car over to the valet and

walked inside with her. Still not speaking, they rode up in the elevator and stepped into her lush hotel room.

Only after he'd closed the door behind them did he speak. "You told me before you wanted to be my wife, but not Mrs. Samuel Logan the Fourth. I think I know now what you meant by that."

She was glad because she wasn't sure she could explain it any better.

"But here's the thing," he continued. "I wasn't asking Paulette Atherton to be my wife. I didn't know at the time she went by Paulie, but she's who I wanted to marry."

"You only ever saw Paulette."

"You're wrong. I never saw you in jeans and a hockey jersey, but I saw you. The real you."

She wanted to believe him—wanted to believe the man she'd loved had seen the real her—but it didn't seem possible. "The real me was pretty well hidden, Sam."

"Do you remember the fundraiser buffet for the senator at the Yacht Club?"

"You're proving my point. I displayed perfect Stepford wife potential that day."

He snagged the front of her jersey and pulled her close. "I'd forgotten something in my car so I was outside when you arrived. I saw you driving too fast with the top down and the music too loud. You were belting out the lyrics like you didn't care who was listening. Then I watched you use the rearview mirror to fix yourself up so you'd look respectable, and when you were all spit-polished and perfect, you gave the mirror the finger."

She remembered. "You asked me out on our first date that night."

"I wanted you. The fact you cleaned up nice was a bonus because the truth is I'm a businessman and that's the circle I run in. But I wanted the woman who drove too fast and sang too loud. I thought the pressure of the wedding and being in the spotlight had you kind of uptight and, after we were married, I hoped I'd see her again. Now, I wish I'd said something before it was too late."

"But this is the life you lead."

"I'd give it up for you, but I can't. Too many people depend on me. But it's only part of the life I lead, and don't kid yourself. As long as I send a check, they couldn't care less if I show up or not, especially since I'm off the market."

Hope filtered into her emotions, despite her best efforts to block it out. "Are you? Off the market?"

"I haven't really been on the market since that day at the Yacht Club." He slid his hands down her back to settle at her waist. "I'm not going to lie to you, Paulie. It would mean a lot to me if you'd occasionally show up on my arm, looking spectacular. But I want the life we've had for the last few months. I'll commute, you'll serve beer. We'll have sex…a lot."

"That sounds like a good plan." She wrapped her arms around his neck. "I can do that, too—the function thing—sometimes. A few, maybe. It'll be easier, I think, since I know you don't expect it."

"I love you, Paulie." He lowered his mouth to hers.

She reveled in the kiss—the first kiss they'd ever shared free of doubt and personal hang-ups and false expectations. When it was over, she smiled up at him. "I love you, too. I never stopped."

He let go of her waist and pulled a small box out of his coat pocket. Tears sprang into her eyes, and she wondered if she should tell him she still had the ring he'd given her before—the monstrous diamond solitaire—tucked away in her drawer.

But then he opened the lid, and she saw the two gold bands. They were intricately carved, but still elegantly simple. "Something low-key, I thought, this time. Might fit into your lifestyle better than a big rock."

She sniffed, swiping at the tears on her cheeks. "They're beautiful. And so perfect."

"Paulie Reed, will you marry me? Not everybody or everything else. Just me."

She nodded, her heart in her throat, and then he was kissing her again. It was a very long time before he stopped.

BETH DIDN'T CARE WHAT the calendar said. She was ready for her pregnancy to be over. If the baby wasn't born soon—and to hell with twenty more days—she was going to lose her ever-loving mind.

She wanted to see her feet again. She wanted to sleep on her stomach and not have heartburn and not worry about the elevator plunging three floors under her considerable weight. Then, just for grins, throw in the fact they were only one week into June, and she was already miserably hot.

Mostly, she wanted people to stop hovering over her and checking on her and insisting on doing things for her. She wanted to be left alone.

"Just wait a few hours and I'll take you."

She glared at Kevin, barely resisting the urge to stomp her foot. "I don't need you to take me to the store. Pregnant women go shopping all the time."

He reached into his pocket and pulled out his keys. "At least take my Jeep, then."

"I don't want to climb in and out of your damn Jeep. I'm going to take a cab. Which is also something pregnant women do on a regular basis, by the way."

He crossed his arms, and she watched his jaw set into a familiar stubborn line. "I don't like it."

"I don't care."

"Beth."

"Kevin." She shook her head, sick of the conversation. "I only came through the bar as a courtesy—to let you know I'm leaving and where I'm going."

"I just don't think it's—"

"I've made it very clear, from the day I moved in here—or from the day you decided to move me in here, I should say—that I won't let you take over my life."

"And I've made it pretty damn clear from day one that worrying about you and your safety and well-being doesn't mean I'm taking over your life. It means I care about you. I'd have this same conversation with Paulie if she was three weeks shy of giving birth and wanted to run off by herself."

"And Paulie would tell you to kiss her ass."

He shrugged. "She might."

"She would, and so am I." She turned around to

walk away and realized more than half the patrons were staring at them.

"Beth, if you don't want me to take you, then take Paulie with you."

She would have whirled back to face him, but she wasn't exactly graceful on her feet at the moment, so she settled for calling over her shoulder. "Back off."

The cab was waiting at the curb, and she slid into the backseat as quickly as she could manage in case Kevin got it into his head to come after her. He didn't, though, and, as the taxi accelerated away from Jasper's, she leaned her head back and closed her eyes.

She'd have to apologize to him later, and he'd be all understanding and they'd start the cycle again. Friends. Then he'd start pushing a little. Then a little more, until she had to back him off. Then she'd feel bad and try to make him understand. He'd claim to, and then off they'd go again.

It was chafing on her nerves. The baby was chafing on her nerves...literally. She just wanted to feel normal again. When she wasn't hugely pregnant anymore, Kevin would stop hovering and they could stop bickering. Maybe they could start exploring what kind of relationship they really had, or if they had one at all.

Assuming they didn't strangle each other before then.

The squeal of brakes made her open her eyes just as the cab seemed to explode in a shower of glass and screeching metal. She barely had time to wrap her arms around her stomach before the lights went out.

KEVIN WORKED BEHIND THE BAR. Serving, pouring, wiping. Fuming. Glaring.

He knew from having four nephews and a niece that very pregnant women could be irrational. Even downright unpleasant at times. And with only twenty more days until her official due date, Beth was *very* pregnant.

Maybe he could still tie his own shoes and find a comfortable position to sleep in, but he wasn't exactly tiptoeing through the worry-free tulips, either. And he was sick of getting kicked in the balls every time he tried to make things easier for her.

He was sure she was right. Very pregnant women probably went shopping alone all the time. They probably even took cabs. But the big difference between all those other very pregnant women and Beth was that they weren't Kevin's.

But, according to her, she wasn't Kevin's, either, so what the hell did he know?

The phone on the wall rang, and since nobody else made a move to answer it, he clapped a hand over one ear so he could hear. "Jasper's Bar and Grille."

"Hey, Kevin. It's Officer Jones."

He turned toward the calendar on the wall, trying to guess which game the cop wanted tickets for now. "Jonesy! What's up?"

"There's been an accident."

Beth. And just like that Kevin forgot how to breathe. His knees wobbled, and he slapped his free hand down on the bar just to give him something solid—something not spinning—to hold on to.

"A bus ran a red light and hit the cab Beth was in."

She got hit by a goddamned bus? Kevin opened his mouth three times before hoarse words emerged. "How bad?"

Please don't tell me, "I'm sorry, but she didn't make it."

"Don't know. She's on her way to the hospital, and I just turned onto your street. I'll be out front in thirty seconds."

He hung up, explained to Paulie and asked her

to call his mother, then stepped out onto the sidewalk just as Jonesy pulled up in his cruiser, lights flashing and siren blaring. He'd barely gotten his feet in and the door closed before the cop banged a U-turn and sped toward the hospital.

"Have you heard anything?"

Jonesy shook his head. "I was late to the scene. Supposed to help with traffic control, but I heard Beth's name and offered to get you to the hospital."

"The cab…you said it was hit by a bus?"

"It wasn't going fast, so it's probably not as bad as you think, but it hit her side of the car."

Kevin couldn't respond to that because his stomach seemed to be clawing its way up his throat. *Her side of the car.* Beth had to be okay. And their baby, too.

He doubled over, his arms wrapped around his stomach. Would the baby be okay? Beth was far enough along so even if she went into labor, the baby would survive. He was almost sure of it.

But not so sure he could suck in a full breath.

He was opening the door as Jonesy slid the cruiser to a stop at the emergency-room entrance. "Thanks."

"Good luck, man."

He sprinted through the double doors and straight to the admitting desk, barely refraining from slapping his hand on the glass when the nurse took a few seconds to slide the window open. "Beth Hansen. She was in a car accident and—"

She held up a hand to cut him off. "Are you family?"

"Umm…" Kind of?

"I'm sorry, sir. You'll need to wait in the waiting room."

She started to close the window. "Wait! She's pregnant. I'm the father. I'm the baby's family."

Her expression softened, and she took her hand off the glass. "You can't go in right now, but I do know the baby's heartbeat was strong."

"And Beth's?" Because the baby—he loved the baby—but right now it was just a bundle of dreams and possibilities that kicked his hand when he touched Beth's stomach. But Beth—Beth was real and right now and…he loved her.

God, he loved her.

"They're working on her now, sir. Is there anybody else who should be contacted? Her family?"

His throat contracted, and he shook his head until he could speak again. "Her parents live in Florida. I'll call them. She doesn't have anybody here, though. Just me. She had to fill out some preregistration forms for having the baby, and I'm listed as her contact. All she has is me and I promised her she wasn't alone anymore so if you'd just let me go back there and—"

"The doctors are with her right now. I *promise* somebody will come talk to you as soon as there's news."

It felt like hours that he sat in the hard chair, his elbows propped on his knees so his hands could hold his head up. He stared blindly at the ugly tile floor until he felt a hand on his back. He jerked upright, but it was only Terry.

He was still hugging her when Mike and Lisa walked in, thankfully sans children. No doubt the rest of the family would descend upon him shortly because the Kowalskis didn't go through anything alone. Thank God.

"Do you know anything?" Lisa asked, rubbing her hand up and down his arm.

"No. The nurse said the baby's heartbeat was strong, but that they're working on Beth. I don't know what that means."

Joe and Keri showed up five minutes later with his parents in tow, so he had to do the hug and lack-of-news routine all over again. Then he sat and resumed staring at the tile.

Ma sat next to him and squeezed his knee. "I called Shelly and Artie. They're on their way to the airport, but there's a storm going on and...well, they'll be here as soon as they can. And I've been praying for her since Paulie called."

"Thank you, Ma."

"Figured I should since we all know you're not very good at it."

No, but he was doing his fair share of bargaining with whatever higher power might be listening. He left the form of address open, though, because now wasn't the time to risk alienating anybody up there who could help.

An old-fashioned clock hung on the waiting room wall, and he listened to the *tick tick tick* of the second hand until he thought he'd go mad. His family wasn't helping. He knew they meant well, but when a boisterous group like the Kowalskis were so silent a person could hear a clock tick…it scared him.

Too many ticks of the clock later, a doctor entered the waiting room. Tall and graying around the temples, he exuded an air of confidence, but it was the fairly grim set of his mouth that Kevin focused on. He stood, barely aware of his family standing with him, his mom's arm hooked around his waist.

"I'm sorry," the doctor said, and Kevin's knees buckled. He would have hit the floor if Joe hadn't pushed him backward into his chair. "But the nurse didn't get your name."

The breath whooshed out of him, and all he could do was stare up at the guy.

Joe cleared his throat. "When a family's waiting to hear about a loved one, maybe you shouldn't open with 'I'm sorry.'"

The doctor looked startled. "Of course. My apologies."

"My name is Kevin. Kevin Kowalski. How's Beth?"

"Stable. No serious injuries, thankfully. Bumps, bruises, some lacerations from the glass."

He crumpled into his mom's embrace, unshed tears of relief blurring his vision. "And the baby?"

"Vital signs are stable. As sometimes happens, the trauma kick-started the labor process, though, and since the baby's full term, we're going to let it progress naturally. Once the baby's delivered, we can give Beth some pain meds. Are you the father? Her labor partner?"

Holy shit. "What?"

"Yes, he is," Mary said.

"You need to come with me, then. You're about to become a daddy."

The world swam for a few seconds and then went dark.

CHAPTER NINETEEN

KEVIN CAME TO on the waiting-room floor with his head in his mother's lap. She shouldn't have been sitting on the cold, dirty tile floor like that, so he struggled to push himself up.

Mike grabbed his arm to help. "Take your time, Scarlett."

"Screw you, Mikey."

"Hey, it's not every day I get to see one of my brothers swoon."

"Swooning implies some kind of feminine grace," Joe said. "That was more like watching a cement truck blow a hairpin turn and fly off the side of a mountain."

"Assholes."

"Boys," Mary snapped. "Enough."

The doctor cleared his throat. "This isn't uncommon for new fathers, especially considering the circumstances. We'll get you some orange juice and you'll be good as new."

He felt about as good as a newborn foal, trying

to stand on wobbly legs. "I'm good. I just want to see Beth."

"You just sit here," the doctor said. "We'll get her moved upstairs, and in a few minutes the nurse will bring you up."

"I'm having a baby." Kevin sat down and leaned his head back against the wall. "Holy shit."

"Okay," Mary said in her *mom* voice. "You're all going to go to Beth's. Kevin, does she have a bag packed?"

"I...don't know. The spare keys are kept in the safe in my office. Paulie'll give you the one to Beth's apartment."

"Theresa, Lisa and Keri, you look for a bag, and if you don't find one, pack one up. Michael and Joseph, you'll bring the bag and Kevin's Jeep back here while the girls make sure the apartment's ready for a new mother to come home to. Your father and I will stay here."

"It could be a while, Ma."

"I do know something about childbirth, dear. But if you need a break or you...go crashing through the guardrail again, I want to be here so Beth isn't alone." Kevin squeezed his mother's hand, willing to ignore the shot at his manhood because she cared that Beth had family with her. "After the baby's born I'll make some casseroles to divide up and freeze. But for now, that's all we can do. I'll call you others if there's any news."

Everybody but his parents filed out of the waiting room just as a nurse appeared with a cup of orange juice and a couple of cookies. He consumed them under his mother's watchful eye, and then the nurse brought them upstairs. After much hugging and a few maternal tears, he left his parents in the waiting room and—finally—got to see Beth.

She looked small and pale and scared in the middle of the bed, with scratches and some bruises on her face and arms. But she was awake and okay, and she even smiled when she saw him in the doorway.

"Kevin. You're here."

"Of course I'm here." He dragged a chair close to the bed so he could sit and hold her hand. "I've been here. Jonesy came and got me in the cruiser and my whole family showed up and I passed out so I had to have orange juice and cookies before I could come up. But I'm here now."

"A ride in a police car and a snack. Sounds like a fun field trip."

He laughed, but only for a second because she sucked in a breath as her grip on his tightened so much he thought he felt his bones grinding. "Breathe, honey. It'll only last a few seconds."

The longest few seconds of his life, but he knew it was only going to get worse. So very much worse.

When the contraction ended, she had tears in her eyes. "I didn't even get the sheets on the baby's crib yet. I didn't want them to get dusty."

"You don't need to worry about that right now."

She gave him a weak smile. "Don't tell me. Your entire family left here and went to my apartment."

"My parents stayed here, but otherwise…yeah. Ma deployed the troops. But nobody's trying to bulldoze you, it's just—"

"Kevin, stop. It's okay. I get it. When I go home everything's going to be ready for the baby, and the place will be spotless and, knowing your mother, my fridge will be full and my laundry clean. Not for any other reason but that they care about me and that's what your family does."

"My family loves you." And he was about to say it—that it wasn't just his family who loved her—but another contraction hit her hard, and the nurses had to check her, and then there was another contraction and the moment was gone. He could tell her later, maybe when she wasn't screaming in agony. For now all he could do was hold her hand, help her breathe and wait.

At some point during the ordeal his mother

slipped into the room. She smiled at him while brushing the hair back from Beth's sweaty face. "The storm's easing up in Florida and your parents hope to board soon. They want me to tell you they love you."

"Part of me hopes they get here in time," Beth said. "But another part really doesn't want this to take that long."

Mary laughed and wiped Beth's forehead with a cool cloth. "Why don't you take a break, Kevin? Go get a coffee or something?"

Before he could tell her he wasn't going anywhere, Beth dug her nails into his wrist. "No. Please don't go. I need you here."

"I'm not leaving." He shifted his arm to gently break her death grip and hold her hand instead. It felt good—her needing him—even if it was under extreme circumstances. "I'm okay, Ma."

She stayed a few minutes, then kissed them both on the forehead and headed back to the waiting room. He knew she'd call everybody and give them an update—no news yet.

He mopped Beth's forehead. Fed her ice chips. Held her hand. Coached her through breathing. Dried her tears. Promised her again and again it would all be over soon.

Six of the longest and most grueling hours of

his life later, the doctor held up a slimy, squalling, squirming red thing and said, "It's a girl!"

"A girl," Beth whispered.

They took the baby away for a few seconds, and then they laid her on Beth's chest. She looked a lot like a startled and unhappy tomato with arms and legs.

Kevin thought she was gorgeous. "Lily."

Lily Ann Kowalski. Beth stroked their daughter's almost bald head and then gave him the most achingly beautiful smile he'd ever seen.

All the frustrations and fears of the past few months fell away, and Kevin simply basked in the warmth and joy of the most perfect moment of his life.

When Beth opened her eyes, it was to a headache, a hospital room and Kevin snoring in the visitor's chair. She thought maybe she was dreaming, but a hazy memory of screeching metal and flying glass dragged her firmly into the present.

The baby. Pressing her hand to her stomach, she found only the deflated and doughy lack of a child. Then the painkiller-induced sleep fell away as she remembered the hours of labor. Of Kevin holding her hand and stroking her hair.

She must have made a sound because Kevin jerked awake. "Beth."

"Lily?"

The smile that lit up his face told her everything important. "She's beautiful."

"Where is she?"

He moved to the side of her bed, sitting gingerly on the edge. "She's in the nursery, probably wondering why a bunch of people who look like her daddy and two who don't have their faces pressed to the glass, staring at her."

Her parents had made it. "Is she okay?"

Kevin lifted her hand and pressed a kiss to her palm. "She's perfect. Loud, but perfect."

Tears blurred her vision, and she was grateful he hadn't let go of her hand. She could use some of his strength. "I feel like I got hit by a bus."

He laughed so hard the nurses came, which meant he had to let go of her hand and get out of their way. But he didn't go far. He sat back in the chair, listening as they assessed her.

She had a lot of pain, not only from childbirth, but aches and pains from the accident. Her head was pounding, for one thing, and the entire right side of her body throbbed.

"Will you have help at home?" the older nurse asked. "You won't be going home until at least tomorrow, but it's still going to be difficult with your additional injuries, so we need to know you'll have assistance."

Kevin winked at her behind the nurse's back. "Trust me, she'll have help."

Knowing his family, she'd be begging for less help before the week was over. Or maybe not, she thought as she tried to sit up straighter in the bed before collapsing. She couldn't be alone with the baby unless she could move without being drugged, so she resigned herself to at least a week of company. Mary probably already had a dry-erase board with a schedule on it up on her fridge.

She'd worry about that later. Right now she just wanted to hold her daughter. After raising the head of her bed and propping her up with pillows, they finally brought Lily to her. She was swaddled in a pink blanket, her tiny face almost serene in sleep. Her cute rosebud mouth puckered a little when Beth caressed her cheek, but she didn't wake.

The nurses left, pulling the door closed behind them. Left alone, she unwrapped Lily and memorized every beautiful, perfect part of her. It was too soon to know what color her eyes would be, but she had her daddy's dimples.

"She's amazing." Kevin was standing next to

the bed, and she hadn't even noticed him moving. "You're amazing."

"You were pretty amazing, too, you know. I was worried after your reaction to the movie in class."

He eased down on the edge of the bed. "It's different when it's the woman you…care about who's in pain."

She didn't miss the hesitation in his words, and her heart picked up the pace as she wondered what he'd really been about to say. Surely not what her overactive imagination assumed he'd been about to say. He was attracted to her, and he wanted to take care of her, but he'd never so much as hinted that he might love her.

While deep down inside, a part of her squealed in delight at the possibility, the rational part of her mind—the part she'd let run her life almost entirely since getting pregnant—was glad he hadn't said it, even if it was true. If he said it out loud, she'd have to question whether it was simply the heightened emotion of seeing their daughter born that prompted the feeling, and she just wasn't strong enough to resist him.

Making any kind of decision at a time like that would be a huge mistake, never mind one that would have a profound effect not only on their futures, but on their daughter's.

"So about this help I'll have at home," she said, in an effort to change the direction her thoughts were taking. Unless, of course, he was about to tell her he planned to move in with her until she was back on her feet. That might help her physically, but it wouldn't do a damn thing for her mental health.

"Ma and Lisa and Terry have it worked out, I guess. Your parents are going to stay with mine, except when your mom's with you. I thought with all the...stuff...that comes after pregnancy, you might be more comfortable having a woman around to help you out."

Why did he have to be so damn considerate all the time? "Thank you."

"I'll still be around, too, if you need me." He scrubbed his hands over his face, and in the seconds after, before he masked it for her benefit, she saw just how exhausted he was.

"You should go home," she said. "Stretch out in a real bed and get some sleep."

"I'm not going anywhere. I slept some in the chair, so I'll be okay."

"Sleeping upright in a chair isn't a decent night's rest, Kevin. Lily and I have an entire crew of nurses available at the push of a button. My mom's going to want to come in. You don't need to stay."

"I know I don't need to. I want to." He looked at her, his face uncharacteristically serious. "I'm not ready to leave you yet. When Jonesy called and said your cab got hit by a bus…"

"I'm okay now."

"I'm not." He took her free hand in his. "When I thought… After the call I realized something."

Please, don't, she thought. She didn't want him to say it then, when she couldn't trust that it came from anyplace other than the emotional roller-coaster they'd been on.

"I love you, Beth." Joy and dismay battered against each other in her mind and all she could do was shake her head. "Don't tell me I don't."

"I was in an accident and then we had a baby, Kevin. After upheaval like that our emotions are obviously going to be out of whack and—"

"Stop." He stood and let her hand slide free of his. "Forget I said anything."

As if she could ever forget hearing those words. "No, let's talk about this."

He shook his head. "I'm too tired to stand here and listen to you tell me my feelings aren't real, but I'm not so much of an asshole that I'm going to argue with you when you just had a baby."

As if on cue, Lily started making squeaking noises she assumed were the sleepy precursors to a full howl.

Kevin bent and kissed the baby's forehead. "I think you're right. You're obviously well taken care of here, your parents want to see you, and I need some sleep. Call me if you need anything. If not, I'll see you later."

He walked out without making eye contact with her, and Beth panicked. She wanted to call him— to ask him to come back so they could talk about it—but Lily made it painfully clear she didn't care what was going on between her parents. She wanted to eat.

Beth rang the bell, and it wasn't until one of the nurses handed her a tissue and assured her being emotional was normal that she realized she was crying.

KEVIN PUT ON HIS BEST HAPPY face—a skill honed by several years of tending bar—just before he turned the corner into Beth's hospital room. Today he'd be bringing them home, and he didn't want the day before hanging between them.

After sleeping like the dead for hours, he'd called her to check on her rather than driving back to the hospital because he was afraid she'd see how badly she'd hurt him. With some more time gone by, he was pretty sure he could fake being happy well enough to get by. For now.

She looked better—stronger—as she sat in a rocking chair, holding Lily and talking to his mother, who'd pulled one of the visitor's chairs up close. Her mother was in the other chair on the other side of the rocker.

"Hey, Ma." He kissed Mary's cheek, then leaned down to do the same to Lily, keenly aware of how close his face was to Beth's. So close he felt her breath across his cheek as he pulled away. "How are my two best girls today?"

A flush brightened Beth's cheeks, but she smiled. "Ready to go home."

"As soon as they give you the all clear, I'll get you out of here." With no place else to sit, he perched on the edge of the hospital bed. "Are you going home with them, Ma?"

"For a while. And we don't want Shelly overdoing it, either, so the girls and I will be popping in now and then to give a hand."

"I feel a lot better now," Beth protested. "I don't want everybody turning their lives upside down over me."

"Don't even start." Kevin gave her a hard look. "When I called at three this morning they said

they'd brought Lily into the nursery because they
had to up the dosage on your pain meds before you
could sleep."

She looked down at the baby, probably so she
wouldn't have to look at him. "I really am feeling
better this morning."

"And you'll keep feeling better because you'll
be resting and letting people help you rather than
running yourself ragged."

He caught their mothers' gazes bouncing between the two of them, matching small furrows between their eyebrows. Maybe he wasn't doing quite
as well at pretending as he'd hoped. Fortunately,
the pink bundle in Beth's arms wiggled, distract-
ing the women from wherever their thoughts had
gone.

"Finally," Shelly exclaimed. "I thought she'd
never wake up."

Four hours later, they had Lily strapped into her
car seat and Beth out of her wheelchair, ready to
hit the road. It made him nervous, her going home
when just the night before she'd had so much pain
she couldn't sleep, but she seemed in good spirits
and didn't hesitate at all when it was time to say
farewell to the nurses.

Mary followed them in her car, and they parked
in the lot behind the bar so they could duck in the

back door, unseen. He took the stairs two at a time while his mother—carrying the car seat—Shelly and Beth took the elevator, so he reached the top floor just a few seconds after they did.

As expected, Beth's apartment was spotless and her fridge fully stocked. The crib was made up and the changing table ready to use. Lily was sound asleep in her car seat, so his mother set it next to the couch and draped the edge of the receiving blanket over the handle to keep out the light. Beth thanked her and went into the bathroom with Shelly supporting her.

Kevin stepped up behind his own mom and wrapped his arms around her shoulders as he kissed the top of her head. "Thanks, Ma."

She patted his hand. "She's family, even if it's taking her a while to get used to it."

"You think she will?"

"I think when her mind settles enough, she'll figure it out. She's been through a lot. Be patient."

He thought he'd been pretty damn patient for a pretty damn long time now, but what else was he going to do? It's not like women you loved were interchangeable and he could simply move on to a more agreeable one. One who didn't throw his feelings back in his face.

"All you can do is wait for her to be ready,"

she said, as if she could read his thoughts. He was pretty sure she couldn't or she'd have kicked his ass frequently during his youth, but it was still unnerving.

"I've been waiting. It's not getting me anywhere."

"What else can you do?"

The bathroom door opening saved him from answering, and Shelly helped her daughter to the couch before going back in. Beth looked pale, and he figured it would only be a few minutes before her exhaustion beat down her relief at being home again.

Sure enough, his mother started shooing him toward the door. "She needs to sleep now."

"I'd like to feed Lily."

"In a while. Let them get settled in first."

Before he knew it, he was in the hall, and the door was gently but firmly closed on him. With his hands curled into fists, he stared at the wood, wanting to kick it in so he could spend some time with his own daughter, thank you very much.

But the memory of the shadows under Beth's eyes made his shoulders slump and his hands relax. She did need to sleep, and she wasn't going to do that with him underfoot. There would be plenty of time for feeding Lily when her mother wasn't ready to drop.

So he'd wait. It seemed to be the sum total of his life now. Waiting.

CHAPTER TWENTY

BETH THOUGHT SHE'D BEEN TIRED before. All-nighters in college before she'd given it up as not for her. Double shifts after not enough sleep. Tossing and turning all night toward the end of her pregnancy, desperate to find a comfortable position.

Now she was tired. Three nights with a newborn and she didn't know what day it was. She wasn't sure she'd put on clean clothes that morning, and she sure as hell didn't have the energy to lift her hairbrush as high as her head.

"Hey," Lisa said, "I'm going to call down and order some wings and fries. We can find a movie on and veg in front of the TV."

"I'm supposed to sleep when the baby sleeps." And the baby, thank God, was sleeping.

Lisa had spent the night, and the company was nice, but Beth was determined to take care of Lily herself. The women couldn't stay forever, and then she'd be alone. Mary and her mother had puttered around the apartment and hovered while Beth fed

Lily, but they'd both respected her wish not to lean on them too much.

When Lisa showed up, ready to get away from her four boys for a while, Mary and Shelly had gone back to the Kowalski house to see what their husbands were up to and relax for a while.

"I know they say that." Lisa grabbed the phone. "But if you only sleep and take care of Lily, you'll get dragged down. You need to be able to enjoy a few minutes of being awake while she's not. A mental break."

A mental break*down* was where she was heading. "Go ahead, but I'll probably nod off and choke on a French fry."

But forty minutes later she was licking buffalo sauce off her fingers and actually laughing at an old episode of *Friends*.

For a few minutes she felt almost human again, and a tightness she hadn't even been aware of loosened in her chest. Lisa had been right. Exhaustion was still fogging her brain and making her body ache, but even a few minutes of normality gave her a glimpse of her old self.

When the episode ended, Lisa gave her a once-over and a kind smile. "Why don't you go take a shower? You'll feel better."

"Lily's going to—"

"I'm not going to sit here and let her cry, Beth. I managed to get four of them old enough to go to school, at least. Your pain's a lot better, but a nice, long hot shower will do wonders."

It would. Steaming away the aches and pains and washing away some of the grimy feeling. But she needed to learn to work around Lily's schedule. She'd still need to shower after the other women returned to their lives. "I should be there when she wakes up."

Lisa blew out what sounded like an exasperated breath and turned the television off. "Look, I get that you're used to doing things alone and you don't like to be dependent on other people. That's fine. You're going to be alone soon enough, but right now I'm here. You're going to take a shower and when Lily wakes up I'm going to change her and feed her and hold her."

Beth opened her mouth to argue, but what came out was, "Okay."

The reluctance and guilt washed down the drain as the first hard pulses of hot water massaged her sore muscles. A couple of the worst cuts still stung, but her bruises were fading to purple and yellow. She shampooed her hair twice and used more than the usual amount of her favorite bodywash, making a rich lather.

She stayed under the water until it started running cold and then dried off and put on a fresh pair of yoga pants with a cheery pink T-shirt. Both maternity, of course, since baby weight didn't magically drop off during labor. She didn't care. Right now it was all about the comfort.

Rather than scraping her hair back into a messy ponytail, she brushed it out and left it loose. There were shadows under her eyes and residual bruising on her face, but she wouldn't go so far as makeup. She felt good enough for now.

When she walked out of the bathroom she saw Kevin lounging on the couch, feeding Lily. While her body couldn't be bothered to offer up so much as a twinge of interest, her heart did a quick somersault at the sight of him cradling their daughter. And maybe a little at the warm smile he gave her.

"Mike stopped by for a burger and a beer. Ma's got the boys so I figured I'd come up and let Lisa have lunch with him. I hope you don't mind."

"Oh. No, of course not." It was the first time they'd been alone since the night Lily was born, and she felt inexplicably shy.

They'd been through something so incredibly intimate and bonding together. Then he'd told her he loved her. And she'd told him he didn't.

"You look a lot better. From the accident, I

mean. Not just because you just got out of the shower."

"Trust me, the shower didn't hurt."

She watched as he set the bottle on the coffee table and lifted Lily to his shoulder. He alternated between rubbing her back and gently patting until she gave up an unladylike burp. Then he settled her back in his arms and gave her the bottle again.

Beth sat on the end of the couch and folded her legs under her. "You're very good at that."

"One niece. Four nephews. Lots of practice." He smiled down at their daughter. "It's not the same, though. I didn't know it then, but it's not the same when she's your own."

She'd never held or fed a baby before her own, but she'd looked into Lily's eyes as she fed her and thought she understood what he meant. "She's so sweet when she's feeding. Or sleeping."

He looked up at her, then, and arched an eyebrow. "Speaking of which, I got a phone call from Ma earlier and I just talked to Lisa a few minutes ago. Why aren't you letting them help you? You won't even let *your* mother get up during the night."

"They *are* helping me. They're making sure I eat and they clean up. I'm lucky if I get to finish my coffee before the cup's whisked away to be washed. They're hovering and…it's too much."

"Let them take a night feeding. Or two. The more you let them do, the faster you'll recover. Your body needs to rest."

And she didn't need another lecture. "If I get in the habit of letting them take care of everything, it'll just be harder when I'm alone."

She knew it was the wrong thing to say as soon as the words left her mouth, and the way his jaw tightened confirmed that. "You won't be alone. I'm five feet away. Number two on your speed dial."

Beth was feeling too refreshed and relaxed to spoil it with an argument. "I'll try to lean on them more. I promise."

His face relaxed, and he pulled the bottle away from Lily as she sucked down the last few drops. He got a couple of burps out of her, and she seemed content to be cuddled against her daddy's chest.

Beth's heart did another annoying backflip, and she turned her gaze to the television he must have turned back on when he sat down to feed Lily. The channel had moved on to a classic romantic comedy, and she tried to lose herself in the banter.

Kevin chuckled at the on-screen antics, and Beth forced herself to relax. She'd enjoy the companionship and take advantage of the extended mental break, as Lisa had put it.

But her eyelids were heavy, and no matter how much she blinked, she couldn't seem to keep them open.

"Sleep, Beth." His voice was low and reassuring. "I'm here. And I'm not going anywhere."

She let herself slide into sleep with his words playing through her mind. *I'm not going anywhere.*

"I'M NOT SURE THIS IS a good idea. She's only three weeks old."

Kevin made the turn into his parents' driveway and killed the engine. "The weather's beautiful, and you need to get out and get some fresh air. You haven't left your apartment since your parents flew back to Florida."

She ignored him, which wasn't a surprise. Not being very happy about his taking the baby out, she'd reluctantly insisted on going along, bad mood and all. He had Lily's car seat unlatched and in his hand before Beth even got out of the Jeep. Most of her aches and pains from the accident had faded, but it would probably be a while longer before she was her old self again.

Thankfully, Beth smiled when his mother opened the door and accepted her hug with no trace of her former irritation. His dad got the same treatment, and Kevin started getting annoyed. Maybe her bad mood was just for him, even though he hadn't done a damn thing to deserve it.

He set the car seat with a sleeping Lily in it on the floor at the end of the couch, so her mother and grandmother could hover over her, and went into the kitchen for a beer. His father followed him in and grabbed one of his own.

"How's it going, son?"

Kevin didn't know how to answer that. If he wanted to know how Lily was doing, everything was great. She'd totally aced her two-week checkup. If he was talking about his relationship with Beth, that wasn't so great. "Okay, I guess."

"She's been on her own a few days now. How's that going for her?"

"She says she's all right, but she wouldn't admit it if she wasn't, so I don't know. I do know she's tired, but I try to help out and take Lily to my place when I can so she can get some stuff done or take a nap."

Leo leaned against the counter, eyeing him over the rim of his beer can. "You don't look too happy."

Kevin shrugged. "I wish things were different between Beth and me, but if I push, she'll just push back harder."

They heard Mary's voice getting louder, so that was the end of the conversation. A few seconds later, the three most important women in Kevin's life walked into the kitchen. His mother kissed his cheek. Beth, who was holding Lily, gave him a small smile, and maybe it was his imagination, but he thought he saw some apology in it.

Lily was awake and squirming, but she wasn't squawking for a bottle yet. He peeked inside the receiving blanket she was cuddled in and brushed a fingertip over her cheek. She wiggled and—in a total shocker—Beth laughed softly.

"She definitely knows her daddy," she said, "even when it's the lightest touch."

Kevin had pushed and prodded Beth into this dinner because he wanted his parents to have some time with Lily and because Beth needed to get out of her apartment, but it pained him. The togetherness without being together was even more pronounced now that Lily was born, and it chafed. Sometimes a little and sometimes, like now, more than a little.

Mary stepped up beside them. "While Lily's content, I want to take some pictures for the family album. You two go sit on the couch with her while I get my camera."

Just like that, the anxiety was back in Beth's

face. He put his hand on her back and guided her toward the living room before she could argue.

"I already know what you're going to say," he said in a low voice. "Let her take a nice picture of you and Lily and then me and Lily. And then, please, let her take one of the three of us just to make her happy."

She sat on the couch and peeled the blanket off Lily to reveal a cute pink dress. "What if some-day—"

"Someday if I find a woman who'll let me in her life instead of slamming the door in my face over and over, Lily still might like having a picture of her parents together."

"Oh." He could tell by the way her cheeks pinked up and how she sucked in her bottom lip that he'd hurt her feelings somehow, but she couldn't possibly believe she could have it both ways. They could only spend so much time in the relationship purgatory she'd sentenced them to.

Mary returned with her camera before Beth could respond to that, if she even intended to. With his parents codirecting the impromptu photo shoot, they managed to get the three shots Kevin suggested, and he and Beth even smiled. They got pictures of Lily with each of her grandparents and then both of them together before she announced she was done by turning bright red and letting out an eardrum-piercing wail.

"She definitely gets her volume from your father," Mary told Kevin.

Beth finished changing and feeding Lily as his mother put dinner on the table, so they were able to eat in relative peace. His parents had a bassinet, and Lily was close enough to Kevin's chair so she could watch him. Her eyes were brilliant blue, and when he grinned at her, she just blinked.

They made small talk while they ate, chatting about Lily and the bar and Joe's latest book. How Lisa was faring with her boys out of school for the summer. What they were going to do about the fact Brian and Bobby kept sabotaging the spinach in Mary's garden and trying to blame it on rogue chipmunks.

It was familiar chatter, and Kevin felt some of the tension easing out of his body. With the stress abating, he could think more clearly. It had only been three weeks since Beth had gone through a car accident and childbirth on the same day. While each of the days since had seemed to drag by for Kevin, they had probably passed in the blink of an eye for an exhausted and slightly battered new mother.

For the umpteenth time, Kevin reminded himself he had to be patient. He'd made his feelings for Beth pretty clear, so all he could do was wait for her to sort through her own.

IT HAD BEEN THREE WEEKS since Kevin first told her he loved her, and he hadn't said it again since.

She'd hated to do it, but she was running low on groceries—groceries she wanted, at least, rather than what Mary and her mother thought she should have—so she'd asked Kevin to stop at the store on their way home from the Kowalskis' house. Now he was pushing the cart along behind her, babbling to Lily, whose seat was latched on to the seat of the cart. They probably looked like a real family to any shoppers who took notice of them, instead of neighbors who just happened to have a baby together.

As she tried to focus on the unit price of diapers, she found herself unable to stop dwelling on the question of whether or not he'd meant it when he'd told her he loved her.

She'd told him it was a knee-jerk reaction to hearing about the accident and then seeing his daughter born, but she had no way of knowing if that was the truth or not. The fact he hadn't said it again since made her believe maybe she'd been right.

The not knowing left her feeling uncertain and off-balance, so she said nothing about it. And she worked harder at keeping a distance between them, just in case his feelings for her really *had* been all wrapped up with her having a baby.

Knowing Mary, though, within a few days she'd be getting a beautifully matted and framed photo of Lily and her parents—an almost perfect family smiling for the camera.

"Are they going to do tricks?"

Kevin's voice jerked her out of her depressing thoughts, and she realized she'd been staring at the shelves of diapers for who knew how long.

"Sorry." She grabbed a package of store-brand diapers in the next size up, because Lily was growing like a weed, and tossed them into the cart.

Kevin took them back out. "Are you sure you want these? One of the magazines I read said these over here are the best. Super absorbent areas specifically placed for baby girls. Soft, stretchy elastic. Good for sensitive skin."

"And the most expensive." She grabbed the generic diapers out of his hand.

He grabbed them right back. "We can afford decent diapers."

We? "The store brand is decent enough. And it's bad enough I let you talk me into accepting a paid maternity leave. I'm not going to waste your money—or mine—on fancy diapers just because the package is pink instead of generic white."

"Fine." He tossed the package back into the cart. "I just want her to have the best."

"Trust me, she's not going to be traumatized because her diapers don't have specially targeted absorbency zones for girls."

He resumed rolling along behind her in silence until she started picking through packages of boneless chicken breasts. "Why don't you just call down to the bar and have them make you something. You don't need to be cooking meals right now."

She wished, not for the first time, she'd left him in the car with the window cracked an inch. "Jasper's has a great menu and the food's delicious, but it's still a sports bar, Kevin. Sometimes I just want a salad with some sautéed chicken on the side."

"I'm sure if you asked, they could make that for you."

Turning around to face him, she put her hands on her hips. "If you think I'm going to interrupt your staff with special-order demands from above, you don't know me at all."

"Okay, so that wouldn't be like you." He gave her a small smile, not at all like his usual ones.

"Maybe I could take you out for dinner one night soon."

"For God's sake, Kevin, I'm perfectly capable of making chicken and a salad with a baby in the apartment."

"That's not what I meant." The smile faded as his mouth tightened. "I was asking you for a date. I just timed it badly, I guess."

Timed it badly? He could say that again. "I have a three-week-old baby, Kevin, and—"

"We. *We* have a three-week-old baby."

"Which is why dating should be the last thing on *our* minds. Besides, I thought you were going to find a woman who'll let you into her life and not slam doors in your face and blah blah blah. Whatever."

She tried to turn back to the chicken in case he could see on her face how much his words had bothered her, but he caught her wrist. "You're jealous."

"Am not."

"Are, too. You're jealous of a woman who doesn't even exist."

She jerked her hand out of his and grabbed the first package of chicken her hand fell on. She put it in the cart with the diapers that weren't good enough and walked away. Maybe if she ignored him, he'd keep himself busy talking to Lily. She was sleeping, but that never seemed to stop him. She was beginning to think the Kowalskis were genetically incapable of being quiet unless they were sleeping, and giving birth to one hadn't done anything to negate that impression.

Sadly, even pushing the cart, he had no trouble keeping up with her. "If you're jealous, that must mean you care."

"Of course I care about you, you idiot. But we're not going to date and I've told you why a million times."

"So let's go back to the whole chocolate cake thing."

Her face felt as if it was on fire, and she kept walking, right past the salad dressings. Maybe if she kept him in motion, the shoppers around her wouldn't be able to grasp enough of the conversation to cause her embarrassment. "Let's not."

"So you're on a diet, but you've got a nice big slab of chocolate cake sitting in front of you. You won't eat the cake because you think it's bad for you even though it's not, and you won't let anybody else eat it, either."

"If somebody wanted to eat the chocolate cake, I'd have to let her because I'm not going to eat it. Be sad for it to go to waste."

"What if nobody else likes that kind of chocolate cake and it was made special for you? If you don't eat it, it's going to get old and stale."

She snorted. "Like you're going to get stale. I hear women who kiss bar napkins are particularly fond of chocolate cake."

"Jealous."

"Not." She circled back and grabbed a bottle of ranch dressing off the shelf without stopping. "You can offer your chocolate cake to whoever you want."

She managed to get the words out in a flippant enough tone, but she was crumbling like stale frosting on the inside.

The thought of seeing Kevin with another woman made her stomach roll over and her throat tighten, but she was too afraid to tell him that. She'd never had a friendship like the one she shared with Kevin, and she was too afraid to risk it trying to take their relationship to the next level. Or to the level it had been at before, as the case may be. And it wasn't just about Lily's parents being friends—though that was important to her. She couldn't bear losing Kevin's friendship.

"You'll cave eventually." He was obviously

going for cocky, but the sadness in his eyes made her look away.

It would be best for all of them if she didn't fall off the wagon again.

CHAPTER TWENTY-ONE

August

BETH WAS HALFWAY THROUGH the pile of order forms on her desk before she realized she had no idea what she'd just read. With Lily napping in her portable crib at the end of the desk, she was having a few focus issues.

She'd been trying to keep up with some of the work in her apartment, but now that Lily was two months old, it was time to ease back into a real work schedule. Thankfully, Kevin had echoed her desire not to put their daughter in day care yet, so a few things had been added to the office. The portable crib. A swing and her floor gym. It didn't leave a lot of room to move around, but it would do as a temporary compromise.

After restacking the order forms, she started over, determined to pay attention. Lily was sleeping, so she needed to be working. That was the only way it would work. She owed it to Kevin who, not surprisingly, had provided a very generous, fully paid maternity leave.

Less than a quarter of the way through the pile of papers, she muttered under her breath and stacked them yet again.

Thoughts of Kevin weren't any more conducive to concentration than Lily sleeping two feet away, and that made her very unhappy.

Her body was apparently well on its way to recovering from the strain of childbirth, and it shared none of her mind's reservations about reviving her attraction to Kevin. And since acting on it would ruin the delicate balance of friendship and coparenting they'd found, she spent more time than she should trying to squash the shivers and the aches and the warm and fuzzies she got whenever he crossed her mind. She didn't even want to think about what happened when she was actually in the same room as him.

It was embarrassing, really. And painful, to fight something she was pretty sure Kevin was willing to surrender to. He still looked at her the way he had before, with that unrelenting open invitation in his eyes. He was less aggressive about it than he'd been before, though.

He'd been unbearably sweet over the past two months, spending time with Lily whenever he had a free minute and making sure Beth had everything she needed without being pushy. He was getting a lot better at the just-being-friends thing, which was good since that was what she wanted.

No, not really wanted. It was what she thought was best for Lily, and that made it the most important thing.

But there were still times, usually when she should have been sleeping, that she wondered what it would be like to be a real family. To wake up next to him every morning instead of him reluctantly saying good-night and going back across the hall when Lily went to bed.

It was too risky, though. There was too much at stake if things went sour, and she couldn't be sure they wouldn't. There hadn't been a point in their relationship, other than one date, that hadn't revolved around Lily, and, even though Beth was no longer pregnant, that remained the truth. She didn't want to be part of a package deal, and there was no way not to be.

When Paulie tapped lightly on the door and then stuck her head in, Beth was as relieved to be dragged out of her thoughts as she was to see her friend.

"Come in. She'll be waking up in a few minutes anyway."

"Things are getting pretty rowdy out front. Joe stopped in, and he's buying rounds for the house. Seemed like a good time to take a break."

Sounded like an odd thing for a guy with a former drinking problem to do, but Joe was in Jasper's fairly often and always had a soda. "What's the occasion?"

"Probably not my place to tell you, so act surprised, but Keri's finally pregnant."

"That's wonderful!" From what Kevin had said, Joe and Keri had been trying to have a baby since they got married. Almost a year now, she mused, since Lily had been conceived on their wedding day.

"I'm happy for them," Paulie said. "They'll be great parents."

"I'm happy for Lily, too. This means she won't be the low man on the Kowalski totem pole very long."

"And she'll have a cousin close to her own age."

Definitely good news all around. "How's Sam?"

"Good." Paulie leaned back in her chair with a contented smile. "He had some meetings in Boston this week, but I'm going to browbeat Kevin into giving me a few days off next week so we can go over to the coast and be bums."

"Be a good time for a beach wedding."

Paulie started to laugh, then clapped her hands over her mouth to stifle it when she remembered Lily. "No wedding for a while. Right now we're just enjoying each other, though I'm sure we'll get around to it someday. When we're ready to deal with our families, I guess."

"I thought things were going better with your parents."

"Sure. Mostly because I can ignore them. But there are some rules even Sam and I can't get around. When we get married there's going to be a Wedding, with a capital *W.* It'll be hell for me, so we want to be totally solid before we go there."

"No eloping, huh?"

"I wish."

Lily stirred in her bed, scrunching her little face and making smacking sounds, and Beth sighed. "I may as well take her upstairs. I've been so distracted all morning, I haven't gotten a thing done."

"Make her a bottle and I'll feed her. Go out front and see Joe for a few minutes. Join the party."

She shouldn't, but the offer was too tempting to pass up. She liked Joe, his down-to-earth nature having long ago overcome her awe of his success. It would be nice to offer her congratulations in person and ask him to pass them along to Keri.

The bar was almost at capacity when she got out

front, and the mood was good. Naturally her gaze was pulled immediately to Kevin, who was drawing a beer and laughing with his brother. She stood in the corner and watched him for a few minutes, trying to settle her nerves.

He was a natural when it came to bartending. Warm and friendly and quick to laugh. Jasper's had a great atmosphere, and even their slow times meant a reasonably steady flow of regulars. This definitely wasn't a slow time.

Just as she was about to step out of the shadows, a tall and very busty brunette in a Red Sox tank top and barely legal shorts handed a napkin to Kevin across the bar. Judging from the fresh coat of paint on the woman's pouty mouth, Beth didn't have to guess what was on the napkin.

Kevin glanced at the napkin, then gave the woman a speculative look that made Beth's stomach hurt. She hated this part of his job the most, no matter how often he claimed he had no interest in the napkin kissers. And, because it was good for business, he gave the woman a fully dimpled grin and a look that could lead her to believe he just might give her a call sometime.

Beth didn't really believe he would, but it was unsettling to see the kind of temptation he faced every day. Especially since more than a few of the baby pounds she'd gained hadn't been baby pounds at all, but Jasper burger pounds. She wasn't in maternity clothes anymore, but she still felt slightly dumpy next to the napkin-kissing crowd.

Once the brunette had swayed her not-very-subtle hips out the front door, Beth joined the celebration. She didn't miss the fact Kevin's eyes lit up when he saw her in a way they hadn't for the napkin kisser. It helped soothe her annoyance but also put her squarely back in conflicted territory. She wasn't willing to risk their friendship on a real relationship, but she didn't want anybody else to have him, either.

She spoke to Joe for a few minutes, her heart warmed by the joy that was practically exploding from him. Then she sat in silence while another brunette slipped Kevin another napkin and he went through the routine again.

"Getting quite a collection there," she said when the woman was gone.

"That's the fifth one since I got here." Joe smirked when Kevin gave him a quelling look.

"You mention babies and the women go crazy." Kevin grabbed a seltzer and set it in front of Beth. "I must look particularly virile."

Joe snorted. "Or particularly desperate."

Beth didn't care for the direction the conversation was taking, so it was time to jump in. "It's a good thing you don't bring Lily into the bar. If they see what a beautiful baby you made, we'll have to double our napkin orders."

He propped his elbows on the bar so his face was very close to hers. "I can't make magic like Lily with any woman but you."

"Oh." She felt the hot flush creep up her neck into her face. Dammit, and she'd been doing so well.

Joe raised his soda in a toasting gesture. "Good one, Kev."

"Shut up, Joe." Kevin shot him a dirty look. "You got your girl. Trying to get mine here, if you don't mind."

The heat in her face spread to her entire body, and Beth cursed the postpartum hormones that had to be to blame for the sudden hot flashes. "I should get back to Lily so Paulie can come back to work. Give Keri my best, Joe."

She fled before Kevin could say any more. Clearly, whatever cease-fire he'd declared when she had the baby was over, and she was fair game again. The assault by his charm, his sincerity and—God help her—his sexuality had resumed.

She needed to keep reminding herself that, if

she surrendered, Lily's happy childhood could be the hardest hit casualty.

"SHE'S NOT EVEN GIVING you an inch, huh?"

Kevin shook his head as Beth disappeared through the door to the back. That was one way of putting it. "She already knows I want the whole mile."

"What's the deal with you guys, anyway?"

An empty mug raised at the end of the bar, but Randy was right on it. "She wants us to be friends."

"More friendly than working together, practically living together and having a baby together?"

"No shit. But she's got it in her head I'm all hot and bothered for a relationship because of the baby, and that if we get together because of that, eventually it'll fall apart and then we won't be friends anymore, which would suck for Lily."

Joe shrugged. "I get being worried about ruining the friendship, but relationships don't come with guarantees no matter how they start. And it's not like you just met. You guys have been together now—kind of—for what? Ten months?"

"No, she's been holding me at arm's length now for ten months, which sucks." Except for that one time in February, which was way too damn long ago. So long ago the memory barely kept him warm at night anymore. "At first she was afraid I'd take over her life, and now she's afraid of ruining our friendship."

"That's a lot of afraid."

"I'm afraid my balls are going to explode." Too late, Kevin remembered they weren't alone, but thankfully nobody seemed to be paying any attention. Wasn't the kind of thing a guy wanted getting around. "She's killing me. This whole thing is killing me."

"Have you told her that? How you feel, I mean, not that your balls are going to explode, because nobody really wants to know about that. Especially me."

"She knows how I feel. I've made it pretty damn plain."

"*L* word?"

"Yup."

Joe arched an eyebrow. "That's pretty damn plain. I'm guessing you didn't get it back."

"No, I got an explanation of how what I was feeling was because she'd been hit by a bus and then had a baby. It wasn't real. Just emotional upheaval. Hell, even before the *L* word came into play, she had excuses for anything I might be feeling. I only cared about her because she was pregnant and shit like that."

"Well, how 'bout now? She's not pregnant, she hasn't been in any more accidents and Lily's two months old."

Now it was his turn to shrug. "I haven't said it again."

"Why not?"

Why not? Because having your emotions thrown back at you and explained away as not being real wasn't something most guys did for shits and giggles. "Not really up for being emotionally kicked in the balls again, thanks."

"A bit hung up on the family jewels there, pal."

"Screw you, Joe. Easy for you to say, since you've got a loving wife waiting for you at home."

"And you think it was easy? That she just magically fell into my arms?" Joe shook his head. "I took a few hits to the sac, too."

"So you know, then. That it's not easy to keep putting yourself out there."

"I know it." He took a long sip of his soda. "I guess the question is whether or not she's worth the risk."

He didn't even have to think about it. "She's worth it."

"Then think about this for a while—if you

haven't told her how you feel since the accident-slash-having a baby, how is she supposed to know she was wrong?"

It was a damn good question, and it gave him something to think about as his fool brother stood and called for another round on the house. The beer and the congratulations flowed again, as did a couple more lipstick-smeared napkins, which he tossed into the basket unread.

The only woman he wanted had made it very plain she'd never kiss a napkin for him.

Two-thirty in the morning and Kevin had his forehead and palms pressed to Beth's door, listening to his two-month-old daughter cry.

Lily had one hell of a set of lungs on her, and as the hours ticked by it became pretty obvious, even from his own apartment, she wasn't in the mood to sleep. There were moments of silence, and then the squalling would start up again—probably when Beth decided it was safe to lay her down again.

He wanted her to be comfortable coming to him for help, but as the time passed it became clear she wasn't going to. She rarely did. No matter what he did or how often he reminded her, she couldn't seem to get it through her damn head she wasn't alone.

Damn stubborn woman.

When Lily's shrieks got louder, no doubt from Beth's pacing near the door, he gave up thinking about what he should do and knocked.

The door opened, and it took every ounce of his self-control not to take a step back. She'd looked better while actually *giving birth* to the kid than she did right then. Her hair was insane, and her face was puffy from lack of sleep. Her eyes were wet and red, and she kept sniffling, as though she was in a constant state of near tears. The look in her eyes brought to mind a trapped, rabid animal.

And Mike had been right. She was still the most beautiful woman in the world, and he didn't want to be anywhere but here.

"I know she's being loud," she said in a wavering voice. "I'm sorry if we woke you up."

When he reached out and took Lily from her, Beth practically sagged in relief. "Why didn't you call me, Beth?"

"I didn't want to bother you. She just… I've done everything. She's fed, changed, she doesn't have a rash. No pins sticking in her. No…anything. She just doesn't want to go to sleep."

"Then you walk across the hall, hand her to me and tell me it's my turn." He repositioned Lily and rubbed her back in gentle circles.

His little princess let out a belch worthy of the blue-ribbon winner of a baked beans–eating contest, then nuzzled against him and closed her eyes.

And Beth totally came undone. Sobbing, she collapsed in a chair and dropped her head into her hands. "I burped her. I burped her and burped her and burped her. I can't even do *that* right. I'm the worst mother ever."

Definitely not the time to laugh at her. "Beth, come on. Babies do that. When the boys were babies, Lisa would burp the hell out of them, and then as soon as Ma took them, they'd let out these hellacious belches."

She shook her head without looking up. "You're just saying that to make me feel better."

"I'm serious. When Lisa cried and said *she* was the worst mother ever, Ma told her it was something about how people are all different shapes, so we push on the baby's belly and diaphragm or whatever differently. Who knows? Anyway, you need to go to bed."

"Yes." She plucked a few tissues out of the box balanced on the arm of the chair and mopped at her face. "I'll go put her down and then go to bed."

"Not a chance. This peanut's going to be starving before you know it, and the last thing you need is to get up again in two hours. Go to bed. I've got her." He was going to suggest she take a shower before she crawled between the sheets, but he was afraid she'd fall asleep standing up, fall, hit her head and drown. "Go. To. Bed."

He knew how deep her exhaustion went when she didn't even argue or claim she was okay and could handle it herself. She just kissed the top of Lily's head, tears running down her cheeks, and staggered off in the direction of her bed.

Leaving Kevin with a warm ball of sleeping baby and a dilemma. He didn't have any formula at his place because it was just as easy to grab bottles from Beth's. But if he put Lily down to pack her a bag and she woke up screaming again, Mama Bear wouldn't get to hibernate in peace.

In the end he stretched out on the couch with Lily cradled in his arms. After nudging a couple of the throw pillows under his arm so he'd be less likely to flop around and drop her, he closed his eyes.

For the first time in quite a while, he felt totally content. Under the same roof as Beth, with his daughter in his arms, Kevin willed himself to fall asleep quickly. He'd need all the rest he could get to keep up with his tiny hellion.

And for the talk he and Beth were going to have in the morning.

CHAPTER TWENTY-TWO

THE SUN STREAMING THROUGH her window woke Beth, and she sat up straight, her heart thudding in her chest.

It was morning. And not the brutal, still-dark-but-technically-morning hours her daughter liked to keep, but actual morning. Eight o'clock, as a matter of fact.

Why hadn't Lily cried?

With trembling hands, she shoved back the covers and slid out of bed. And then she remembered Kevin. Remembered the bone-deep exhaustion and the crying—hers *and* Lily's. The relief so intense tears had streamed down her cheeks as she'd handed the baby over and crawled into bed. He must have stayed so she could sleep through the night for the first time since Lily was born.

Panic at bay, she pulled on her robe and crept from her room. If Lily was sleeping, Kevin was probably crashed on the couch, and she didn't want to wake him. Then she heard his voice and stopped, peeking around the corner into the kitchen.

He was swaying back and forth with their daughter gazing adoringly into his face from the cradle of his arms. "I'm going to do my best to make sure your life is awesome, but it won't always be. Those are the times you need to dance in the kitchen the most. It's good for your soul."

Beth sighed and leaned her head against the corner of the wall, as enchanted as Lily by the soft, tender timbre of his voice.

"You don't even need music," he told Lily. "You can dance to the music in your head. Hopefully not to that country-and-Western shit your mother listens to, though. Oh…damn. Don't say shit, Lily-bean. Or if you do and Mommy hears you, don't tell her you heard it from me, okay? Tell her Uncle Mike said it."

She might have giggled if her throat wasn't all clogged with emotion. Seeing Kevin with Lily always made her feel blessed, but this moment—this was an intensely private moment between a father and his baby daughter, and she shouldn't be eavesdropping.

Backing slowly out of sight, she turned into the bathroom and made some noise flushing the toilet and brushing her teeth. When she walked back into the kitchen, Lily was in her bouncy chair, and Kevin was setting two steaming mugs of coffee on the table. He smiled at her, and Lily kicked her feet, making herself bounce.

"Morning, sunshine." He pulled out her chair for her.

"Thanks...for everything." She sat and wrapped her hands around the mug. "You didn't have to stay. I just needed a good nap, that's all."

"No, a good night's sleep is what you needed. And we had it all under control, didn't we, Lily-bean?"

The baby kicked her feet and blew a raspberry at him.

"Don't listen to her. All under control." He sat in the chair opposite her and took a sip of his coffee. "I should probably tell you there's a diaper out in the hall, though, because I didn't think the trash can lid would hold it. It was...gruesome."

"So you put it in the hallway?"

"It was either there or the freezer."

"Hallway works."

They were quiet a few minutes, drinking their coffee and watching Lily kick her feet. A quiet family moment, she thought. Almost like they were a real family.

And they could be. She knew all she had to do

was say the word and Kevin would have her down at city hall signing a marriage license so fast she'd be lucky if she got her shoes on.

Last night, while she was exhausted and crying and Lily was exhausted and crying, she'd asked herself why she was going through it alone. Right across the hall was a stand-up guy who'd treat them like princesses and shoulder his share of the burden. Hell, probably a good chunk of her share, too, because that's just the kind of man he was.

If only there was some way to separate their relationship from Lily. She wished they'd had more than one date before the baby sideswiped them, changing everything forever. There wasn't any way to untangle him as himself or as Dad, or her as herself or as Mom.

She and Kevin had been bed partners. They were friends. Most importantly, they were co-parents. But were they lovers? Not in the sexual sense, but were they two people whose relationship was based on love? No matter what he said, she couldn't be sure.

"You look better," Kevin told her, and she was startled to realize she'd been staring into the bottom of her empty coffee mug.

"I feel better. The last couple of nights have been a little tough." When he opened his mouth, she held up her hand to stop him. "Yes, I should have dragged you out of bed and handed her over."

"We've been together—or non-together or whatever you want to call it—a long time now, Beth. I don't know what else I can do to make you believe you don't have to go it alone."

"I'm trying."

He looked sad more than anything. Beaten. "A year. It's been almost an entire year, and sometimes I don't feel like we're closer to…anything, than when we started."

"Please don't do this right now."

"Then when?"

"When I'm not a wreck. When I've had more than six consecutive hours of sleep in a month. I don't know, but not right now."

"And then she'll be teething and then it'll be something else."

"I can't do any more than this, Kevin."

"Maybe you could see about my mom watching Lily so we could go out for dinner."

"It's too soon." She stood and walked toward the coffeemaker so she wouldn't have to see his face. "How about I make us some breakfast?"

KEVIN FELT HIMSELF HIT the wall—a big brick wall he couldn't go through and could see no way around. A dead end.

"I can't go on like this, Beth."

Her shoulders slumped as though she recognized the note of finality in his voice. "We decided a long time ago the best thing we could do for Lily was be friends."

"We are friends. But I love you, Beth." There. He'd said it again. "I want to be your husband, too."

He could see by the rising panic on her face he wasn't going to get the answer he was looking for. And once she said no, he was going to have to cut her loose. No more playing at house from across a hallway divide.

He'd find a nice place for rent and make sure his child-support checks covered it so she and Lily could live in a real house with a nice yard. His daughter would come to visit as often as possible. She'd have a special suitcase for going to Daddy's, and he and Beth would make inane small talk when he picked Lily up and dropped her off again.

His gut ached at the thought, but he couldn't stand life on the wrong side of the door anymore. He finally understood that old cliché *so close, yet so far*.

"I'm tired of living across the hall from the woman I love and my daughter. Tired of having two doors and a hallway between me and my family."

"And I'm tired of knowing I wouldn't ever have seen you again if I hadn't gotten pregnant. I'm tired of wondering if anything really holds us together besides Lily. And I don't want to get married and then spend my whole marriage like Lisa, wondering if it's not real under the surface."

"Everything I feel for you is real, Beth." He didn't know how to make it any more clear than he had. "And I think we've proven we don't need to marry for Lily's sake. She's born, she's named, her parents are friends. If we go our separate ways, she'll spend time with us both and be fine, just like all the other kids out there whose parents aren't married or get divorced."

Beth sat back down at the table, and he wondered if she realized her coffee cup was still empty. "What do you mean by go our separate ways?"

"I told you I can't go on like this anymore. And, while it's not a big deal right now, before we know it, Lily will be up and about. She can't live in a third-floor apartment over a bar without so much as a blade of grass to play in. It's time to start looking for a place, and the only question is whether or not I'll be going with you."

Her face paled. "See? I knew this would happen.

Our relationship's falling apart and now I need a new place to live."

Only the fact that Lily was gurgling to herself in her seat kept his temper in check. "Don't do that, Beth. Don't make it sound like I'm throwing you out in the street. I'm talking about finding a decent house for you and the baby that you'll be able to afford with support checks."

"That's not what I want from you."

"Then what *do* you want?"

She only shook her head, staring into the bottom of her cup.

"You want things to continue on as they are, but I can't anymore. I'm sorry. I want more."

"I don't think I have any more to give right now. But I don't want… I don't know."

Rather than sit there and keep beating his head against the brick wall, Kevin took that as his cue to leave. He stood up and, after kissing Lily, turned to Beth, who looked as miserable as he felt. "You need to think about it for a few days and then we'll talk again. We're either going to have a real relationship or we're going to go our separate ways and share custody of Lily. Let me know."

He walked out before he could change his mind—before the sadness in her eyes made him take it all back and tell her they were okay. Because he wasn't okay.

And if she told him it was over—that she'd decided they should go their separate ways—he might never be okay again.

THOSE ARE THE TIMES YOU NEED to dance in the kitchen the most. It's good for your soul.

In the middle of the night, with the radio quietly playing a sad country song, Beth danced with her daughter in the kitchen. It was a song about love and loss and heartbreak, and she tried to keep her tears from dripping onto Lily as she swayed with her in her arms.

She missed Kevin. Even though he was in the same place he was every night, probably doing the same thing, it felt different tonight. He was just across the hall, but so very far away. And unlike the countless other times they'd danced around the subject of their relationship, she wasn't sure he'd come back this time.

That hurt more than any of the possibilities she'd spent the last…well, almost a year considering. She'd spent so much time worrying about what would happen if she let him in and he left her, she'd driven him away.

Now that he was gone, she could see it. Even if

they went their separate ways, as he'd said, they'd make it work. They'd maintain a good relationship, and Lily would be fine, just like he'd said.

Beth was the one who wouldn't be fine. She wanted him back.

Over the top of Lily's head, a square of white on the counter caught her eye. It was a Jasper's napkin, and for the first time since Kevin walked out the door, she smiled.

Ten minutes later she sucked up her courage and dialed his number. He answered on the second ring, his voice heavy with sleep. "What's wrong?"

"Lily's okay. I… Can you come over for a few minutes?"

"I'm already over. Unlock the door."

He was standing in the hall in nothing but a pair of sleep pants, with his hair mussed and the phone still held to his ear. She felt a pang of guilt for calling him in the middle of the night—he must have thought something was wrong with the baby and literally run across the hall.

"What's the matter, Beth?" he asked, coming in and closing the door behind him.

"Nothing." Lily squirmed in her arms, wanting her daddy. "We were…"

She stopped as Kevin set his phone on the table so he could take his daughter, giving her cheek a nuzzle. It sounded stupid now, Beth realized, and she shouldn't have dragged him out of bed in the middle of the night.

"You were what?"

Sighing, she resigned herself to telling him the whole story. "Lily and I were dancing in the kitchen and…we missed you."

"You did, huh?" He moved closer to her, cradling Lily in one arm. He didn't look as if he thought she was stupid for calling. And he didn't look angry or sad, either. He looked hopeful, and that made her feel hopeful, too.

"Yes." She swallowed hard when he stroked her cheek with his free hand. "It didn't feel right without you there."

"I'm here now." He slid his arm around her waist, tucking Lily in between them, and started swaying a little.

She swayed with him. "We made you something."

"Wow. Dancing. Arts and crafts. I had no idea my girls were so busy in the middle of the night."

His girls. Warmth flooded her, and she handed him the napkin before she could change her mind. He had to let go of her waist to take it, but he stayed close enough so she had a front-row seat to his reaction.

She didn't own a Do-Me Fuchsia lipstick, but she had a dark blush color that showed up against the white. Above the Jasper's logo were two lipstick kisses—hers and a tiny, puckered imprint of Lily's. Under the logo she'd painstakingly written her message in the same lipstick. *We love you.*

He looked at it a long time, until anxiety started gnawing at the warm glow she'd had going on. Even Lily started squirming, as though she felt the tension suddenly making her mother's stomach hurt.

Then he looked at her, and the hot intensity in his gaze turned her breathless. "We?"

"I love you." It was so much easier to say than she'd thought it would be. It felt so right and seemed to loosen a band constricting her heart.

"You kissed a napkin for me."

"It must be true, then."

"Just so we're on the same page here, I want it all. I want you to be my wife. I want to find a nice house outside the city with a big backyard."

She looked up into his eyes, almost afraid to believe it. "I want that, too."

"And someday, when this monkey finds a guy willing to marry her, I want to dance with you at her wedding and look at you the way Pop still looks at my mother."

"Yes." She wanted that, too.

Holding Lily in his right arm, he scooped Beth close with his left and kissed her. "Dance with me."

She put her arms around Kevin and their daughter and laid her head on his chest. "Always."

EPILOGUE

BETH HANSEN BECAME Mrs. Kevin Kowalski two weeks later, on a balmy Saturday night in the middle of a playground. She wore shorts, a relatively clean white shirt, a streak of marshmallow in her hair from prewedding s'mores and an accumulation of at least a half dozen layers of bug spray.

She carried a bouquet of wildflowers Kevin's nephews had picked for her in the woods. While she couldn't identify them all, she'd been assured—by Mary, not the boys—that none of the leaves were poison ivy and all the blossoms were insect-free. Lily snoozed in her stroller, the entire thing draped with mosquito netting, and Kevin wore a T-shirt with a fake tuxedo pattern printed on it, a last-minute gift from his brothers.

Her father walked her down an aisle lined with strings of lit Chinese lanterns borrowed from a camper, while her mother sobbed and Paulie, her maid of honor, tried not to swear at a particularly determined horsefly.

Every year the entire Kowalski family made the trip to northern New Hampshire to camp for two weeks, ride their four-wheelers and swim in the pool. It wasn't exactly primitive camping, since they were all bedding down in very nice RVs, but there were s'mores and hot dogs on sticks and plenty of mud. Kevin and Beth's shiny new RV—an extravagant wedding gift from Joe and Keri—was parked by itself in an isolated spot across the pond from the others, on account of it being their honeymoon.

She'd questioned the wisdom of bringing a two-month-old baby camping, but Kevin had pointed out that Lily didn't really care where she was as long as she was fed, changed and cuddled. Plus, he'd said, she was a Kowalski. She could take it.

"I now pronounce you man and wife," the justice of the peace declared. "You may kiss the bride."

She flung her arms around her husband's neck as he lifted her right off the ground to kiss her senseless to a soundtrack of cheers, applause, wolf whistles and what sounded like a few groans and gags from the juvenile male crowd. That was followed, naturally, by a very unhappy squawk from Lily, who didn't particularly care for having her naps interrupted.

Kevin set Beth down, but Paulie—who wasn't camping but had made the drive up with Sam—was already at the stroller, lifting the baby out. Kevin and Beth were hugged and kissed as they made their way down a makeshift receiving line—more like a gauntlet, she thought—and then she was able to take Lily.

"At least you know how you'll be celebrating your anniversary every year," Paulie said. "The Annual Kowalski family camping trip."

"Of Doom," Beth and Kevin said together and everybody laughed.

Then there was food and more food and then the cake. Or the cakes, rather, because there were three sheet cakes to accommodate the family, their friends and pretty much everybody in the campground.

Lily was fed and changed and eventually, after a round of pass-the-baby, she finally went back to sleep in Shelly's arms. Stephanie plugged her iPod into a set of external speakers somebody had provided, and a sweet country song drifted across the campground.

Kevin pulled Beth into his arms, and they danced for the first time as man and wife. She laid her head on his chest, tears brimming on her lashes. She wasn't sure how he'd managed to stumble across the Tim McGraw and Faith Hill duet, considering his taste in music, but it was perfect. His love definitely did something to her.

"I thought I'd never get to dance with my wife."

She loved the sound of that. "You sure know how to show a girl an interesting time, husband."

His hands slid down her hips—not far enough to be indecent in front of the family, but far enough to promise he'd get indecent later. Beth preferred to think the warm tingle spreading across her skin was the thrill of the moment rather than the high concentration of DEET eating her flesh.

"Are you going to be sorry someday you didn't get the dress and the flowers and all that crap?"

"I'll never be sorry. And I had flowers. Special flowers picked just for me."

"Umm…were you able to identify all of them before you touched them?"

"No, but your mother checked them for poison ivy and bugs."

She rested her head against him as he laughed, and she felt the rumble through his chest. His hands slid up to her back, and he rested his cheek on the top of her head as they swayed together through the rest of the song. As the last notes faded away, he tipped her chin up and kissed her again. Then he moved his mouth close to her ear.

"I can't believe I'm going to say this," he said so quietly nobody could hear him but her, "but I'm glad you made me wait. Made *us* wait. For this, I mean."

So was she. This marriage wasn't going to be chased by doubts. No staring at the ceiling in the middle of the night wondering if her husband had really wanted to marry her. "I love you."

"And since you wrote it on a napkin, it must be true."

True to his word, Kevin had framed the napkin she and Lily had kissed in the middle of the night and hung it over the bar. She was hoping that, along with the wide and shiny gold band on his finger, would cut down the number of napkins in the basket.

"Do you want your present now?" he asked.

"Right here in front of everybody?"

"Everybody helped. Joe just finished up his part while we were dancing, as a matter of fact. I think they'd like to see you open it."

She let him lead her over to the table set up for the gifts, and she laughed when he handed her a flat package wrapped in newspaper and secured with what looked like an entire roll of tape.

"We either forgot the extra wrapping paper or it's hiding in one of the campers," Keri explained.

"I wrapped it," Brian said.

Bobby shoved him. "I helped!"

"It looks wonderful." Beth turned the package over in her hands until she finally found what looked like a weak point in the tape. It wasn't easy, but she managed to get the flat box unwrapped without using her teeth.

When she lifted the lid and peeled back the tissue paper, her breath caught in her chest, and tears sprang instantly to her eyes.

It was a collage photo frame, identical to the one she'd given Kevin for Christmas. The picture Mary had taken of them with Lily when she was three weeks old was in the center. There was a photo of Beth playing with the boys and Stephanie at Christmas. A shot of her and Paulie laughing together at Jasper's she'd never even known was taken. A photo of her parents with Lily, taken while they were still at the hospital. A group shot of the entire family, with her at the center in her tiara, taken at her baby shower.

And there were two from that very night. One taken as they looked into each other's eyes and said their vows. Another of them in each other's arms when they danced as husband and wife.

That must have been Joe's part, she thought. He had a laptop and a small printer with him, so he must have printed the last two pictures while they finished their dance.

They were all there in candid moments captured forever under glass. Her family. "It's beautiful."

Kevin put his arm around her waist and pulled her close. "They'll look awesome hanging together in the new house."

There wasn't a new house yet, but Kevin was pretty determined Lily would spend her first Christmas in a real house with a yard she wasn't old enough to play in. "Yes, they will. In the meantime, they'll hang together over your—I mean *our*—couch."

He kissed her again, until Bobby's voice broke into the moment. "Time for the Wedding Garter Toss of Doom!"

Beth and Kevin broke apart, and she laughed when she saw the game they were setting up. Instead of horseshoes, they'd be tossing rings painted to look like wedding garters at the stakes. The kids were already arguing over who was on which team, and the guys were surreptitiously switching out paper cups of Kool-Aid disguised as wedding punch for beer and sodas.

Her family, she thought again, and there was no hesitation. No pangs of regret or longing for Albuquerque. Hell, she even had her eye on a late-model minivan for sale down the street from the bar.

This was her home, with the people who cared about her. She loved them all, especially the tall one arguing with his brothers about how many paces should be between the stakes and whose paces they were going to use.

"I love you," she mouthed when he looked in her direction.

He grinned, flashing full dimples at her. "You might love me right now, but the kids said we have to be on opposite teams. The groom's team and the bride's team."

Beth laughed and joined her family, ready to kick her new husband's ass at the Wedding Garter Toss of Doom.

* * * * *

A new generation of cowboys stake claims to
their land—and the women they love....

Three classic tales from #1 *New York Times* bestselling
author and *USA TODAY* bestselling author

LINDA LAEL MILLER

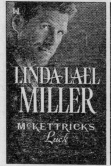

Available now!

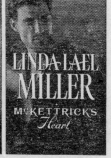

Coming in March 2012.

Coming in May 2012.

"Linda Lael Miller creates vibrant characters
and stories I defy you to forget."
—#1 *New York Times* bestselling author Debbie Macomber

HQN™ | HARLEQUIN®
www.Harlequin.com

PHLLMT2012

REQUEST YOUR FREE BOOKS!

2 FREE NOVELS
FROM THE ROMANCE COLLECTION
PLUS 2 FREE GIFTS!

YES! Please send me 2 FREE novels from the Romance Collection and my 2 FREE gifts (gifts are worth about $10). After receiving them, if I don't wish to receive any more books, I can return the shipping statement marked "cancel." If I don't cancel, I will receive 4 brand-new novels every month and be billed just $5.99 per book in the U.S. or $6.49 per book in Canada. That's a saving of at least 25% off the cover price. It's quite a bargain! Shipping and handling is just 50¢ per book in the U.S. and 75¢ per book in Canada.* I understand that accepting the 2 free books and gifts places me under no obligation to buy anything. I can always return a shipment and cancel at any time. Even if I never buy another book, the two free books and gifts are mine to keep forever.

194/394 MDN FELQ

Name	(PLEASE PRINT)

Address	Apt. #

City	State/Prov.	Zip/Postal Code

Signature (if under 18, a parent or guardian must sign)

Mail to the **Reader Service**:
IN U.S.A.: P.O. Box 1867, Buffalo, NY 14240-1867
IN CANADA: P.O. Box 609, Fort Erie, Ontario L2A 5X3

Not valid for current subscribers to the Romance Collection
or the Romance/Suspense Collection.

Want to try two free books from another line?
Call 1-800-873-8635 or visit www.ReaderService.com.

* Terms and prices subject to change without notice. Prices do not include applicable taxes. Sales tax applicable in N.Y. Canadian residents will be charged applicable taxes. Offer not valid in Quebec. This offer is limited to one order per household. All orders subject to credit approval. Credit or debit balances in a customer's account(s) may be offset by any other outstanding balance owed by or to the customer. Please allow 4 to 6 weeks for delivery. Offer available while quantities last.

ROM11

shannon stacey

77678 EXCLUSIVELY YOURS   ___ $7.99 U.S. ___ $9.99 CAN.

(limited quantities available)

TOTAL AMOUNT $ _____
POSTAGE & HANDLING $ _____
($1.00 FOR 1 BOOK, 50¢ for each additional)
APPLICABLE TAXES* $ _____
TOTAL PAYABLE $ _____

(check or money order—please do not send cash)

To order, complete this form and send it, along with a check or money order for the total above, payable to HQN Books, to: **In the U.S.:** 3010 Walden Avenue, P.O. Box 9077, Buffalo, NY 14269-9077; **In Canada:** P.O. Box 636, Fort Erie, Ontario, L2A 5X3.

Name: _____

Address: _____ City: _____

State/Prov.: _____ Zip/Postal Code: _____

Account Number (if applicable): _____

075 CSAS

*New York residents remit applicable sales taxes.
*Canadian residents remit applicable GST and provincial taxes.

HQN™ | HARLEQUIN®
www.Harlequin.com

PHSS0212BL